"Good girl, wha
of her head.

"Damn, Tom, how can you say that? We're lucky she's even with us tonight, not down in a secret hideaway nobody knows about." Alex slammed his fists into his jacket pockets.

"Nobody needs to lose their cool," Dillon warned.

"She's okay, Alex. Take it easy. Now tell us again what you told Reggie." Her brother waited until she pulled out a dining room chair. She plopped down and unbuckled her shoes.

"Look, you told me to be intentionally vague. He knows Alex is getting paid for something on Friday. Right now, he thinks he might get his hands on a diamond necklace. But as soon as he puts two and two together about a delivery like you boys think he will, he'll be after the bigger prize. The whiskey. So all the other little stunts you have planned must fall into place."

"They will. They have to. But I think he'll stick with Friday. Ole Reggie will want our truck even more now. He'll realize he must move the hidden whiskey before anyone else, besides you, finds out about his hiding place." Dillon looked straight at Kit.

"Exactly. Reggie knows she knows." The veins on Alex's neck stood out.

"Well, I'm headed to bed." Maybe Tom would drop the big brother act for once and not mind Alex sleeping with her instead of down the hall in the guest bedroom. You never knew. Men.

Praise

Joy Allyson's Whiskey Secrets will have you falling for a time when men were real and women brought them to their knees... follow the impact of prohibition on a family's whiskey empire based against the backdrop of the Roaring Twenties. You'll laugh and cry as Tom Tanner's Tennessee Whiskey heirs work their way into your heart. You won't be able to put this one down!
~Kim Turner, author of The McCades of Cheyenne series

Whiskey Secrets

by

Joy Allyson

Whiskey Secrets

Cover Art by *The Wild Rose Press, Inc.*

The Wild Rose Press, Inc.
PO Box 708
Adams Basin, NY 14410-0708
Visit us at www.thewildrosepress.com

Publishing History
First Edition, 2023
Trade Paperback ISBN 978-1-5092-5244-2
Digital ISBN 978-1-5092-5245-9

Published in the United States of America

Dedication

To my husband, Hal, and our two daughters Wren and Ashley for your unwavering love, encouragement, and patience. Without with-there would be no writing journey for me.

Acknowledgments

Many thanks to my editor Judi Mobley for her marvelous editing and unlimited patience and to Karen Ford for finding new and creative ways to do more research.

Chapter One

Oak Hollow, Tennessee, July 1924
Tom

"Do you want to take a last look?" Tom Kittrell narrowed his eyes, scanning his father's face for any uncertainty about what they must do.

"Nah. What's the point? Already decided. Can't afford to find one more dead body on the rick house floor." His father slapped his hat on his leg before yanking it back on.

"Hard to believe another person was idiotic enough to think barrels of whiskey were hidden in the rafters," Tom scoffed.

Boarding up the building did not discourage roving vagrants from breaking in. They'd put out a horrendous fire earlier in the year, started by drifters whose abandoned campfire damaged a third of the property.

A flock of starlings flew from the roof, vacating the three cupolas they nested in for generations. The giant distillery was a second home for his cousin, Dillon, sister Kit, and him. A site they played in as children, worked at in their first jobs, and finally where they took on their roles as heirs apparent of a whiskey empire. Tom scrubbed his shirt sleeves.

The county sheriff, standing alongside his father, glanced toward the small crowd gathering across the creek, then to the sign painted on the building: Penland Kittrell Whiskey Distillery. "Had no choice after you found the second body. Got the summons right here in my pocket for allowing public endangerment."

"Damn, the entire country is going to hell in a handbasket. It's 1924 for God's sake. So much for the 'noble experiment' bringing civilized behavior back." Pen kicked a *No Trespassing* sign. "Might as well throw in these too, son. Useless."

The sheriff shook his head. "Well, I've seen enough. Prohibition's turned regular folk into lawbreakers overnight."

Tom rolled his tired shoulders and stared at the darkening skies.

The lawman cleared his throat. "You use enough kerosene? Dad-gummed rain has soaked everything."

"Should go fast. We stacked a good size tinder pile inside." Tom jerked off his work gloves and wiped his forehead with the back of his hand. "It'll burn. The interior's bone dry."

"Built with hewn cedar and oak," his father added. "Seems like a hell of a way to outlast insanity. Burn down half my business."

"Might keep them temperance folks at bay. They get riled up pretty easy."

Tom agreed with the irrational statement. Distillery owners in the city warned them, the Eighteenth Amendment, including those who supported it, was no passing storm. It still stuck in his craw to do something that went against everything he believed in.

His mother and sister crossed the footbridge over the shallow brook and walked their way.

The sheriff raised his hat. "Sorry you ladies have to

see this, Mrs. Kittrell, Miss Kit."

"We should feel blessed as a family. At least Tom Tanner Tennessee Whiskey was awarded a medicinal contract." Chloe Tanner Kittrell gripped her husband's arm. "We're lucky, sheriff. We have friends in Nashville who closed their businesses and moved away."

The resignation in his mother's voice did not surprise Tom. Although he read no emotion in her eyes, he sensed her unhappiness.

His sister was not as stoic. Kit wiped a tear from her eye. When he handed her his gloves, she clasped them tightly. "For once, I'm glad Dillon can't be here."

"Won't be long, sis," he told her. "Sorry, soon as this fire takes off, I will hightail it out of here. Rain set me way back. Can't stay a minute longer."

"Be careful," she whispered.

"I will."

"Go ahead. Light the fire," his dad ordered.

He dug in his pockets for a match, then hefted the staff from the empty whiskey barrel. One scrape against the barrel's rusted iron band set the torch ablaze. Carrying it high, he strode past former workers and townspeople gathered to witness the spectacle for no greater reason than proof prohibition was permanent.

"There she goes!" A solitary voice shouted when he hurled the torch on the prepared pyre.

A loud swoosh bit the cool evening air. The fire took hold and raced up the wooden beams onto the one-of-a-kind crafted racks that once held some of the finest distilled whiskey in the Americas. Flames leaped toward the rafters. They wicked their way 'round the storage rack tiers and roofline trusses, then darted and

3

dashed across the triple roof openings.

Sparks sputtered and crackled. The blazing inferno shot through the roofline. Timber collapsing punctuated the deafening roar of the engulfing fire.

"Prohibition can't last forever," his sister said as they watched the orange madness burn.

****

A slick dark blue Marathon convertible drove up beside Tom, passing him on the narrow two-lane road. The driver hit the horn. Honk. Honk beeped through the quiet. Tom steered his truck to the right as much as he dared. The three soaking-wet men laughed boisterously. Not a care in the world for their custom leather bags and shining golf clubs tossed in the back seat.

That should be me. He shook his head. A young unmarried man, twenty-nine years old, should enjoy a Sunday afternoon on the golf course. Not be driving a five-ton truck loaded to the gills, down pot-holed roads, and looking over his shoulder for nosy county cops. *Yes, I'd like to finish on the back nine somewhere and get ready to take a pretty Sheba out for a good time.*

Two golfers held up their silver flasks as the car zoomed by. Their driver tapped his horn again, giving a final happy salute. Tom reached across his seat and grabbed his flask, toasting them with a healthy slug as the convertible roared past him and the Model T traveling in front. The steady rain stopped, but mist still obscured the black Ford he'd been following the past few miles.

Tom tightened his fists and banged the steering wheel. Highway Seventy's bridge washout in Mt. Juliet cost them an entire day. Southwest winds brought moisture from the gulf and produced monsoon-like rains throughout the entire region. It was a record-wet July in Middle Tennessee, normally their hottest and driest month of the year.

As he approached a curve, rumbling started. The intense thundering amplified. A boom exploded, reminding him of artillery shells blasting around him while hunkered down in the trenches in France during the war. A deafening roar followed. The entire truck rose and then slammed back to the asphalt. Grabbing the steering wheel tight, he shot a look in the rearview mirror—his crew's car skidded to a stop. Tom swiveled his head forward. Then he saw it. Mudslide.

The automobile's brake lights ahead flashed. The side of the mountain heaved, then mud, boulders, rocks, and trees flowed downward, devouring the hapless blue convertible. Nowhere to go. Tom hit the brakes and shifted gears into reverse. Damn. His men blocked him from behind.

As clods of earth hit the windshield, Tom ducked. The violent explosion shoved his truck across the road, the left wheel dipped into the soft shoulder. He held his breath. His body went rigid. He prayed gravity and a shifting load didn't pull him down the mountainside. He shifted gears again and inched forward. The saturated terrain oozed, then settled. An eerie silence menaced over the ridge-top. The car in front had turned to the left side, taking the brunt of the impact.

Tom switched off the engine, opened the driver's side door, and peered down a twenty-foot drop. The hair on his arms rose. He eased out of the truck. He made his way toward the vehicle. Rubble covered the car. A bushel size boulder landed through the driver's side windshield. The left side of the car was obstructed, but there was a figure on the right. The quick-thinking driver saved his passenger.

Avoiding rocks and clumps of earth, Tom hiked to the right side door. The occupant was draped over the dashboard. With a hard yank, he wrenched the door open.

"Are you all right?" Anxious, he leaned in and pulled the slumped body back into the car seat. Long brown curls framed a pale heart-shaped face. It was a woman. Alive!

She was young and couldn't be much older than his sister. He took out his handkerchief and dabbed the dripping blood off her forehead. When he removed the cloth, her eyes opened.

Beautiful violet eyes, the color of the ocean after a thunderous storm passed, and fluttering black lashes stared at him, uncomprehending. She licked her lower lip, stanching the blood from where she must have bitten herself on impact. Full pink lips begging to be kissed.

Tom stepped back. *I've met an angel.*

"Can you move?" he asked. "Let me get you out. Take hold of me."

Her right arm grasped his shoulder, and her left hand gripped his forearm. No telltale ruby-red nail polish flappers relished, just a diamond and a gold wedding band on her left hand. She was married.

"Miss… Ma'am. Look at me while I lift you out." Afraid she'd turn and see the trapped body of the driver, most likely her husband.

"I'm stuck—my foot." Her distressed voice held a musical lilt. Of course, his angel.

He stretched his hand across the floorboard.

"Excuse me." He raised the long skirt of her black dress to check her foot. A slim ankle protruded from an indentation in the surrounding surface. After scooting her free leg out, he leaned in to dislodge her left foot.

"Your shoe is caught."

She winced as he pulled her foot free, minus her shoe. "Place your arms around me. I'm going to carry you to my truck."

His companions, following behind him, approached the buried vehicle and assessed the best way to remove the boulder jammed into the windshield.

"Alex, open my passenger door so I can get her inside." Following his best friend, Tom carefully carried the heavenly body in his arms. He felt her feminine curves and featherweight while trekking on the scattered rubble. She held tight. Both arms about his shoulders. Her breasts pressed against him when he stumbled. He gently lifted her onto the seat.

"Thanks, Alex. Better go check on…"

The woman stared at the accident from the elevated position. The enormity of the slide and the damage it did sank in. She leaned her head back, giving a soft whimper.

His other friend motioned a thumbs-up from the car. "We got a pulse," he called.

"Ma'am, your husband is alive," Tom told her.

She bolted upright. "My husband is dead."

"No. He's alive…"

Chapter Two

Tom

The angel's face transitioned from pale white to ghost white. Her eyes started rolling to the back of her head. *My God, she's going into shock.*

Tom pushed her across the seat and crawled in beside her. He wrapped one arm around her and slapped her hands with his free hand.

"Breathe, take a deep breath." Her eyes shut, then opened, staring unfocused. Her pulse seemed normal, except her hands were cold and clammy. He smoothed her cheek, brushing brunette curls from her face. "Stay with me now. Gonna be all right."

She shook her head as if ridding it of cobwebs, then took a deep breath. Her shoulders shuddered and her whole body shook. He reached past her, across his seat, and grabbed his flask. He twisted the lid off the container, tilted the young woman's head up, and pressed the flask to her mouth.

"Here, you need to take a sip. It'll warm you up." She swallowed hard, sputtering, coughing, and spitting. Her color returned at once. "Sorry, I didn't have a cup," he said, immensely relieved she hadn't fainted.

She sent him an accusing glare, her bright eyes glistening with tears. She pushed his chest and scooted away. "Was that whiskey?" She wiped her lips, mouth, and complete face with her hand as if she committed a mortal sin.

Tom breathed a deep sigh of relief. "Are you okay for a minute? I'm going to see if I can help your…"

She stared, animosity shining in her eyes. Her forehead stopped bleeding, yet the cut on her mouth still bled. She licked her lower lip. Oh, to kiss that swollen lip. *Damn.*

He turned, climbed out of the cab, and scrutinized her before trekking to the smashed car.

"I think we can still get him out." Alex climbed off the hood. Shoving the boulder off was impossible.

"We've pulled him across the car seat. I believe we can free him. The engine is pressed against his legs, though," Alex said as Tom approached.

"Okay, let me get a board from the truck. We'll leverage it under the steering wheel and hopefully dislodge him." On his return, Tom glanced into the cab. The young woman watched their progress. *Well, we can't hide how grim it is for her husband.*

They attached two more boards, constructing a makeshift stretcher. Once they freed the victim from his wrecked car, the trio heaved him across the boards and carried him to the back of the wood-paneled vehicle. Tom jumped on the back bumper and lifted the canvas flap.

"Are you sure about this?" Alex checked the truck's bed. All twenty-four barrels of Tom Tanner Tennessee Whiskey remained undamaged and secure.

"Can't worry about it now. The only place to put him." Tom scrambled about, moving what he could. "Okay, I made enough space to lay him out flat. He won't fall off. Too crowded by half. Best we can do.

We can take him to the Little Creek clinic. Hurry. Let's get out of here before the law shows up." He gave a wry smile.

It was a dangerous, some might say, unwarrantable enterprise his family operated these days. One forced on them by unbelievable circumstances of the crazy times they lived in. Prohibition brought the Tanner Kittrell clan, once at the top of whiskey distilling, to its knees.

His cousin Dillon, sister Kit, and he were positioned to take the reins of the whiskey-making empire and guide it into even greater glory in the new century. Instead, they were forced to save their livelihood and face the Temperance Union's fanatical zeal and the Volstead Act's forcefulness.

Hiding whiskey was not illegal. Making spirits without a license, selling, or transporting was criminal. Well, his family, like it or not, was now in the bootlegging business. Tom didn't waste time on resignation, regret, or wishing things were different. His family still had dreams and desires. Hell, it was no secret one of the richest women in Nashville played both sides during the Civil War. She'd have her southern supporters take her cotton to New Orleans, then pay off Yankees to slip it past the blockaders to England.

He checked one last time before jumping down. Removing barrels of Tom Tanner Tennessee Whiskey from underneath the burned-out flooring of a Kentucky barn took an entire night. The whiskey had been safely hidden away, across the state border, when Tennessee inexplicably instigated prohibition ten years before the rest of the nation. Then a lightning fire destroyed the secret hideaway.

Tom received an urgent phone call from his friend. "Get here fast."

He strode to the smashed car the man and woman traveled in and grabbed a small suitcase from the back seat. He opened the front door and extracted the woman's shoe.

"What about her?" Alex asked.

"Doubt if she'll much care." Tom tossed the suitcase in beside the man and then lowered the tarp. "Who is she gonna tell? The hospital workers?"

He climbed behind the steering wheel and handed her the shoe. "I'm Tom Kittrell." He adjusted his rearview mirror and shifted the truck into reverse. "We're taking your husband to Little Creek. They have a small hospital there."

"He's not my husband."

Tom screeched the gears. Before he could ask the obvious question, he concentrated on maneuvering the narrow road without teetering over the shoulder. The slow journey back down the steep hillside took every bit of his attention. A county police car sped by them. Tom did not flinch. He knew they'd pass him to check on cars in the mudslide.

He stole a glimpse at his passenger. She stared out the side window, then turned and asked, "The blue car, the convertible that passed us right before the…"

He shook his head. "No. We were lucky."

She took a deep breath, looked at her hands, and twisted her wedding band.

"If you don't mind me asking, if the man we rescued a few minutes ago is not your husband, who was he?"

"My uncle."

"Uh…" He paused before asking. "Where is your husband?"

"He's dead. He died in the war."

Tom's foot slipped off the gas pedal. He shifted gears. "Sorry." Damn. Even if he died in the war's last year, that'd be almost four years ago. Maybe he suffered from lingering wounds or was shell-shocked. Didn't die right away. Still. He peeked again at the beautiful lady sitting beside him. Long time… He squirmed in his seat, trying to concentrate on the road.

"Do you have anyone you can call once we drop you off?" *Like a new sweetheart?* "I wish I could help more—but we have to get this load…"

"Yes, my aunt. She has a telephone. I hope you can stay until she arrives—she'd want to thank you for rescuing her husband."

"Can't. Sorry."

"Well, in that case, I'll say thank you on behalf of us both."

"You're welcome. Mrs.…."

"Johnson, Camille Johnson."

"Where were you and your uncle headed, Mrs. Johnson?"

"Oak Hollow."

"No kidding. That's my hometown. Maybe I know your aunt."

"Her name is Beatrice Givens."

Reflexively, Tom slammed on the brakes and shot his right arm out to keep Mrs. Johnson from falling forward. "You've got to be sh…" Beatrice Givens. Otherwise known as Beatrice the Bitch. The woman was Oak Hollow's rendition of "claim to fame Carrie

Nation." Carrie Nation, the woman who almost single-handedly brought prohibition to the United States. The woman whose very presence waving a hatchet struck terror in the bravest of men.

Mrs. Givens was one of the League of Nations Prohibitionists' self-appointed marshals and a major confederate. And an ax to grind, no pun intended. With Tom Tanner and Penland Kittrell distilleries both headquartered in Oak Hollow, "the nation" deemed it needed its own personal steward to ensure strict enforcement of prohibition laws. The Eighteenth Amendment struck a deadly blow to the tiny town.

Most states refused to appropriate money for additional law enforcement, so compliance fell on local communities. Still, fear of prosecution, loss of private property, or one's business closure was a solid deterrence.

Yes, he smirked. He doubted her aunt would look up Thomas Tanner Kittrell and thank him!

"Yes, ma'am. I wish I could hang around until your aunt arrives. It'd be something to have her thank me in person."

She brushed a curl behind her ear, gave him another penetrating look, then straightened her back.

"Reckon you seem about my sister's age. She's twenty, in her last year at college. Her name's Kit. You ever met her?"

"I've never been to Oak Hollow. I'm kinda tired. Do you mind if I close my eyes?"

"No. Hell—sorry, 'scuse my French. It's what the Brits said when I was overseas on the front," he said, smiling. Why was it important to let her know he was in the war too? "Sorry this ole truck's not more comfortable. We've ordered a new one."

His friend, Alex, who was helping him on this expedition, funny word to call it, sent the exhaustive designs to Detroit. He supervised the unique modifications of the special vehicle.

Damn. He looked at his passenger again. She'd lost a husband, and he'd lost two buddies in the war. There were so many needless deaths. Through luck or was it good fortune, both he and his best friend Alex Stooksbury emerged from the war unscathed? He'd never forget the day a captain pulled his soaking-wet body from the trenches and ordered him back behind the lines to the field hospital. The general surgeon emerged from the operating room, his hospital apron soaked in blood. He surveyed Tom with a keen eye before removing the appalling covering and addressing him.

"I have it on direct communication you worked in a distillery before the war?"

"Yes, sir."

"Thank God. I'll not lose another patient because these damn orderlies can't measure out morphine accurately. Get washed up. We'll be going back to surgery in thirty minutes."

The closest he found himself near the trenches again was if they were short of ambulance drivers and needed him to transport casualties from the front to the makeshift hospitals. On one transport, he ran into his best friend. His enlistment records listed him as a mechanic. Once his commanding officer learned this, they transferred Alex to his squadron without delay. He and his best friend worked from behind the lines for the remainder of the war.

Camille laid her head back. *Guess she's avoiding answering any more of my questions.* She dozed while he motored down the detoured route. After he took a curve too sharply, her head fell on his thigh. She moved about on his upper leg, repositioning her head in his lap. It was an effort to keep both hands on the steering wheel.

Two hours later, before dusk descended, Tom reluctantly shook his passenger's shoulder. "Wake up."

Camille sat up, rubbing her eyes. Disoriented for the moment, she frowned at him as if determining if she'd seen him before.

"We're checking on your uncle. If he's awake, we'll give him some water."

Tom gave a hand signal out his open window and then pulled over to a picnic site on the side of the road, making sure his pals followed.

"Be back in a minute." He jumped from the cab and walked behind the truck.

Alex leaped on the bumper and raised the tarp off the wood panels to check on the young woman's uncle. "He's all right. Still got a pulse."

"Ooh."

All three men turned to see Camille. She had clambered out of the cab and followed Tom. Her eyes widened as her gaze moved from her uncle to the contents of the truck. She stared at the oak barrels stamped with the unmistakable word: Whiskey.

"Good time for a stretch. We have at least another hour before we make Little Creek. Alex, do you have any fresh water?" Tom walked back and pulled out his empty thermos to refill.

"Those were whiskey barrels," Camille said after

they stretched and had a water break.

"Yes, they are. Medicinal exemption. Contract from the US government." Tom helped her back in.

"I saw the stamp. Tom Tanner Tennessee Whiskey. Do you work for them?"

"Yes." He was thankful she did not ask if those barrels had a medicinal contract.

"I don't believe in medicinal purpose whiskey. It's abused to high Heaven and used to pacify alcoholics."

"Might be. But I can assure you, folks drinking medicinal whiskey saved a lot more lives than those who drink poisoned hooch because they can't afford bootlegged spirits."

She stared at him. Her mouth open. "Do you believe that, or is it just something you tell yourself to justify what you do?"

"I don't need convincing. I've seen it. Farmers, working-class men, and soldiers desperate for swill, who couldn't afford to buy liquor from reliable bootleggers, would drink anything. Take your pick—hair tonic, toxic household products, even nasty concoctions of Sterno and end up with alcohol poisoning, blindness, or even die."

Camille shook her head. "It's disgusting to advance your living on those illiterate souls' backs."

"Well, how about the literate souls who make tens of millions of dollars in the black market? I'm trying to combat them too. The crime rate in these United States has soared since prohibition."

"There will always be men who skirt the law."

"Men! Sweetheart, some of the best bootleggers around are women."

She pursed her lips, not willing to argue anymore.

"Hey, are you one of those suffragettes who has run out of causes to support once you got the vote?"

She glared at him, unable to not take his bait. "What does that have to do with anything?"

"Well, I figured if you were—it'd explain things."

"Like what?"

He chuckled at her piqued interest. "Just how passionate you are about this whole prohibition thing? Or dedicated, should I say?"

"You are insane."

"Well, if you are a suffragette, you should be happy. Prohibition has liberated women. Before the Eighteenth Amendment took place, I never saw a woman in a bar unless she was a prostitute."

Camille gasped.

"Nowadays, you can go into any old speakeasy from Nashville to about anywhere and see lots of women drinking. Yes, sirree. Respectable women. And young ones too. The country's number of women drinkers must have quadrupled in the past five years."

Camille scooted away, placing distance between them.

"And the most remarkable change in the 'war between the sexes' is in bootlegging. In most states, police officers won't stop a woman they suspect bootlegging. Women know this and use it to their advantage. Can't search her, police say. No, wouldn't be right. But I hear in a few places they don't care anymore. They'll search a nice-looking woman whether they suspect her or not."

She put her hands to her ears.

"And whose side are you on for children who've been swept into bootlegging too, just to help their

17

families survive?"

"How dare you try to use innocent children in your defense of making alcohol?"

"Well, I've seen the children's side of it firsthand too, sister. Children used and abused." He tilted his head toward her, raising his eyebrows. "Don't tell me it's never occurred to you the collateral damage such a law created?"

"People have a choice. The law's the law."

"I like the fact you say people have a choice."

Camille's eyes glistened. As much as Tom hated seeing her unhappy, he was glad he took her mind off her uncle. A man who might be a corpse in the back of his truck right now for all he knew.

Within the hour, he pulled into the little hospital's parking lot.

"Wait here," he told Camille. Tom returned with two orderlies pulling a gurney. As they removed her uncle from the back, he reached in and retrieved her small suitcase.

"They will take good care of your uncle."

Her eyebrows furrowed as he handed her the bag. A flush crept up her cheeks. "Thank you. Thank you for your help today."

"If you think you'll be okay, we're shoving off. We've lost a ton of time already."

He would have liked to stay. He wished he could take her to Oak Hollow himself. A light misted rain fell. Water droplets sprinkled on her wavy hair and glistened on her cheeks.

She opened her mouth as if to say more, yet only nodded.

He walked away with an image of her face, pale and still, imprinted in his mind.

Chapter Three

Dillon

The heavy metal door clanged shut behind Dillon Tanner. After nine months at Brushy Mountain Federal Penitentiary in Morgan County, Tennessee, he was a free man. He surveyed the process room and then walked to the counter. A guard pushed a small package forward. Dillon unwound the twine and poured out the contents. He gathered his wristwatch, then scooped up the coins and pocketed them along with the small roll of bills.

"Don't know whether you being a war hero or your famous whiskey name got you out of prison early." The officer behind the counter gave a nasty smirk.

My name? Did the man seriously think his name helped spring him early? *Hell, no.* His name ensured the feds sentenced him to prison in the first place. To make an example of Dillon. And the sugar on top, he was removed from the scene, allowing the true criminals to operate freely as corrupt officials gave a wink and a nod.

Dillon snorted, then curled his lip, scrubbing his hand through his thick wavy hair. Hell, he wasn't even a legitimate Tanner. If his grandmother hadn't insisted he take his biological father's name, he'd still be ignominious Dillon Brown.

Dillon gave the warden's assistant a bitter scowl, then walked out the penitentiary doors hatless. The warden sent his assistant to complete his discharge. Guilty conscience? Hard to say. But Dillon already knew who set him up. V. L. Stonecipher. The man behind the operation.

Almost a year in jail gave him lots of time to think. If an "honest" thief or one of those Chicago south side want-to-be thugs stole his Tom Tanner Tennessee Whiskey with its authentic government exemption seal, he could have lived with it. And taken his losses. Out-and-out theft was one thing.

But reliable, hell, more than reliable word passed to him through the prison grapevine delivered a different story. Turned out it was some silver spoon, smarmy, cake-eating, country club smart-ass—who paid for the hijacking of his load of legal medicinal whiskey. The same smart-ass had his henchmen cold-cock him, leaving him in his truck cab, so when they called the law—Dillon was going to jail. Impossible to prove "hijackers" replaced his legit whiskey with the "rot gut" spirits they found him with. The law was the law. Transporting illegal whiskey was a federal offense.

"For whatever reason, Dillon, they wanted you out of the picture," his lawyer said after they denied his appeal.

Stealing his whiskey wasn't the exclusive goal. The whiskey theft disguised a more devastating consequence. A takeover of Tom Tanner Tennessee Whiskey. Dillon's white-hot anger and killing rage had cooled, only to be replaced by a more dangerous cold, calculating desire for revenge.

Kicking his boot toe in the mud, Dillon gave a

fleeting look at the penitentiary's granite walls and matching cloudy gray skies. Two hundred and seventy days to plot and plan. Stuck in the state pen with the orneriest men he'd ever been around. His payback, Dillon made use of his time and befriended a handful of those fellows. A good many reminded him of the troops he led through the damn trenches in France. Decent men. Dependable men.

He whistled, then waved for a taxi. A private car drove to the gate. He glanced in the car window. Tom sat behind the wheel. He swore under his breath after spying Kit in the back seat.

"Thanks for picking me up. But why'd you bring Kit? She didn't need to come within fifty miles of this place." Dillon looked back at his cousin.

"Dillon, don't act like I'm a ditsy baby vamp." Kit Kittrell ignored both men's eye rolls, leaned over the back seat, wrapped her arms around his shoulders, and hugged him heartily. "Missed you too." She kissed his cheek.

"I'm taking her back to school; she's helping with freshmen orientation. Whatever that is. Big senior now. Besides, we need her."

Dillon shot another glance at Kit. He believed he was being watched. He knew this from the two men he already had working for him on the outside. It didn't do for lowlifes trailing him to know he had a looker like Kit as his cousin. She brushed her long blonde hair from her shoulders and batted her green eyes at him.

She was a little spitfire, a mite impulsive with a stubborn streak, but as brave and as tough as girls came. As prohibition reached its menacing tentacles into the hills and valleys of their up-to-now undisturbed stomping grounds of Middle Tennessee, new survival strategies were put in place. Kit worked tirelessly alongside her brother and him. The three became thick as thieves. They met with farmers and neighbors and located barns and caverns where whiskey could be stashed.

"Look, Kit," Dillon warned, "most households in the county know half our family business operates under the government's legal license, and the other half salvages hundreds of whiskey barrels we've hidden. But it doesn't mean one day someone's going to come along who's not okay with how we do business. I'm evidence of that. Don't trust anybody."

"I know. I pray every day that prohibition ends soon." She sighed.

"Tom, how much does she know?"

"Enough. She'll get your measurements and order tailored clothes for you in Nashville so you pass as a swell. Gotta look the part." Tom eyed Dillon.

"I have jewelry too. Grandpa's cuff links and rings, and there's a diamond stickpin." Kit patted her cousin's shoulder.

"Just so y'all know, our stolen whiskey hasn't shown up anywhere. Unless you've heard otherwise. Don't understand what the hijacker is waiting for. But the SOB is going to pay." He clenched his jaw, and the vein in his neck pulsed. He turned toward the window and studied the passing scenery, unwilling to allow Kit to see his hardened face.

"Dillon, Father's left for Mexico." Kit leaned forward, placing her arms on the back seat, and laying her head on her arms.

"I figured as much."

"He wanted to see you, except there wasn't time. He's getting our new distillery running." She scooted back in her seat, rubbing her wet eyes.

"Dillon knows." Tom glowered at his sister in the rearview mirror.

"I want to help Dad," Kit said. "I'm learning Spanish. You and Dillon can stay in Tennessee and help Mother run the distillery."

"The best way to help Mother is by staying in school. One less thing for her to worry about."

"Mother doesn't need to worry about me, Tom." Kit kicked the front seat, crossing her arms. "I'm going. As soon as I can."

"First things first. Don't do anything to screw up Dillon's plan," Tom said.

"Okay, I'll stay here for now. One of my college friends said her uncle gets liquor from Canada and supplies half the speakeasies in Nashville. I bet he'd know who set you up. I met him on Parent's Day. I could ask him for help."

Dillon jerked around in his seat. He drew in a deep breath before speaking. "Kit, I just got out of a place where you wouldn't believe what men did to other men. I can't imagine what those felons would do to a woman if they had the chance. Absolutely no interference on your part. Do you understand me?"

Kit slumped back in the seat. "Okay, okay. I'll get your tuxedo and other stuff. You will look like the 'Bee's Knees' and the 'Cat's Pajamas.' I promise."

"Not sure what they mean, Kit, but I'll take your word for it. Kit, not a word to anyone. These people are dangerous. I mean it. I would not put murder past them," Dillon warned.

A honey bee flew into Dillon's open window. He batted it away. First one he had seen in months. He took in the green trees, tall grass, and wildflowers hugging the edge of the road. It had been a miserable cold day in November when he was locked away. He inhaled deeply, and a sharp twinge pierced his chest. Was he too fixated on revenge? He gave a short, ugly laugh. *Hell, no.* And his plan to snare VL into a second hijack would not be complete until that man faced the insides of a jail cell himself.

One thing was for certain, if no one took the fight to these criminals, they'd do what they damn well pleased with the rest of us.

Chapter Four

Kit

"Someone's a very lucky man."

Kit Kittrell jumped back, dropping the gentleman's dinner jacket sleeve she was inspecting in Cherry Street Haberdashers. She took a bracing breath and peered at the man, close to her brother's age, around the mannequin. A broad smile filled his face, his light blue eyes, intense, and so much pomade in his center-parted hair that it was difficult to tell how blond he was.

"Kenneth Woodard at your service." He bowed from the waist. "My clerk alerted me that he spied a lady customer requiring assistance with evening wear selections. He failed to inform me the lady was exquisiteness and loveliness personified."

A prickle of a blush rose into her cheeks. She was used to compliments, but none so blatantly over the top. Taking longer than she should, she studied the man before her. Was he just trying to please her?

"I'm shopping for my cousin. He needs a tuxedo for an upcoming dinner dance." She tugged her sea-green hobble skirt as his gaze perused her.

"Will your cousin be joining you?" The manager stole a glance outside at window shoppers scurrying past.

"No. I'm placing the order. I like the style the

mannequin is wearing."

"Excellent choice. If you'll come this way." He led her to a section of the store away from the entrance. "Let me show you these samples." He pulled a sample board from the shelf behind him and placed it on the glass counter. "Feel the suppleness of the material."

Kit lifted a square fabric swatch and rubbed it between her fingers.

"This lightweight wool is like a second skin. It breathes as it slides and molds against your body. You can appreciate the composition's luxuriousness."

He breathed those last words in her ear, touching the fabric as she examined it.

Snatching her fingers back, she made a pretense of studying the wool and silk worsted mixtures.

"May I recommend this solid black? The sheen is very subdued. Will you be attending the dinner dance as well, Miss…?" the manager asked.

"Kittrell. Miss Kittrell. No, I'll be back at college."

"And you are on an errand for your cousin." He gazed at the piece of paper she clutched to her chest. "What an honor you chose our fine establishment to patronize."

"My father is a longtime customer here. We have an account. Penland Kittrell."

"Ah… of Penland Kittrell Whiskey?"

"The same."

"A superior spirit, I'm sure I have been told. Alas, closed, I presume."

"Only in the US. My father is in Mexico as we speak, building a new distillery."

"Interesting." He arched one thin eyebrow upward. "Have you ever been to Mexico?"

"No. But I plan to go soon."

"I have a great-aunt who lives in Amarillo, Texas."

"You do." It piqued her interest. "Have you visited her?"

"Many times." He copied swatch numbers on his order pad.

"Is the town near the border?" She wet her lips, careful not to appear too eager. Perhaps this man could be helpful.

He looked up from his order form.

She waited for his response.

"It's close. You'll require a dress shirt, bow tie or ascot, suspenders, and did you prefer the satin stripe on the trouser legs?"

"Oh, yes. Is it a long trip?"

"To Mexico? Not so much, anymore. If you know the fastest way—you can travel there in a day."

"I must purchase other items of clothing as well," she said, recalling her task.

He reached out and touched the paper with Dillon's measurements, grazing her hand. "Let me give your list to my assistant. May I offer you a cup of tea while he selects items for your perusal?"

"So kind." She wished she still held her list to fan her face.

"Will your cousin be coming in for a fitting, or will we be sending the tuxedo to your address?" He motioned her to a sitting area in the back near the dressing rooms.

"No, Dillon, my cousin, lives on the opposite side of the Wishbone split in Oak Hollow. Just south of here. I'll return to pick it up." Why was she revealing so much? She took a seat by a small table set for tea.

"Your great-aunt you said you visit—did you take the Southern Railroad route or the L&N? I don't mean to be intrusive."

"My dear. Never." He left the sitting area, then returned with a hot pot of tea. As he poured her a cup, the bells on the front door jingled. Kenneth looked up; however, he did not leave her side.

"And the train tickets? Horribly expensive?" she asked.

"I've only ridden coach. Do you come to Nashville often? Perhaps we could meet at the train station for tea."

"Oh?" She cocked her head to the side, furrowing her brows.

"The Union Station has a charming tea room. All the fashionable people meet there. While there, I could show you the shortest routes to Mexico and help search for the best ticket prices—if you plan to visit your father," Kenneth said.

"I do. And that would be very nice," Kit answered.

"And your mother, does she live in Mexico as well?"

"No. She's still here in Oak Hollow."

Had she ever shopped in the city without her mother? Chloe Tanner Kittrell. A classic beauty, this man would say. Despite hearing for her entire life she was her mother's mirror image, Kit knew better. Her mother never stamped, stomped, or skipped like she did and never lost her patience. And she married a man who worshipped the ground she walked on.

Kit sighed. Her mother was married and had a baby on the way by the time she was Kit's age. She did not even have a suitor. She peeked at Mr. Woodard. A year ago, she lost her only boyfriend when he married her best friend. Her college roommate tried to soothe her hurt feelings, telling her he dumped her because she wouldn't sleep with him.

She inhaled and shook her head. Anyway, good girls didn't think about things like that...except that Christmas with...Alex. Since then everything had changed. She sighed. Now, the family had one goal. Everyone was duty-bound; "work the family business," except she felt like the odd man out. No true purpose. How was she helping by staying in college?

Well, she'd be twenty-one in February, and she held her own bank account. If she made it to Mexico, her dad would not send her back. She knew the ins and outs of a distillery like the back of her hand. Whatever was needed, she could do it, would do it, watch gages, do paperwork, stick labels on bottles...

She took another sip of tea. "Mr. Woodard, do I detect a nip of something stronger than orange pekoe?" She had not grown up in a distillery for nothing.

"Kenneth, please, or Ken. And guilty as charged. I felt comfortable sharing a little drop with a like-minded spirit."

She giggled. This was fun. How different to be the lady about town. A brief flirtation was just what she needed. "Please, call me Kit."

Her hour of shopping sped by. Kenneth completed Dillon's custom-tailored tuxedo order with his measurements and boxed the other selections by the time her brother drove up. As Tom jumped from his car, Ken, and his assistant, carrying Kit's packages out the door, met him.

Kit left smiling breezily, excited, and flattered. She

had exchanged addresses and phone numbers with Kenneth Woodard and agreed to meet him for the tuxedo pickup and an afternoon tea date.

****

A week later, Kit strolled into Nashville Union Station's ornate lobby after departing her train. Stained glass, wrought iron, and ornamental sculptures highlighted the vast room's decor from its sixty-foot-high barrel-vaulted ceiling down to the ceramic tile floor. Glimpsing toward the south end, maiden statuary flanked the clock above the stone fireplace, representing Louisville and Nashville. She checked the time.

"Looking for me?"

Kit jumped at the tap on her shoulder. "Ken, oh my goodness, so many people. I'm so glad you found me."

"Call me Kenny, please, as you did the two times I telephoned you. And I could find you anywhere." He gave her a lazy smile. "I stored your cousin's boxed tuxedo at the front desk, so we're free to walk around. Would you like refreshments first? Or are you too eager to plot your way to Mexico to enjoy cake and tea?"

"I must be mindful of my time. I have to be back in Oak Hollow at five thirty. I can't be late. My cousin's driver is picking me up. Thank you, Ken…Kenny, so much for delivering my order."

"Ah. But I'll not abandon you here. You are entitled to special delivery. I am riding with you on the train."

"You are?"

"Yes. I will escort you back. That will allow us more time to get to know one another. I'll return on the evening train. Let's go look at the schedules, shall we?"

31

He took her arm and proceeded to the grand staircase. "I have already been resourceful and hand-picked ticket pricing sheets from the cashier's office." He passed her the packet.

They walked through oak double doors and entered the travel office section. When Kit saw the destination posters hanging on the paneled walls, she forgot to question Kenny concerning his plan to ride the train back home with her. She studied the images. California, Niagara Falls, Canada, and Florida. She moved from one picture to the next and marveled at the iconic landmarks featured. Her heart raced as she daydreamed about visiting and exploring the sites featured in the colorful placards.

She strolled to a poster. Mexico was pasted across it in bright orange. It featured a view from the porch of a Spanish-designed house overlooking a pristine blue bay. *I hope Father has time to enjoy a view like this.*

Hanging beside it was a large map illustrating the routes of L&N. Starting in Nashville, she followed the line to Memphis. From there, it appeared there were multiple choices to be made to reach Corpus Christi. From that city, her father took a local trunk line to the Mexican border and then drove on to Reynosa, the tiny town he selected to build his distillery.

Kit turned to Ken. "So, if you were traveling to Reynosa, Mexico, which route would you take? Where did you say your great-aunt lived?"

Ken studied the map. "It's close. A little town called… See." He pointed to a dot on the map. "Right about here." He pressed his finger to the map. "You must let me accompany you if your cousin is not available. It's safe to travel to Corpus Christi. However, you would need an escort from there."

"Oh, no. I could never ask you that. Out of the question. I think I have enough information. Tea and cake do sound delightful."

She and Kenny entered the terminal's dining room with its brilliantly colored skylight designs and crystal chandeliers illuminating bas-relief figures on the walls. The host seated them at one of the elegant white linen-covered tables next to the expansive windows fronting Broadway. Taxis, cars, motorcycles, and people on bicycles whizzed past on the congested street. Trucks heavy with sacks of flour, cornmeal, and roasted coffee beans stopped at the red light. They turned into the depot to be loaded on the trains beneath the station, rumbling in and out along the arteries tying Nashville to the nation's other railroad centers.

Barrels of whiskey should be readied to load on those trains. Kit shook her head. How long would prohibition last? She looked at Kenny's face. He was studying her. It was a while since she had such attention from an unattached male. Self-conscious, she ran her hand through her hair.

"Tell me about your week," he said.

"Not very exciting. Just deciding what to pack for school. When I was a freshman, I was so excited about how I decorated my dormitory room. It seems so frivolous, so unimportant now. Certainly not very exciting."

"Have you ever been to a speakeasy?"

"Lord, no. I mean I went to a place once last year that was definitely illicit. It was in a cave. I paid admission to get in and they served liquor while there.

"Oh, my, Miss Kittrell."

Was he panning her innocence? This time she did not even blush.

"Do you have a college chum in Nashville? A girlfriend you could stay with, so you need not return on the night train?" he asked.

"Well, there's Evie. She was not my roommate. She lived across the hall from me at school."

"Next time you come to Nashville, make plans to stay with her and I'll take you both out. There's a classy speakeasy downtown connected to one of the nicer hotels. They don't serve bathtub gin. Their bar selections are genuine labels, the real stuff."

"How do you know that?"

"I know the manager." Kit raised her brows at him. "You don't believe me? I'll introduce you," Kenneth said, then glanced about the room. "I bet you could meet anyone of these persons there any night of the week."

Kit looked at the patrons in the restaurant. It was an impressive array of Nashville's finest, affluence, and culture on full display. There were, however, enough young people in the crowd whose fascination with automobiles, planes, music, fashion, and forbidden liquor Kit felt sure matched hers. She wanted to share in their youthful exuberance, their pursuit of fun in this new age. She wanted to be a part of every bit of the excitement.

As absurd as it seemed, she didn't object when Kenny bought a ticket to accompany her back to Oak Hollow. "It seems like an enormous waste of money," she commented as he assisted her into their train car. However, having such a handsome gentleman carry her package was nice.

"If I had taken you to a picture show and dinner, the cost would have run the same. Besides, it will allow me to visit your hometown."

During the train ride to Oak Hollow, they made plans for her stay-over in Nashville with her friend Evie.

"I'll take both you girls to the swankiest speakeasy in Nashville. I'll call my friend Martin and we'll make it a foursome," Ken promised.

"Evie will jump at the chance to go. Summer has been so boring."

Ken dropped his arm from the back of her seat to around her shoulders. Not wanting to appear prudish, she pretended to straighten the tuxedo box, shrugging off his embrace.

She peeped at Kenneth again with half-closed eyes. If what he said was true about knowing the Nashville speakeasy manager, maybe she could find out if any of their missing Tom Tanner Tennessee Whiskey had made its way to their establishment. Dillon would like to know this.

"You said your ride will be waiting when we arrive. It seems your family doesn't allow you much independence." Ken squeezed her hand just as the train stopped. He walked her outside Oak Hollow's train station, carrying her package to the waiting cars and taxis in the parking area.

"What will you do while you wait for your return train?" Kit asked.

Ken looked up and down Oak Hollow's town square. "I'll take a walk. You have a hotel. I can get a good meal there."

"Oh, I wish I could dine with you and then give

you a tour. But Marcos is waiting for me. He's my cousin's driver. Come." She clasped his arm. "I'll introduce you.

"Marcos, this is my friend, Kenny Woodard." Ken handed him the boxed tuxedo. "He has an aunt who lives close to Father, in Amarillo, didn't you say?"

"Did I?" Ken stood back as Marcos lifted the trunk lid.

Marcos placed the box in the trunk. "You must mean another town. Amarillo is far from the border," he stated. "Annaville. You must be thinking about Annaville, Texas, close to Reynosa?" Marcos opened the car door for Kit, never taking his eyes off Ken.

"Yeah, that's it. Annaville. Well, goodbye, Miss Kittrell. I'll call you this week."

Kit waved enthusiastically from her window and sat back comfortably in the car's leather seats. As she turned toward Marcos, he adjusted his rearview mirror, watching Kenny with a strange look on his face before he sped off.

Chapter Five

Cammie

"Excuse me. Excuse me. Sorry."

Camille Johnson recognized the voice before she heard the shuffling back and forth in the pew behind her.

"You're fine. We've got plenty of room. We'll just squeeze you in here."

She could almost see the welcoming smile on the woman's face as she made space for Tom Kittrell. Cammie turned her head over her shoulder. It was him. She dared not meet his eyes.

"Please rise. Join us in singing..." Members of the packed Methodist church rose in unison.

"Holy, Holy..." the congregation sang. Goose bumps rose on her arms as a rich baritone voice sang from behind. *Oh, Mother of Pearl.* She felt her cheeks redden even more after realizing she had sworn in church. It was a brief church service. The town's inhabitants were taking part in the church's bazaar that afternoon to raise funds for the Sunday school addition.

Refusing to look at Tom Kittrell, she kept her chin pressed to her chest as she exited the front doors of the church. Her aunt greeted the minister, whose solemn face spoke volumes as he patiently listened to recommendations for a future sermon. The clergyman looked up, spotted Tom, and reached out his hand.

"Tom. So nice to see you this morning. And how is your fine mother? I haven't seen her in a while."

She and her aunt moved on. "Cammie, I'll be a minute." Her aunt walked toward acquaintances on the lower sidewalk, leaving her behind.

Determined to not avoid him any longer, she turned Tom's way and greeted him. He was dressed in a three-piece black suit, with an exquisite white linen shirt and collar, and a black and purple striped silk tie. She smoothed down her navy serge outfit with white piping. Pastel blue and rose tulle and chiffon dress clusters gathered on the church steps made her feel out of place on the warm August morning.

"Hello, Mr. Kittrell." Involuntarily, she touched her reddening cheeks.

"Mrs. Johnson. So nice meeting you again. Will you be attending the bazaar this afternoon?"

"I'm afraid not. I'm assisting my aunt later in the evening setting up for the revival meeting sponsored by the Save Our Country Crusaders."

"Your uncle? How is his health progressing?"

"Quite well. We brought him home after one night in the hospital. Thank you once again." She peeked at the group her aunt was conversing with. "I must go."

"Wait." Tom extended his hand. "I want to thank you for not saying anything about what was in the truck I drove into Little Creek."

"It wasn't for me to say. I have to go."

****

That evening, after the crowd exited the revival meeting, Cammie stayed behind to gather hymnals tossed on cane-back chairs. When she reached the third row, her gaze confronted a pair of polished oxfords and a neat set of pleated trousers. She glanced up. Tom Kittrell stood in the middle of the empty aisle, blocking her way.

"You never told your aunt who rescued you at the mudslide either?" A relaxed smile crossed his face.

She stared at the immaculately dressed and handsome man in front of her before looking around. Two other people remained in the room. All the other participants had exited, seeking cooler air.

"You never told me you were the heir to two of the largest whiskey distilleries in the state, Tom Tanner Kittrell."

"Actually, it's just one now. We closed Penland Kittrell, burned it down, in fact. And as I recall, you just asked if I worked for them." He looked right at her. With eyes so deep blue, dark, and intense, not wavering when she looked back into them.

"No wonder you argued so vehemently. And the whole time you knew who my aunt was." Frowning, she stacked the hymnals on the end chair.

"Speaking of which. Do you not have other relatives? Someone in your former husband's family in Richmond?"

"How did you...?"

"It's a small town, easy to pick up gossip, wouldn't you agree?"

"You want me to leave?"

"Here you go, Mr. Kittrell. Two strawberry cones as ordered." A young boy scampered toward them, extending both his hands. Tom took one of the ice cream cones from the youngster and passed it to Cammie.

She took a step back, holding her hand up. "No. No, thank you."

The boy's grin vanished. He looked from Cammie back to Tom. "Please, ma'am. I'm promised another dime if you'll take it."

Cammie's pursed lips opened into a huge smile. Chuckling, she gave a sideways glance at Tom. "Under those circumstances." Reaching out with her right hand, she took the proffered cone.

Tom dug into his pocket and tossed the young man a dime. The youth touched his forehead and scurried off.

Cammie licked the dripping cone. "Do you bribe people all the time?"

"Only when it benefits me."

Two laughing children ran up the steps of the municipal building and twirled their sparklers. Firecrackers sounded on the street. "Looks as if you're finished in here. Let's go outside and enjoy the fireworks." Tom took Cammie's elbow and escorted her out before she could protest. A sizable crowd gathered in the town square.

"After the revival has ended, what will you be doing?" Tom asked. "Do you take your hatchet and find more saloons to bust up?"

She pursed her lips. "Yes, we have a quota, five a week."

"Ah, touché. Nice to know you have a sense of humor. And once you've filled your 'quota,' then what?"

"More questions, Mr. Kittrell?"

"I think you can call me Tom now, especially after napping for nearly two hours on my thigh."

40

"I did no such…" She turned away. Three multicolored fireworks exploded overhead.

"You're awful pretty when you blush." He finished his cone, never taking his eyes off her.

"And you, Tom Kittrell? Will you be trucking any more 'medicinal' whiskey in the near future?" She threw the barb back to change the subject.

He flashed a smile and then cocked his head back. "No. I must be out of town during the week, but Friday a new Charlie Chan movie is screening at the Palace. Would you like to go to the picture show with me?"

She flinched, swallowing the rest of her cone. "I'm sorry. I don't go out."

"You're not still in mourning, are you?"

"No. I just…"

"Is it because of who I am?"

"No. Yes. No. I just…" She gave him a wan smile.

"Tell me you'd like to go."

"I'd like to go."

"Great, I'll collect you at seven."

"That doesn't mean I will go."

Why, oh, why? Of all the men she met in Oak Hollow, would the one she hoped to avoid the most be Tom Kittrell? He followed gossip, finding out she was from Richmond. Well, she had followed gossip too. It was easy in a small town like Oak Hollow—one simply started a conversation and let it play out. And everyone from the grocery store clerk to the nurse at the doctor's office shared a story about Tom. And most involved women and or whiskey.

She had done a small calculation. Under thirty. Eight years older than she. Unmarried. Without a doubt, multiple chances to do so, with every young woman in town throwing snares his way. So why did he pursue her? Was she a personal challenge—to see if he could bring her to his side? See if he could convince her to renounce her beliefs about the benefits of prohibition. Small chance.

More probable because she was a widow. Fewer complications for a man determined to remain single.

"It must be comforting, growing up in a small town. Is that what makes you so confident in yourself?" She laughed as youngsters scattered after lighting firecrackers.

"Even though Oak Hollow is my hometown, I haven't lived here my entire life. When I was fourteen, my parents sent me to Scotland. My sister Kit was a handful, and my mother was having a tough pregnancy. Prohibition was in full force in Tennessee and my parents wanted me to apprentice in the whiskey-making industry without my mother fearing I'd be hauled away to jail."

Two children scurried by, and Cammie stepped back. "What happened?"

"My parents thought prohibitions might last a couple of years, then be repealed. Of course, it wasn't. Things got worse. The Eighteenth Amendment passed. My mother miscarried. And I ended up living overseas for three years. I came back when the war started in Europe. Got drafted and shipped right back across the Atlantic."

"Being away from your family had to be hard."

****

Tom

"They visited me twice. And I sailed back once. I was lucky," he said. "I enjoyed a surrogate Scottish family. The Templins. Sarah Gayle Templin, besides my mother, is the most courageous woman I've ever met. A woman to admire if there ever was one."

"And why is that?" She asked as a Roman candle exploded across the green.

"She stood up to the British government. When the war started, they wanted to draft her distillery workers and then ordered her to double her spirit's output for medicinal and military purposes. She insisted she must keep her best workers to meet their requirements. She saved thirteen men's lives, maybe more."

"Does she still run the distillery?" Cammie asked.

"Not anymore? She is a full-time member of Parliament now. Got elected right after the war. Represents her entire district. Sarah Templin. Now there's a woman who works for her community's good. Not trying to rip it apart at every opportunity."

He gave her a huge smile. If whatever crossed her brain was a reason to think highly of her aunt, he wanted her to know other women worked just as tirelessly. And on more important causes.

She pressed her lips in a fine line, sensing his obvious reference. For several seconds, neither spoke.

"What about you? Did you always live in Richmond? Did you meet your husband there?" Tom asked.

She sighed heavily. "If it's okay with you, I'd rather not talk about it."

He wished she would. Maybe do her some good. She'd definitely suffered a few hard knocks. Losing her husband couldn't be the only one. Anyone choosing to live with Beatrice Givens must have gone through hell. He desperately wanted to ask her how long she was married. Kinda like asking outright how long she slept with a man. Wouldn't be polite. But if she got engaged and married the next day, the same as so many of his pals had before they shipped out, she might have only one night—her wedding night.

"Well, if you will not talk after all the beans I've spilled, at least go to the picture show with me. We won't have to talk then. You owe me. No excuses."

With a loud bang, fireworks bursting above their heads lit the night sky.

"Friday night," he said. "I'll be at your doorstep at seven o'clock."

Chapter Six

Kit

"I'm coming." Kit yanked her trailing shawl to keep it from dragging across the pavement. Quickly, she wrapped her sparkling covering around her new blue slip-on sleeveless silk evening gown with its kerchief scarf hemline.

Words failed Kit when Ken Woodard pulled his car in front of Nashville's Cumberland House. She stared open-mouth. *No way a speakeasy is in this hotel.* This was his promise to take her to a "reputable" speakeasy. *Wow!* He and his friend, Martin, picked up her and Evie at her college mates' house without revealing their destination.

Kit pushed through the revolving glass doors; her pulse jumped as she entered the luxurious hotel's palatial lobby. In her mind, it reeked of refinement. The hotel's sophistication and elegance spoke volumes from the massive marble columns to its Greek-inspired statuary, effervescent fountain, and giant spiral staircase. Even the patrons appeared as part of the hotel's grand décor. Gentlemen in white ties and tails smoking Cuban cigars bowed over exquisitely gowned ladies lounging on burgundy velvet upholstered sofas. A woman draped in diamonds feigned boredom while her companion sought to light her dangling cigarette from a ten-inch ebony holder.

Kit pulled her gaze away long enough to see Evie and Kenny dart into a long hallway past the elevators. Breathless, she caught up with them after they stopped at the rear staircase entry to the upper floors.

"Come on." Ken grabbed her arm and swiveled her to the left down a narrow staircase.

Steamy humidity and a strong floral smell overwhelmed Kit as soon as she reached the lower level. The tropical lily and orchid scent assailed her nostrils. Kenny led her around a massive water pipe fabrication and rows of foliage under huge incandescent lights. Kenny's friend, Martin, lifted his arm to a gas-lighted sconce and tilt it forward. A paneled wall unfolded. Other joy seekers joined their party and strolled with them through the dimmed hallway past the piping and plants.

The next moment, two metal doors flung open, and Ken pulled her inside. A jazz saxophone wailed a welcome into a darkly lit cavern. Sparkling lights twinkled overhead. Two footlights illuminated the center chamber on a small stage. Cigarette smoke clouded her view, but as they pushed through, Kit made out an elliptical bar with a real brass rail and mirrors snaking the length of a basketball half-court.

Other musicians joined after the sax player's solo. Trombones and trumpet players, a drummer, and a pianist teased out versions of the Charleston, Bunny Hop, and Black Bottom songs. Martin and Evie grabbed a vacant table near the dance floor. Kenny joined them, holding fancy drinks in each hand. He plunked them down and returned to the bar.

"How does the hotel get away with this? They must

know what's down here." Kit scooted her chair around to see the stage. Her whole insides vibrated. The pulsating energetic scene heightened her senses.

"They do. But tell me when you crossed the lobby, did you hear anything?"

"Yes. The Fountain."

"It buries the sound coming from here." Martin grabbed another chair for their table. "And the flowers, did you notice them? It's their cover. It's an artificial greenhouse. That's how it got its name, *The Greenhouse*."

The bar in full swing floated cocktails from one end to the other. She took a sip of the drink Ken brought her. She coughed and tried not to sputter. It was a rendition of a gin fizz. The alcohol surely was a closer relation to the moonshine she tasted on her fifteenth birthday than to any reputable gin distiller. She gave Ken a sideways glance.

"Be back in a sec," he said as he left her again.

Laughter spilled from every quarter. Giggling girls dressed in sequined concoctions skipped by their table and then plopped on men's laps, kicking their heels high in the air. A woman with a backless dress waylaid Ken as he wove his way back to them with more drinks. He laughed at something she said before she kissed his cheek and let him pass.

There was a momentary hush after the band director rapped his baton. In a flash, an array of a dozen scantily dressed showgirls spilled from behind curtains as the band burst into a rat-a-tat-tat melody. They performed a loosely choreographed dance as if they were in tryouts for the *Follies*.

Martin brought the second round of drinks,

47

prompting Kit to do more than nurse hers. She leaned back in her chair, bouncing her crossed leg to the music. Did she hear water plunging or was it her reaction to the gin fizz? Jazzy tunes reverberated and the twinkle lights danced. When Ken left her side a second time, a man sitting at the table behind them moved his chair in to join theirs.

"A wonderful band." He placed his arm on the back of Kit's chair. "They play at the Four Corners every Friday night. You can dance there."

Kit leaned closer to her table and raised her drink to her lips. *Where is Kenny?* He'd promised to introduce her to the manager. There was no shortage of alcohol. Where did it all come from? The man pressing toward her appeared to be by himself. His breath reeked of cigar smoke, and his eyes glossed as he perused her body.

"I have a sneaking suspicion you like to dance. All Woodard's women do." He cocked his head toward the bar.

"Who? What?" She squeezed her body tight into the table's edge, her giddiness deserting her.

"Bet you'd fancy taking a twirl on the dance floor." The sozzled man placed his hand on her knee.

She stood. "Evie, let's visit the powder room. Better yet, maybe it's time to vamoose?"

Evie smiled understandingly. At that moment, a cigarette girl approached their table. "Here comes the best part of the show," the woman announced.

"We just got here," Martin fussed. Evie stayed in her seat when he said he was not ready to leave.

Kit sat, moving her chair away from the man pestering her from behind. She crossed her fingers, hoping he'd be distracted enough to leave her alone.

The stage lights dimmed. A single spotlight focused on the heavy curtains. A woman materialized, adorned in a huge fan of feathers. She swayed provocatively to the drum's sensual beat. Plumes swished with the hypnotic tempo. Kit sat mesmerized as the woman gyrated her hips and plucked one giant feather at a time from her minuscule costume. One such wave of a feather revealed a bare breast covered by strategically arranged beads and bangles.

Without warning, Kit felt a hand skulk up her skirt and squeeze her bare thigh. She swung around, shoving the man who'd harassed her earlier. She took her drink and flung the contents in his face. He jumped up, knocking his chair down behind him.

"What's going on here?" Finally, Kenny was at her side. The reproached fellow pretended to wipe his face before swinging his right fist at Ken's jaw. Ken ducked, sending the unbalanced man over the table next to theirs. People's drinks spilled and a woman squealed when her date stood with his hands fisted, ready to take on the next instigator.

Suddenly, a loud, shrill whistle pierced the air.

"It's a raid!" someone shouted.

Chaos reigned. Tables and chairs were flung left and right as patrons scrambled. Glass shattered and women screamed. The show's band and star scurried behind the stage curtain.

"Come on." Ken grabbed her arm and followed the band members. Too late. Blue-coated police officers blocked every single back exit. In the scramble to find another way out, Kit became separated from Kenny. Her heart jumped in her throat as the sudden crush of bodies suffocated her.

"Women first, line up," a woman police officer shouted shrill directives. Kit stood gawking. She heard Nashville had hired women since prohibition to serve in the police force but had yet to see a uniformed female.

Somebody shoved Kit, tripping her as she tried to catch her breath.

"This way, now," the woman officer yelled, waving a flashlight.

Police pushed the female customers and speakeasy dancers through a rear exit. Kit emerged, gulping fresh air. Her heart pounded her insides as she took in the unfolding scene. Two police paddy wagons waited on the hotel's back grounds, plus a multitude of baton-wielding officers. Clusters of patrons stood staring at the clamor, away from the police, but close enough to fill their curiosity. An omnibus was driven forward, and a policeman ordered the women to board.

On wobbly legs, Kit mounted the bus steps and miraculously found Evie sitting near the back. Evie trembled and her teeth chattered as the two huddled in a seat together. Kit roped her arm around her friend. Her shoulders stiffened. Getting caught in a raid like this never entered her mind. Thoughts of Dillon's warnings flashed before her. She tightened her arm around Evie and fought back her urge to cry.

Men marched out with their hands on top of their heads; Kit squinted her eyes, searching for Kenny among them. What happened to him? The bus jerked forward, driving them to city hall.

****

Cammie

Early the following morning, on her walk to the

Oak Hollow post office, Cammie Johnson encountered Tom Kittrell again. He drove past her in a new model black Ford as she hurried ahead.

After turning his car around and parking, he jogged down the sidewalk to join her. "I was just heading to Nashville. I need to pick up my little sis ..." He paused, never finishing his sentence.

She clutched the letter close to her chest. He'd asked last night about folks she knew in Richmond. She had no relatives in her former home, but one of her former student's mothers befriended her. It was a lifeline to which she was desperately clinging. She prayed the opportunity came through. An offer to support herself rather than continue to depend on a woman who, despite supporting her beliefs, treated her more like a servant than a niece.

"I had fun being with you last night, Cammie." He twirled his hat brim. "Is it okay if I call you Cammie?"

She glanced around nervously. Surely, this man would not continue to accost her on the sidewalk. What if her aunt spotted her? Worse yet, what if her aunt asked how she knew Tom?

"Yes, fine. I'm on my way to the post office." She hurried her steps. Tom kept in stride with her. The morning was bright and clear, with a slight breeze rustling the nearby hickory tree leaves. She jumped when two squirrels ran out in front of her path.

"Squirrels rounding up nuts this early lets us know we're in for a tough winter," he said.

She stopped. Fleetingly unsure how to respond to the man's innocent small talk. She gifted him with a full-blown smile. "I hadn't noticed. The squirrels. I was walking so fast."

He reached toward her head. Instinctively, she stepped back. He plucked a piece of thistle from her hair, touching her cheek as he removed it. Standing close, inches between them, his gaze fixed on her. She lowered her gaze, unable to meet his intense stare. Her heart pounded. Her skin tingled. She clutched the letter close as if it were a shield. Why, oh why did she feel this way around him?

She frowned at him, pulling her dark brows together. "I must go."

"Don't forget, Friday night. Seven o'clock. Our date."

He turned and left, walking to his car without securing her response.

She shook her head at his hopeless pursuit of her. Stepping out with a man on the wrong side of prohibition, not on her life. In particular, Tom Kittrell, a man who traded his charm, tempting innocent people to partake in the demon's brew. A poison guaranteed souls depended on the devil drink for life. No need to remind herself, she'd experienced those results firsthand. Well, she, for one, resolved not to be taken in by Mr. Kittrell's handsome face.

She closed her eyes. Her insides vibrated. Last night, she promised herself she would not see him again. In her heart, she knew she was attracted to him. But she would not fall in love. Far too many obstacles. She was not foolish enough to let that happen. *Yes. Avoid Tom Kittrell at all costs.*

****

Kit

"Tom, I'm sorry." Kit crawled into the front seat of her brother's car parked outside the Nashville police station and rubbed her arms. She had lost her shawl in the melee from the night before. Her dress was ripped in the hem and her bodice had a grapefruit size stain on it. She reeked of a barroom, which was only fair since that was where she was last night. There and the city jail.

"You're just lucky all they wanted was a fine."

"Tom. I wouldn't have called you for the world. But I had no money, and I couldn't ask Evie. It was my fault she was there. Please don't tell Mother or Dillon."

"Kit, you'll be fortunate half the town doesn't know about your little escapade by now. Do you think the Oak Hollow telephone operator hung up and didn't listen in on a call from the Nashville jail?"

"Oh, my God. I didn't think about that."

"Hell, it doesn't look like you thought at all." Tom scrubbed his hair. "Kit, I get it. You want to have fun. It's just, well, things are different for us."

Exhausted, Kit possessed little strength to argue or explain her lost cause of discovering if the speakeasy had bootlegged Tom Tanner Tennessee Whiskey on site.

"Tom, you'll just get mad at me, but wouldn't it have helped if I found out that place had some of our whiskey?"

"Is that what you were trying to do?" He gave her a thoughtful expression and squeezed her hand.

"Well, where did our whiskey go?"

"I'll tell you what, I'll ask Dillon if you can help him again, but not with anything that will get you arrested!"

She leaned back in the comfort of Tom's car seat and scrubbed a lone tear from her cheek. Never had she felt so worthless. *I'll make amends somehow.*

"Mother's at the distillery today. I'll run you home. You can shower and change before she gets back." Tom leaned in and patted her knee.

Kit's eyes fixated on the gaping hole in her torn stockings, her fingers tracing the rough edges of the tear against her bare skin, unable to gulp back a hysterical laugh.

Chapter Seven

Tom

Four days after rescuing his sister, Tom and his mother pushed through the crowd surrounding the Oak Hollow courthouse building. On the sweltering Friday morning, young and old men stepped aside, clearing a path for his still-beautiful mother. The vast Gothic-style courthouse was the setting for the county's most momentous summer trial. Their family's attorney saved a pair of seats on the defense side. Tom helped squeeze the two of them into the tight row.

He peered at the balcony, every seat there taken as well. Every cross section of citizen showed up for the trial of young Wilber. Wets, drys, in-betweens, and plain curious. Fifteen-year-old Wilber Dobbs was arrested for illegally transporting alcohol on one of the back roads to Nashville in early June. Alcohol made by a notorious hoodlum gang of moonshiners from Georgia.

"County had no right to take his family's car before a trial," a man sitting behind him grumbled.

"And offer no bail. Can't imagine a boy sitting in the county jail for sixty days," his seatmate added.

Tom agreed wholeheartedly with the gentlemen. Thank goodness they assigned the trial to a district judge who moved its date, citing the overwhelming public interest.

Obvious hisses echoed throughout the chamber as Beatrice Givens entered the courtroom. "Thank you again for coming with me," he whispered to his mother as they settled into their seats.

He noticed the direction of her gaze as Cammie sat down with Mrs. Givens. "I'd like to introduce you to Camille Johnson except I think her aunt would take exception."

Tom had raced back to Oak Hollow after bailing out his sister and taking her back home. When he met his mother later at the Tanner family distillery, he'd asked her to accompany him to today's trial. Later he dropped a riveting hint, telling her he'd like her to meet someone he hoped would be in attendance.

He hugged his mother's shoulder. Drawing in a strong, settling breath—if everything went well—tonight, he'd take Cammie to the picture show.

Every soul in the county knew about today's proceeding. Cammie's aunt, along with prohibition vigilantes wanted to lock up Wilber Dobbs forever and throw away the key. The vigilantes lost no sleep on their side. It made no difference knowing the juvenile had no previous altercations with the law and was simply caught in a sting to nab bootleggers. The tall, gangling young defendant didn't appear as if he'd started shaving yet.

Tom was instrumental in bringing in the same doctor who helped the family earlier in the year. The doctor would be a witness for the defense. Wilber's mother was a bottler at Penland Kittrell's until the distillery closed. With no job, she could no longer support her family. A family which included a younger sister and brother.

"Hear ye, hear ye. All rise," the bailiff announced. Instantly, the hum of conversations ceased as the judge walked in. A gavel sounded. "Please be seated." Reporters from the press, a few as far away as Louisville and Memphis, sat with their pencils poised, ready to fill in their blank pages before them. No one moved.

"The prosecution calls Officer Dilbert Headrick." The officer took his place on the witness stand and, after swearing in and stating he was the arresting officer in the case, took his seat.

"Mr. Dobbs admitted free and clear what he was doing. The gentleman, the defendant, didn't deny it at all," the officer replied. It became clear the prosecution had no intention of portraying Wilber as a boy.

The next officer called worked for the federal arm charged with conducting the Volstead Act. The officer looked at his notes. "When questioned, Mr. Wilber Dobbs stated he did not know he was transporting liquor," he answered.

"Do your notes also state young Wilber Dobbs declared he did not know the people who would collect the spirits once delivered because he did not ask?" the defense attorney questioned during his turn.

"Yes," the officer concurred before stepping down.

"Going to the Police Benevolent Fund." A man hollered from the back. The court's solemnity evaporated as the galley responded with loud guffaws and snide comments.

The judge pounded his gavel, and in a clear voice, announced, "Order. I'll have an order in the court."

"Your Honor," the prosecuting attorney said. "I'd

like to call my next witness. Mrs. Beatrice Givens."

Cammie's aunt strode confidently to the stand. She majestically laid her hand on the Bible as she swore to tell nothing but the truth, so help her God.

"Those who covet the devil's drink shall perish in the flames of hell," a zealous supporter yelled.

Spontaneously, another voice called out, "There's blood on your hands."

"Order, order." The judge pounded his gavel.

"Mrs. Givens, could you please tell the court, as an officer of Prohibitionists United, why the county should prosecute even the youngest among us who choose to break the law?" the prosecuting attorney asked as the galley remained on the edge of their seats.

"When the law passed, no one considered who might break the rulings and who would not. Liquor-law violators are criminals, as our leaders in the Anti-Saloon League have expressed, should be 'arrested, fined, sent to prison, and justly punished.'

"We've witnessed mothers pushing baby carriages loaded with spirits. Persons dressed as nuns in their flowing habits concealing spirits, and children, yes, children used. Entirely to evoke sympathy and evade the law. But I ask the court. How do we stop lawbreakers if a handful are allowed to go free and others are jailed? Those perpetrators and their guardians altogether must be punished. These lawless elements should be brought to justice immediately." She jabbed her finger in the air. "We must send a message!"

"Send it, Beatrice!" More shouts emanated from the back seats.

"Send prohibition to perdition!" another voice cried out.

"Thank you, Mrs. Givens. The prosecution rests." The lawyer returned to his seat after his witness stepped down.

"Unpatriotic!" a deep male voice bellowed. The judge pounded his gavel once again.

The defense attorney stood, letting the last calls subside. He regarded the empty witness stand before taking a few measured steps to face the jury.

"As Mrs. Beatrice Givens, so eloquently expressed lawbreakers should be 'justly punished.' And she praises the work of an Anti-Saloon leader. A leader who rose to prominence fostering the message of saloons doing devil's work. These 'Vice Saloons' exist—he insists—to break up and destroy the family. They have built an entire crusade on this mantra. The prosecution failed in today's court proceeding to reveal young Wilber Dobbs' age. Gentlemen of the jury—Wilber is fifteen years old. His father died during the Spanish flu epidemic—a time many in this community lost loved ones. His mother worked at a local distillery as a bottler until prohibition forced the distillery to shut down.

"Wilber Dobbs' appeal to near neighbors' charity was the family's lone way to sustain themselves. However, within months of Mrs. Dobbs losing her job, she contracted consumption. As her condition worsened, her son, desperate to supply medical care for his mother and provide food for his little sister and his brother, made an unfortunate decision. He agreed to drive his family's car loaded with corn liquor to Nashville for a fixed payment.

"Yes, young Wilber should have asked what they placed in his car." The defense attorney looked at each member of the jury. "Yes, young Wilber should have checked himself to see what he transported. The oldest ploy in the book was used to assure young Wilbur did not check the crates. He was told if anyone tampered with the crates in the least, they would charge him with stealing. So, I ask you, jury, what did this young man on trial today, witness at the time he made his crucial decision?"

Dobbs' attorney bowed his head after the last question. He raised his head and then faced the judge. "The defense calls Dr. Rupert Frayser."

Once sworn in, the lawyer asked, "Dr. Frayser, could you please state your occupation and relation to the defendant?"

"I am a resident physician at General Hospital, in Nashville. I have a family practice as well. An Oak Hollow resident, who had not seen Wilber Dobbs for several days and did not know of his arrest, contacted me. Because of concerns for the Dobbs family, I made a house call.

"I heard a young child crying as I entered the house. I observed two children, a boy, and a girl, both suffering from malnourishment. The mere skeleton frame of a boy sat on the floor surrounded by excrement and flies. The young girl was immobile and lying across her mother on her bed.

"Once I removed the child, I saw blood. Blood-soaked clothes, blankets, nightgowns, sheets, and towels. I was uncertain as to the little girl's condition. Was she injured? Her mother was scarcely alive. Then, the mother coughed, and when she did, I saw the blood's origin. This is what hastened young Dobbs' decision to take that delivery to Nashville."

"There. There's the true blood on your hand, Beatrice Bitch," somebody yelled from the balcony.

"Evil liquor is the veritable devil," another voice rang out. A scuffle arose in the balcony, chairs overturned. A woman screamed.

The judge pounded his gavel. "Order, order in the court. Any more outbursts and I'll have the entire court cleared. Officers, please escort those disrupters from my court."

The judge stood and pounded his gavel again as the fracas continued. Torn bits of paper floated from the balcony. Screams and shouts echoed from the gallery.

Cammie rose from her seat and clambered across the people sitting next to her before scrambling to the side door and pushing it open.

Tom looked at his mother. "I'll be back."

In the hall, Cammie leaned against the pink marble wall, her face in tears. When Tom approached, she wiped her red face with her tiny handkerchief and took on a stoic expression, trying her best to not lose any more dignity.

"Don't say I told you so," she uttered. "Don't remind me you were telling me actual stories the day of the mudslide."

"I won't."

She moved away from the wall, her back stiffening as more outbursts echoed from inside the courtroom. People streamed out of the gallery. Reporters scurried to the nearest phone banks.

"I didn't know." She bit her lip. "I didn't know it was a doctor you were bringing from Nashville. A doctor whom you must have sought to check on the family. My aunt said you were providing the chief witness. I assumed it was another one of your cohorts telling everyone about the tax money the state was spending on prosecuting these crimes. Or how much money the state was losing by not taxing whiskey. Which is no excuse."

She stamped her foot in frustration.

"Cammie, I will do more. Can do more." Did the gap between them narrow or widen? His ribs tightened.

"Can't everything stop altogether?" she pleaded, her violet eyes turning a deep shade. "Can't you stop what you do? And the prohibitionists, can't they stop too…?"

At that moment, Tom's mother reached his side. She took one look at Cammie and went to her, placing her arms around her. "The judge dismissed the case. He gave credit for the time served. Young Dobbs is free to go. The family will have the remaining days with their mother together. In peace."

Cammie turned into Chloe's arms and wept.

More clamor echoed throughout the public rooms. Doors slammed open. All at once, Cammie's aunt and her flock of followers marched down the hall. Tom stood in front of his mother and Cammie, blocking them from view. The enraged mob paraded past behind Mrs. Givens, several with fists in the air and clamoring about the legal system's injustice. Shouts continued as the rowdy entourage exited through the courthouse's rear doors.

Tom stood in the hallway watching the last of the throng exit. "I'll take Cammie home. But first, I need to thank the attorney and sign off with the bailiff to collect Wilber."

"We have groceries and other items in the car we

need to deliver to the Dobbs' house. Don't be long," his mother reminded him.

"I'll go with you. You don't need to take me home first," Cammie volunteered.

Tom looked at Cammie, then at his mother. He nodded, then took his mother's elbow and walked with her to the courtroom door. "Are you sure that's a good idea, taking her with us?" he asked in a lowered voice.

"You know, your father and I were at extreme opposites over how and who was attempting to take control of the distillery businesses in these parts before we were married. If you can believe it, he was trying to court me in the middle of all our troubles. I wasn't interested in any of his obnoxious attention."

Tom's mother's cheeks reddened. "What happened?"

"Your father suggested we join forces and solve the problem together. Working alongside him allowed me to see how dedicated he was, how honest his feelings were…and I don't mean about me. Just a suggestion. Think about how you can help the Dobbs children. Ask her to help." She glanced at Cammie. "She will not be alone in seeing the enormous impact of spending our time and resources on banning alcohol while ignoring wider societal evils."

Tom patted his mother's arm. "You go on ahead with Cammie. Here's my car key. Our attorney can drop me and Wilber off."

Chapter Eight

Dillon

"Thanks for driving over. Read this." Dillon handed Tom a folded letter. The two cousins stood on the family's expansive wrap-around porch the morning after the Dobbs trial.

"Any idea who's behind it?" Tom pursued the document again.

"No. Had a Nashville postmark. Was in yesterday's mail to our lawyer. The only address is the one in the letter, a post office box number. Never heard of CBA and Associates."

"Hmm. 'Offer substantial remuneration for a majority interest in Tom Tanner Tennessee Whiskey.' Don't beat around the bush, do they?" Tom handed the letter back.

"It's addressed to the both of us, even though Kit's a minor, she's still one-third owner," Dillon said.

"They might not know that. Even so, they did some digging. It's been six years since my parents transferred ownership of the distilleries to the three of us. Had to be a ton of those changes in the courthouse, with everyone scared shitless over the Spanish flu." Tom cleared his throat. "Have to ask. Should we connect this offer to your lockup at the penitentiary? Your imprisonment just being a shot across the bow?"

"Hell of a shot across the bow. Almost a year in the state pen." Dillon stared across the front lawn.

"Yeah, pretty drastic. But could be a stiff warning of their capability."

"So transporting whiskey from Canada or shipping it from the Bahamas is getting too expensive. They just want us to distill it here, using our medicinal contract as cover."

"Looks that way."

"I'll get Deane to decline it and track down CBA in the meantime. Find out who they are. They'll expect a counteroffer before they try anything more drastic."

"You hope."

"Let's keep our plan in place."

"All right." Tom ran his hand through his hair. "I'm sure Mother told you Wilber Dobbs was released yesterday."

"Yeah, I heard it was a pretty long night in town too. Some folks got arrested."

"I was going to the picture show. But they shut down the box office early. Crowds roamed Main Street past midnight."

"Sounds like feelings ran high."

Look, I know the last thing we need is to add another person to the payroll, but young Dobbs needs a job."

Dillon laughed, his eyes crinkling at the corners the minute his cousin made the unusual request. Not commenting, he pushed his hat back off his head.

"The boy could help sweep up the charcoal spillage—the old-timers hate to do that," Tom suggested.

"Very benevolent of you, Tom. Wouldn't have

Joy Allyson

anything to do with trying to impress a certain pretty widow I've heard about?" Dillon teased.

Tom took the jab in a good vein. "I don't think 'impress' is the word I'd use."

"Yeah, I think we could find something. Speaking of making new hires, let's head around to the back."

They walked side by side around the three-story Victorian home's porch to the flagstone area between the primary residence and the washhouse. A Hispanic woman hung linens across the clotheslines, and a muscular man of the same ethnicity carried another basket load to her.

"Marcos, Tena, I want you to meet my cousin, Tom Kittrell."

"Ah, the culprits I've heard about who are helping my sister learn Spanish." Tom nodded at Tena and extended his hand to Marcos.

"They incarcerated Marcos and me together. Your mother hired Tena as a housekeeper and Marcos, who is a hell of a cook, will work in the kitchen. However, most of his work will be on our other project."

Tom shook Marcos' hand. His giant mitt swallowed Tom's with a sure grip. The man looked like a professional heavyweight boxer. "Nice to meet you both."

"Let's head across the creek. Marcos was my cellmate at Brushy Mountain. Guess they figured he'd pummel me to a pulp in the first twenty-four hours we were together." Dillon laughed. "Just the opposite. Turns out we have a lot in common. Marcos got nabbed above Memphis in a roundup of people hired to pick tomatoes and grapes. He'd been making wine in a handcrafted still and the locals didn't care for the competition."

Dillon and Tom walked down to the crossing bridge toward Tom Tanner Tennessee Whiskey's distillery. The building had changed little in the past fifty years. The crucial difference today was the two guards stationed at the entrance and another patrolling the perimeter. A requirement once nationwide prohibition was enacted. Not for federal statutes, but for protecting the distillery against lawbreakers wanting the whiskey for themselves.

The other pain in their side was prohibition forces were becoming increasingly vigilant. At distilleries across the nation—law enforcement agents entered federally licensed distilleries and destroyed what they deemed excess production for medicinal and military needs. Tom Tanner Tennessee Whiskey Distillery or any other contracted distillery was subject to unannounced visits by government goons. Dillon had witnessed the act firsthand. The subsequent count to determine overage was what the agents found first, then confiscation. What followed afterward was a rollout smashing barrels and draining whiskey into the nearest gutter or creek.

So vilified by this action and the confiscation of whiskey from citizens in rural communities across Tennessee, he and Tom had a running list of former whiskey suppliers pleading for them to buy their barrels dirt cheap. A handful needed the money to survive, others simply took the loss rather than see their life's blood, their craft, and their art destroyed.

And it was like art, Dillon reflected. Destroying aged whiskey was like slashing a rare painting because you were personally offended by its presence.

"I have the rest of the barrels I brought down from Kentucky ready to sail tomorrow," Tom said.

"It's a good thing. We're due. Those inspection thugs haven't shown up here since I was released from prison. I can feel it. Something's about to happen," Dillon warned.

"I'll get these barrels to Mobile before anyone can trace them to us. I sent the first last week. I'm taking the rest down myself. Might be a month before I get back." They entered the distillery and climbed upstairs to the offices. Tom circled behind his desk and entered the walk-in vault. He grabbed two bullet cartridge boxes.

"Damn, hate you'll be gone a whole month." Dillon eyed Tom as he took his pistol out and rotated its cylinder. "I have Marcos helping me and another man working on the inside. He can get me more info on where they hid my whiskey after they stole it."

"You know for certain who took it?" Tom asked.

Dillon nodded his head. "I have an unbelievable lead. Got a few more things to put together before I act, but I have a check and the name of the man who bankrolled the job. The bribes alone had to cost a pretty penny."

"It shouldn't take me longer than a month. In the meantime, is there any way Kit can help you out that won't land her in a hot mess?" Tom asked.

"I'll think on it," Dillon said.

"I promise I'll be back to help. It's personal to me too—what happened to you."

"Nothing has changed since I was released. We'd know if the stolen whiskey surfaced. This leads me to believe it's still hidden until things cool down. My plan stays the same. Going to get my whiskey back and someone's going to get their 'just desserts' handed to them."

Chapter Nine

Tom

A funny feeling coursed through Tom's belly, standing on the wharf the next morning at sunrise. An unexplained premonition. Late August or early September was a perfect time for rafting. The river ran low and calm. He had transported whiskey barrels down the Duck River to his longtime friend's waterfront dock near Centerville, Tennessee, since he came back from the war. Hugh Thibodeaux owned the largest lumber mill in the state. Barrels of whiskey were easily transported in the trucks entering and exiting the mill property daily. From there, they trucked the whiskey to Mobile and then shipped it across the gulf to Galveston.

In Galveston, they shipped the whiskey to the California markets. They paid top dollar for genuine Tennessee whiskey. Thirsty clients were clamoring for unadulterated whiskey. Assuring quality and quantity was the only way to preserve their brand for when prohibition was repealed.

The Wilber Dobbs' trial delayed this last raft trip. He wished he'd had time to visit Cammie before he left. *When I get back.* He ran his hand through his hair. His mother planted a seed, an idea. Meet Cammie in the middle. Perhaps it happened that afternoon at the

Dobbs' house? A way for them to put their differences aside.

He hoped he had made inroads, changing Cammie's opinion of him. She worked alongside his mother that afternoon, bringing some normalcy to the Dobbs' household. She helped clean, cook, and even played with the little girl before his mother suggested he take her home before her aunt missed her.

He blew out a deep breath. If nothing happened in the meantime, to screw up the journey.

Tom slung his knapsack over his back. He secured everything for his three-man crew and one teenage son for their trip down the Duck River. A journey they made half a dozen times before. With a bit of luck, his last trip. One he hoped would not be any different from the others.

Vern, his chief oarsman, and young son stood alone at the pier's end. His twelve barrels of whiskey were loaded, secured, and covered with tarp on the handcrafted cottonwood and poplar flatbed vessel, which was more barge than raft.

Blue jays cawed overhead, and a large fish jumped in the calm waters beyond the dock. He speculated this trip might be more dangerous. A sour taste was left in a few mouths after losing the court case against Wilber Dobbs. The unrelenting determination to spike a dent in those fighting against prohibition like him had increased. If authorities could upend this trip down the river, they would. If that were the case, someone squealed.

"Where's the rest of my crew?" Tom asked.

"Don't reckon I know," Vern said as a truck's engine roared up along with another loud vehicle.

"Guess it's them now."

"Hell, I've told them not to drop off right here at the dock." Tom gritted his teeth, then jumped on board the raft and started untying the ropes.

At the sound of tramping footsteps, he turned around. Eight men dressed in federal agent blue trekked through the bank of cedar trees. Rifles pointed at him. Another car could be heard driving up and its doors slammed. The minute he raised his hands in surrender, Cammie and her aunt came through the same tree line.

Beatrice Givens marched between the uniformed men and pushed herself in front of the squad. He had never seen a woman so furious. Furious and triumphant. Cammie tried to pull her aunt back behind the gun barrels, but Mrs. Givens insisted on being at the front.

"Bennie, fetch me my ax," the woman demanded.

A boy, not over twelve, scampered around the uniformed troops and handed Beatrice a twenty-inch hatchet. The metal-edged blade glimmered in the morning sun.

"I reckon I'll be doing the first honors here. How nice of you to position those devil barrels over the water. We won't have to soil city streets by hacking them in town." She raised her ax threateningly.

The lead officer lifted his firearm in the air and stepped forward, exhorting his authority. "I'll be getting these criminals off the barge first."

"I just might give that there varmint a whack too." Beatrice sneered, not stepping out of the way.

"No, Aunt Beatrice." Cammie pleaded, grabbing her aunt's arm.

Tom turned to Vern. "You and your son stay here. Don't leave the raft."

Tom nodded his head at the officer and leaped back onto the dock. He walked cautiously down the dock, with his hands still in the air, keeping a watchful eye on Beatrice. As he drew even with her, he winked.

Infuriated, she spat in his face, then slashed the hatchet downward.

He dodged her weaving arm, then circled her and grabbed Cammie around the waist. With his other hand, he pulled from his jacket a Colt 45 and brandished it in front of the armed men.

"Anyone make one sudden move and she's dead." He pulled Cammie to his body and walked backward to the barge, his pistol barrel lodged under her chin.

"Vern, you, and your boy untie the ropes and get ready to shove off. We are taking us a little trip."

The federal agents remained stationed; their guns trained on Tom. They stared in open amazement as he dragged Cammie on board and stood in the raft's center with his arms still around her.

Vern and his son let loose the last rigging tethering them to the dock.

"Captain, you are not going to let them get away!" Beatrice Givens screeched.

"Shove off, boys," Tom shouted.

"They're headed to the fireboat. Gonna try to chase us down," Vern hollered.

"Let 'em try. Took care of that last night. Figured they might try and follow. Ain't got enough fuel to reach the channel."

Within seconds, they were in the river's main current, moving downstream at a good clip.

"Damn glad you came with your aunt. Not so sure if I had taken your aunt captive the feds wouldn't have 'accidentally' shot her," Tom chortled as he released Cammie.

Cammie whirled on him, shoving against his chest. She stepped toward the raft's edge scanning the receding shoreline.

Damn, not going to try and jump off. For a moment, he was frightened she might just do that. "Don't even think about it," he warned edging closer to her.

"Just let me off at the next bend. I'll walk back." She extended her arm palm up to create space between them.

"Sorry, sister." He grabbed Cammie's forearm and yanked her to the center of the raft. "With this current, the strongest swimmers would have a tough time making it ashore," he warned.

She gave him a scathing look and jerked her arm back. She stomped over to a wood plank stack and plopped down.

Tom occupied himself steering the tiller, making sure they stayed in the middle of the river. While Vern used the pike pole to push away driftwood, his son ambled toward Cammie. The normally quiet boy introduced himself. Maybe he was putting in a good word about him to relieve her fears. As if she'd believe anything good about him at this stage.

"Will you be letting me go ashore soon?" she asked when they had traveled at least two miles. "You're far enough away from the authorities. You know I won't tell anyone where you're headed,"

"Yeah, one thing I know about you. You're not a snitch. But, sweetheart, everyone up and down the river knows where these barrels are going. Mobile." He heard her deep intake of breath. "Don't worry. Don't plan on keeping you on board long."

He stocked the flatbed raft with provisions for a makeshift camp of five men. No women. There was a tarped area for sleeping or staying dry. In the center hull was a miniature cooking pot and stove and no bathroom facilities at all. Tom observed Cammie checking the "accommodations" and left her to do her own thinking while he spoke to Vern.

"Once we get to Crow Island Bend, I'll send Vern to get a lay of the land. If it looks okay, I'll release you there," Tom explained as he coiled the tow ropes into a neat pile. "But it looks like you'll have to spend the first night on board with us."

"No. Just let me off now." She scanned the shoreline. "I can find my way back. I'll not stay another hour on this raft." She slammed her hands on her hips.

"Why so anxious to get back? I'd not be eager to be around a woman who weaves a hatchet about."

"You just held a gun to my head!"

He nodded his head in agreement. "Yeah. Still…"

"I have. I plan…"

"A plan?"

"I was going to leave Oak…What does it matter? You know you'll go to jail. They'll catch you and people like my aunt will be the least of your worries." Cammie clamped her lips together and crossed her arms over her chest.

"Federal troops come and go. Six months from now, there won't be a witness in sight to recount what happened today except you and your aunt."

"You could have run away when those officers showed up. Everyone knows it was you who helped

Wilber Dobbs get released from jail. They would have looked the other way. No one would shoot you. They just wanted to bust these barrels."

Leaning in closer, he propped one arm on a whiskey barrel, drawing in a breath before speaking. "If you think that's all that would have satisfied your aunt, you're not as smart as I think you are.

"Do you mind filling in the gaps, since we have a while to chat? How'd your aunt find out about my trek here and how'd she muster troops so fast?"

Cammie shrugged her shoulders and held her floral cotton dress' hem when a stiff breeze blew. She looked at him, shading her eyes under her straw hat. "I overheard my aunt talking to a handful of men last night. They were at the house pretty late. Their meeting wasn't out of the ordinary. It happens a lot. This morning she woke me early. She told me to put on my prettiest dress. Said it was a special day."

Cammie smoothed her hands down her sides, clasped her hands, and twisted her wedding rings. "I had no idea where we were going."

"Did you know those men you saw her talking with?"

"No. They came in on the Nashville train."

"Just need to know if there's a swamp creature out there playing both sides."

Tom thought about Dillon and his plan for revenge on the man who set him up. The minute he could, he'd warn Dillon there must be a body snooping around their distillery, looking to make an extra buck by turning in their movements. Or was it more serious? Was it linked to the same person or people who set Dillon up? And was it related to CBA and the offer to buy them out?

****

They breached a little island at dusk and let Cammie off to relieve herself while they tied up. That evening, Vern's son helped set up a cot beneath the tented tarp for Cammie to sleep on. She seemed oddly resigned at being taken hostage, but Tom sensed her uncertainty about the situation he placed her in.

"Do you mind if I stay out here with you?" she asked, biting her lip. "It's hot beneath the tarp."

"Not at all. Vern's taking first watch." He covered their frying pan and pot with a tarp. Patrols cruising up and down the waterway at night would check anything reflective.

"I'm grabbing some shuteye myself before I relieve Vern." Tom dragged a canvas roll from a pile and covered the wood planks, making a pallet. He sat down on the edge and leaned his head back against a barrel leaving room for Cammie. She wandered over and crawled next to him, facing away, her back almost touching his. Gentle waves lapped against the hull, swaying the raft. Within minutes of shutting her eyes, she nodded off to sleep.

Shortly after midnight, he shook her shoulder. "Come on, it's my shift. Let's get you inside the tarp. It's cooler now."

He helped her to her cot and then joined Vern on the port side lookout.

"You hear it?" Vern asked.

"Yeah." Distinctive motor sounds echoed along the river, then Tom caught the outline of a patrol boat cruising the main channel. The two men hunkered down and watched as the river patrol boat shone a threatening beam in their direction.

"They'll be back." Tom glanced at the lean-to. If Cammie woke, would she try to alert the authorities? He had no idea where her sympathies lay.

By the time she came outside the next morning, they had already pushed off. The boat and its contents rolled with the swift current the entire day. Cammie held onto the ropes that secured the barrels as they moved along. It freed him to navigate without worrying about her actions.

The sun grew lower in the sky in the late afternoon, but the heat did not lessen. As the sun set in the evening, they moored in an isolated inlet. Vern and his son disembarked and trekked to the nearby town.

"It will be a few hours before they hike back from Crow Island, but Vern's checking about finding you a way back. He told me there was some leftover ham he cut up at lunch. You haven't eaten all day."

Tom took a long look at her before striding across to their canteen spot. Her hat had blown off sometime during the day. Her hair tangled in bunched strands. Her cheeks turned pink from both the sun and windburn. "Gonna fix you a sandwich."

"Thanks, it would have been kinda hard to eat and hold on to a rope today. We were moving so fast."

"All good. The sooner this trip is over, the better." She had no clue how badly he wanted this trip to end.

She gave him a haughty look. "If your company has a medicinal contract, why are you taking whiskey to Mobile?" Cammie asked.

"First off, no one believed prohibition would be the law of the land. These barrels were stored in Kentucky. Took them there when Tennessee adopted prohibition early. They're the ones you spotted in the back of my truck. If I took them back to our compound now, they'd bust them up during inspection because we'd be over our quota. We've cut back our production as much as we dare. Can't put everyone out of work."

"So, are you hiding them in Mobile?"

"No." Tom handed her a sandwich. "Selling them. Guess that makes me a bootlegger in your mind too, not just a whiskey maker."

Cammie climbed on top of a barrel. "Could you hand me some water?"

Tom ambled over, holding a tin cup of water. "Every business needs capital. We don't make enough with our government contracts. Times are not good for country folk either. Corn was the cash crop around these parts for years. When the demand dropped to almost zero after the war and the Eighteenth's passage, folks started showing up in the middle of the night at Tanner House. They begged us to buy their barrel or two they had stored away just to make money to feed their family. We couldn't turn away.

"So some of these barrels..." She ran her hand across the barrel tops.

"Yeah. We're the middleman." Tom finished his sandwich and then wrapped the leftover ham. "You finished? Let me help." He extended his hand.

Cammie took his hand and jumped down.

Tom did not let go. Dusk took what little light there was away, and it was difficult to see her eyes. He slid his thumb across her wrist. Her pulse jumped, then she pulled her hand free.

"Guess it's time for you to turn in." He smiled to himself.

Chapter Ten

Dillon

"Mr. Dillon, this is Tena. Please, is Marcos there? May I speak to him? Your aunt had me cleaning Miss Kit's room, and her college trunk is still here."

Dillon passed his attorney's office phone to Marcos. He was meeting with his lawyer to see if the mysterious CBA and Associates had made a counteroffer to buy their distillery. Marcos had returned to pick him up at the law office after dropping off Kit at Oak Hollow's train station.

"No, I didn't forget." Marcos spoke into the telephone. "She said nothing about a trunk. Can't we just send it tomorrow? Okay. I'll drive back and see if her train has left yet."

Dillon sent Marco a questioning look. "Is something wrong?"

"For some reason, Tena has an uncomfortable feeling about Kit. Something about her trunk. It was shoved in the back of her closet. Like it wasn't meant to be found."

"I'm done here. I'll go with you to the station." Dillon grabbed his hat and headed toward the door with Marcos. "What time was her train leaving?"

"She told me five forty."

"Good. We've got time. Let's go."

It was near nightfall when Marcos swung Dillon's car into Oak Hollow's train station parking lot. Kit, carrying her small suitcase, skipped down the platform's stone stairs. A man Dillon had never seen before welcomed her with open arms. The couple jumped into a blue Dodge and sped off.

"There is no Annaville, Texas," Marcos said. He slammed his foot on the car's accelerator, skidding out of the parking lot, and followed the car.

"What the hell are you talking about? And do you know who the hell that fellow is?" Dillon demanded.

"Met him the day Miss Kit came back with your tuxedo from Nashville. I can tell a two-bit liar and scoundrel from a mile off. Told me his aunt lived on the Mexican border. I just made up a town, Annaville. No such place. He agreed a little too fast."

"Catch them. Make them pull over. They're going north, not south. If he was driving her back to school, he's driving the wrong way."

Marcos gunned the motor and pulled alongside the Dodge sedan. The other car's engine could not outrun Dillon's Packard.

"Get in my car, Kit," Dillon shouted when both cars pulled to the shoulder.

Dillon glared at Ken. He swallowed hard, restraining his anger. Marcos opened the car door and grabbed Kit's bag from the sedan's backseat.

"Get out," Dillon ordered Ken.

"Why did you stop us?" Kit's eyes widened. "Dillon, no. Don't hurt him." She opened her door and raced around to Dillon.

"Stay in my car." Dillon shoved Ken into the wooded area off the side of the road. "Get moving.

We're going to have a little talk."

Marcos followed. The two men returned minutes later without Ken. Neither said a word as they climbed into Dillon's Packard. After starting the engine, Marcos turned the car around and sped back to Oak Hollow.

"You didn't hurt him?" Kit asked.

"He'll be okay in a couple of days. Don't think you'd recognize him if you ever saw him again, though. Which you never will."

Kit gasped.

"Your Mr. Dandy was sure willing to throw you under the bus, missy, in case you think he's some big hero. Told us it was your idea to go to Mexico. Said he was only going along with it because he didn't want you traveling down there by yourself. And he added you didn't want to leave on the train from Oak Hollow in case someone spotted you taking off with him.

"I'm half intended to believe his story." Dillon rolled his shirtsleeves back down. "Care to elaborate on why you decided to run away with a man you just met to God knows where?"

"We were going to his aunt's home. Kenny said she lived near the border where Dad is. He had a nice letter from her agreeing to my visit."

"That pleasant letter was most likely as fictitious as the town he said his aunt lived in. There's no Annaville, Texas. You ever see this letter, Kit?"

****

Kit

If Kit answered truthfully, she'd have to admit she'd read only one letter. And it was from Kenny. He wrote apologizing profusely for involving her in the Greenhouse speakeasy raid. His apology came with the offer to assist her in traveling to Mexico if she still wished to go. His proposal was like a soothing balm to her bruised ego.

"I just wanted to help." She sniffed. "I could be of help to Dad. I've disgraced Mom. Made an idiot of myself with the speakeasy episode. We don't know what's happening with Tom taking that widow lady with him down the river. And Dad was counting on him helping once you were released from prison."

"Kit, your brother is like a cat. Has nine lives. Don't worry about him. As for your father, we have an idea in mind that will help him. Can you, for once, just promise you'll go back to school? Give your sweet mother one less thing to worry about. Can you promise me that?"

She sniffed and nodded her head.

"Let's get you back to school. I've got a way you might help me from there."

****

Dillon

Just when he needed him the most. *Damn it, Tom.* Dillon didn't know the last time he'd been this pissed off at his cousin. He glanced at his wall calendar. He should already be back and helping him. Not on a boat trip down the Duck River with the river patrol to every tenpenny whiskey bootlegger after him! And all because he lost his head over that widow. How stupid could the man be?

Since forever, he believed his cousin Tom, Alex Stooksbury, and he were the only men left in Oak Hollow with any brain cells. A man who'd tie himself to a woman during prohibition must be out of his frigging mind. Once tied down, he'd be more worried about her than his business operation. It took every minute of the day to scrape together a living in a community whose major income provider was being decimated by a bunch of lunatics at the state capital and Washington, DC.

He observed from his office window three distillery workers' kids jump in the nearby creek. He spied overturned buckets. The quarter each child was promised for a full bucket of hickory nuts was forgotten. He shook his head, thinking of Tom again. Last thing his plan needed was to come up a man short.

He checked the phone directory on his desk. Kit had returned to school for the fall semester. He called the dorm number listed. After waiting for five minutes listening to girl gossip, the dorm monitor found Kit.

"Hello?" she answered.

"Kit, have you heard from Tom? A call, a telegram?"

"No. I was hoping you were him. Mother told me the trip down the river became complicated and Tom forced a woman to go with him."

"He's lying low I hope. I thought he might call you and not risk being heard on the party line. The Anti-Saloon League is breathing down our necks. They've been here twice this month."

Dillon glimpsed out his window again, craning his neck, searching beyond the fence they constructed four years ago. At least two guards should be on patrol this afternoon.

"I know you need him to get the whiskey back. What are we going to do, Dillon?"

"He'll be back soon," he said with more enthusiasm than he felt. "Might not need him if I can track down who's got my whiskey."

His initial plan was to snare whoever hijacked his truck by getting that same perpetrator to try a second holdup and catch him in the act. But that might not be necessary if he caught who exacted the heist and found his whiskey first.

His outside contact made another important discovery while he was in prison. Recent hijackings of alcohol deliveries were finding their way to regional country clubs. Before he was released, they followed one hijacked truck to Hillside Country Club in the prosperous quarry town of Lassiter, only a couple of hours from Oak Hollow. And only one hour away from Kit's college.

However, his hope that the offender hid his whiskey at Hillside looked doubtful. Another cellmate he befriended in prison, Luis Zalatoris, took a job as a dishwasher at the country club. Luis alerted Dillon the club had an underground cellar but said no Tom Tanner Tennessee Whiskey, legal or otherwise, was found in the storeroom. If not there, Dillon wondered where the thief hid the stolen liquor cache with a street value of half a million dollars.

However, Luis passed on another significant piece of information. A bronze plaque in the grand entry hall of the Hillside Country Club listed the club's founders. The fifth name was Lucas Stonecipher. Similar to the name he held close to his vest, V. L. Stonecipher, the crook who exacted and funded the whiskey heist. The man who sent him to prison was turning out to be an elusive character. Neither Dillon nor the men working for him had located him yet.

The Stonecipher name was easy to track. It was

engraved on most buildings' commemorative plaques and monuments about the town of Lassiter. Lucas Stonecipher, a prominent member of the community, now deceased, could have a son or grandson and be the V. L. Stonecipher Dillon was looking for. He glanced once more at his calendar. He had circled the date of Hillside's Country Club Founder's Day Dinner and Dance.

"Kit, here's how you can help me."

****

Dillon locked his office door and drove east, two hours and three counties over. He cruised by the Hillside Country Club to survey the property and study its layout, then returned and parked his inconspicuous black car on the other side of the road. The Hillside's boundaries were a hundred and fifty acres of prime real estate, with the club situated on a knoll overlooking the river below. The sprawling half-timbered stone, brick, and stucco exterior of the club with its steeply pitched slate roof, peaked gables, and dominant arched front entrance spoke volumes about old-world charm.

Taking his time, he sat with a bag of peanuts observing matrons meet for their noontime lunch and bridge games. Their husbands and sons soon followed, attired in golf knickers, argyle sweaters, and socks for eighteen holes of golf.

When the country club concept was first introduced to the upper echelons of American society in the last century, affluent Americans used them as social centers surrounded by swimming pools, tennis courts, and golf courses. The perfect place where one's sons and daughters could meet "the right kind of people."

Dillon knew their popularity had soared since

prohibition, with membership off the charts. The perfect place where one could imbibe one's favorite beverage without interference from authorities. These clubs were private property and, as such, an extension of a man's own home. So while the metropolises touted their "speakeasies" at top-of-the-line City Clubs—the heartland of America boasted their "Country Clubs."

While big-city mobsters supplied their neighborhoods, country clubs furnished the suburbs with their favorite spirits. The slickest of hoods couldn't make inroads into society's upper-crust layers. Transactions were much safer and more lucrative if one of their own conducted those business activities.

It was "one of their own"—Dillon determined who hijacked a truckload of Tom Tanner Tennessee Whiskey on its way to safe harbors after being bottled, tagged, and licensed with its official medicinal whiskey stamp. This same person made sure the secret of who he was and how he stole the whiskey stayed safe by putting Dillon Tanner away. That was his biggest mistake.

Dillon started his car and turned onto the main road, heading north. Twenty minutes later, he turned into a gravel drive. Camp Red Oak. Dillon had completed his basic training at the camp before being deployed overseas. It had changed little. Since the war's end, the county repurposed the property with upgraded utilities and turned it into a summer camp. The deserted camp would serve as his plan's base of operations.

He parked his car outside the old officer's barrack, now used by the camp counselor. After retrieving his suit carrier and duffle bag from his trunk, he unlocked the building with the key he had made. Inside he hung his tux, then glanced at the small mirror above the bureau. Definitely needed to tie his tie on right if nothing else. He placed a leather pouch in the top drawer, then removed a pair of handcuffs from his bag, plunked them in the drawer beside the bag, then shoved it closed. He took a last look around the spartan room, checking for any means of escape. No one would leave this place on their own.

Chapter Eleven

Tom

In the wee hours before morning, Vern and his son returned from scouting Crow Island to the flatbed raft. They handed Tom the parcels and parted for good without taking Cammie with them.

Tom pressed his lips together and rubbed the back of his neck. A full moon bathed the raft as it bobbed on the glimmering water, presenting a tempting target. He set aside the bundle Vern delivered, then shuffled to the lean-to. Drawing the tarp flap back, he peered inside. Cammie sat up with an expectant look on her face.

"Well, the good news is we've fresh provisions." He studied her from the opening's frame. There was just enough moon to see she had slept in her dress. "The bad news, at least for you, is you'll have to stay onboard with me a little while longer."

"What?" Cammie sprang off the cot and pushed past Tom. She scanned the raft. On bare feet, she tripped across the rough floorboards. No one climbed the hill in the moonlight. She tottered to the raft's edge. They were no longer tethered. Tom stood at the stern, steering their raft from the shore.

"Why? Why did you not let me go?" She turned stormy eyes toward him.

"Vern said the town was crawling with feds and the

biggest bunch of wicked ne'er-do-wells he'd ever seen. Folks got wind of a story involving whiskey barrels on a raft floating down the river. They have boats ready for a search at daylight. Damn. Used to be a nice little fishing village, but now it's an out-and-out pirate's lair. No one safe there." Tom pulled hard right on the tiller, then took the paddle to push them further out. "So you see, little sister, you're my key insurance now. I guess you're stuck with me all the way to Centerville."

So upset this time, she failed to chastise him for calling her "little sister." "But you can't. Just let me go. Get me close and I'll swim to shore," she pleaded.

"Forget it. Who the hell will believe you're not a flaming dockside doxy who got tossed overboard after a drunken sailor grew tired of you? Bet you'd be a pretty picture in a soaking-wet dress plastered to your skin."

He laughed, then cleared his throat. It was an image he didn't want to contemplate. Pulling hard on the oar, he maneuvered the raft back into the channel. "Vern brought you oranges and eggs."

"That was very kind of Vern." Her hand touched her heart. Squinting at him in the pale moonlight, she asked, "Did you let him and his son go, so authorities would not arrest them in case they caught us?"

Tom ducked his head and concentrated on steering. "Guilty."

Cammie brushed her hands down her dress. "Where're those eggs? I don't trust you to put them in a safe space."

Tom laughed. "Here, hold the oar a minute." He scrambled to a spot behind a barrel where he stashed his things and returned with a small pile. "Put these clothes on first. Don't want anyone spotting us and seeing a woman on board."

Cammie lifted a man's cotton shirt and trousers as if weighing their practicality. "Okay, I'll change."

Minutes later, she reappeared dressed in his shirt and pants.

Tom grinned. From a distance, she'd appear a man, but up close he was very aware of her curves.

"Come here." Tom pulled a piece of thin leather off the oar lock. "Turn around." He tried his best to scoop her hair into a knotted bun. As his fingers grazed her neck, she flinched. "Be still. I've done this for my sister before. I'm just trying to tie your hair up."

When he finished, Cammie ran her hands down the back of her head. He turned her to face him.

"If you pull your straw hat over your hair, you'll look like a boy."

He brushed his fingers across her cheek as he secured an escaping tendril behind her ear. His hand ached to caress her, to smooth her furrowed brow, and to kiss the frown away from her beautiful lips.

"That should work from a distance." He exhaled deeply before stepping back.

****

Tom's greatest fear traveling down the river was passing Frog Jump. The known hangout for bootleggers and rumrunners was north of Linden, where the Duck River meandered around a shallow sandy river deposit. The loop's narrow neck let unsavory characters spot rafts traveling down the river, and then waylay them on the other side.

Hoping they were in the clear when they first approached the loop, Tom scanned the peninsula. A few shacks and duck blinds lined the shore, but he didn't see anyone.

As they rounded the oxbow, Cammie hissed, "Someone's under the blind."

"Here, take the tiller. Keep it steady."

Two men threw off the duck blind and paddled their small raft toward Tom and Cammie.

"We need help," a man shouted.

"Oldest trick in the book." Tom raised his hand's palms as if he were helpless to change their course.

Frustrated, the shouting man reached inside his jacket. The gleam of a pistol reflected across the water. He waved it menacingly. They were closing in. Fifty feet away.

"Cammie, get behind the tiller box. Duck down."

Tom scrunched up next to her. "We're sailing through," he shouted. He shot once in the air, letting them know he was armed.

The bandit ignored Tom, and without warning, fired. The shot went wide, hitting the port side. Tom aimed and returned fire. The shooter toppled into the water. His partner lifted his oar, navigating right. Tom aimed again and shot the oar, rendering it useless.

Suddenly their raft jolted to a stop, throwing Tom and Cammie to their hands and knees.

"Sandbar!"

Tom looked at the raft chasing them. The man he shot surfaced and then dove into the chest-deep water again.

"He's looking for his gun. Here, take mine." He handed Cammie his pistol and jumped into the water. He pushed the starboard side, but the heavy vessel barely moved. Cammie dropped the pistol onto the floorboard and grabbed the pike pole. She angled it in the water and pushed the sandy bottom.

"They're coming this way," she said.

"Get the gun." Tom pushed hard again, and the raft broke free. The current caught them, and the vessel floated away. He dove into the water and swam to catch the raft.

"Grab the pole," Cammie shouted as she extended the stick.

He grabbed hold and held on, drifting with the raft. Hand over hand, he dragged himself to the raft. Cammie tossed the pole and grasped his shoulders, pulling with all her strength. Half a minute later they dropped to the wooden floorboards. Their bodies pressed to each other, gasping to draw air into their lungs, their faces just inches apart. His eyes lingered for a brief moment on her lovely passionate mouth, then he frowned. His arms weak, he pushed her away and crawled to retrieve his pistol. He thought his chest was exploding.

"We're safe now." Tom peered above the stern. Their raft glided on the swift current. He stood. The other vessel faded into the distance.

"Are you sure?" Cammie asked, her voice shaking.

"Yes." He turned his pistol in his hands. "Why didn't you use my gun?"

Cammie stared at him, her huge eyes sparkled, and she unexpectantly laughed. It was a joyous, youthful laugh, full of relief and happiness. No tears or hysterics. She pulled into a sitting position and rubbed her hands up her cheeks. "I've never touched a gun in my life. I thought I'd have more luck trying to save you than guessing how and where to shoot."

Tom looked at his firearm again. He stuffed it in

his back waistband, then extended his hand.

"Good choice." He chuckled hoarsely, conscious of more than admiration for her courage.

He released her hand sooner than he wanted. Her hair was undone and hung about her shoulders. The shirt he had given her was wet and molded to her body from where she had dragged him to her. He didn't care for her to know how frightened he had been. His heart pounded hard inside his chest.

If the two men had ambushed them, they'd want more than whiskey. He squeezed her shoulder and then ambled over to check where the stray bullet landed.

Chapter Twelve

Tom

In the late afternoon, two steam-powered boats going in the opposite direction passed Tom and Cammie on the river. No ambushes, no searches, and no seizures. A newfound sense of optimism found Tom. The tension in his face and body eased as the raft glided peacefully and the morning's incident faded away.

The sun blazed as the day wore on and Tom watched Cammie struggle to cool herself. Her tiny straw hat gave little protection. Beneath the cramped tarp, heat soared. She couldn't stay under it. She searched to find shade among the stacked whiskey barrels, the heat stifling all her efforts.

Pointing to an abandoned buoy marking a channel change ahead, he said, "I have an idea." He steered toward the buoy and once the raft bumped against it, he tied up the front. We're safe out here in the middle. "Why don't we go for a swim.?" He sat on the edge and unlaced his shoes. "The water's calm, and you can climb up and down the raft's wooden rack."

He stood and lifted his shirt over his head.

****

Cammie

Cammie felt the color in her cheeks deepen. Almost two months had passed since Tom carried her body from her uncle's car to his truck. But she still recalled his powerful arms enveloping her. Of her breasts pressing against his muscular chest. And his masculine scent as she wedged her face under his neck. She craved, wanting something she wasn't sure of, or unsure she even wanted if she had it. An aching sensation traveled throughout her body.

She had been safe in her little bedroom at her aunt's house with these disturbing thoughts. But now, facing him twenty-four hours a day and in a twenty-foot square raft was driving her insane. When she thought about Tom, which was more time than she cared to admit, her heart hammered. It was impossible not to notice how his gorgeous blue eyes sparkled, how his beautiful smile melted her insides, or how his hair never stayed in place after he brushed it back with his slender fingers.

For those brief seconds when they lay next to each other after she pulled him aboard, she had an overwhelming impulse to take his head between her hands and draw it to her own. Not prone to daydreams, she shook herself. Why, why was he forcing these emotions on her? Emotions she had never felt before. And for Tom Kittrell, of all people.

Her eyes fixed on him, and he flashed a playful grin. His gaze was like a physical touch, sparking warmth deep inside her that radiated outward. She whirled around, her back to him until she heard him dive into the water. She stepped to the raft's edge. He had left his clothes in a neat pile. Did she dare throw them overboard?

No. There was no point. He'd come out and remain naked for the rest of the trip just to aggravate her. She shook her head, disgusted with herself.

"Water feels great. Come on in." He waved.

Was she a woman who would cut off her nose to spite her face? Ridiculous. Her body craved nothing more at this moment than a cool dip. Grabbing a soap bar from the cooking area, she scrambled to the edge.

"I'm coming in." In a hurry, she stripped down to her shimmy. Rather than dive in and risk losing the soap, she took the wooden ladder. She let go, ducking under the water and holding the soap high in her hand. When she surfaced, she couldn't help but laugh. The water lapping her feverish body was deliciously cool and refreshing. While treading water, she soaped her body first, then shampooed her hair.

"Gonna share?" Dillon swam around her, watching her ministrations.

She handed him the soap. While he washed, she swam twenty yards past the buoy before returning.

Tom finished washing, never taking his eyes off her. Did he think she would swim away?

"If you're done, hand me the soap. I'm getting out." He swam toward her and handed her the bar. She placed the soap on the raft's edge and felt for the ladder and climbed up.

"I want to swim a bit more," Tom said before he swam away from her, circling the raft with giant strokes.

****

Tom

Did Cammie think he could climb up after her with her smooth bottom almost pressed in his face as he helped her find the rungs of the makeshift ladder? Her soaking-wet combination camisole and underwear might as well have been invisible. After an exhausting five laps, he scrambled aboard.

Holy mackerel. Cammie lay on a piece of canvas, sunning. Her translucent undergarment clung to her wet body. Rose-tipped breasts rose and fell with each breath while lacy underwear veiled a dark triangle at the top of her thighs. Smooth, long legs stretched out weakened him at the knees. He hobbled to his clothes pile and yanked on his trousers in case she opened her eyes and noticed his appreciative stare.

That night, Cammie baked potatoes while he cut pieces of ham for their dinner meal. They sat and ate in silence. He didn't know what she was thinking, but he was mapping out their journey in his mind. *Where can I leave her?* He racked his brain to pinpoint a place where he was positive she might be safe. It was dawning on him she would be much safer off the raft and for sure safer from him.

She gave him a questioning look. "I never told you how kind you were, helping the Dobbs family."

He shrugged his shoulders. "Anyone could have done it."

"That's just the point. They didn't." Her violet eyes glistened as she raised one hand to her chest. "You, I …misjudged…" A slow smile appeared.

Tom stood. "You done?" He reached for Cammie's plate. Their hands touched.

He looked across the water, then back to her, taking a deep breath. *One more day.* If they sailed early tomorrow and caught swift water, might make it a day early. He tipped his head back in frustration, noting the incoming gray clouds. *Well, gives me something else to concentrate on.*

"Looks like we might get rain tonight." He stood

and took their plates to the side, scraping the remains into the water. "If you'll finish clearing up, I'll throw an extra tarp on the lean-to, so it won't leak."

He tied their raft as securely as he dared to trees on the shoreline, but the raft rocked incessantly in the shallow water. In no time, the rain began. Tom tied Cammie inside her tarp tent. At least she would stay dry. With her secured, he crawled under the temporary tent he'd made.

After midnight, winds ripped away the covering he'd constructed for himself. A lightning bolt flashed in the distance and rain pelted him. Shivering, he abandoned his plans to wait it out. Kicking the soaked canvas, he raced to Cammie's tent and grabbed the tie, unclasping it. The tarp tossed open from the inside, and he collided with Cammie. He fell into her arms, grabbing onto each other.

Tom wrapped his arms around her, lowered his head, and pulled her into a kiss. The tarp fell behind him. He pressed an open-mouth kiss to her lips, neck, and chest, her skin soft and smooth against his. Her heart beat a response. He covered her face with more kisses. He broke away long enough to yank off his wet shirt. They stumbled into the lean-to, kissing while Tom held her tight. He felt for the cot and pulled Cammie onto his lap.

He kissed her lips, her collarbone, and the top of her camisole. The single garment she wore. He yearned for her. A primal urge to claim her possessed him. He grasped her buttocks, then slid his hands over the curve of her breasts, then down again. She curled her arms around him, threading her fingers through his wet hair, answering every kiss. He plundered her sweet mouth, sending his tongue to meet hers, to explore, inviting her to do the same.

He closed his eyes and inhaled deeply; sensations rippled through his body. He curved his hand around one breast, then pulled at her chemise opening, desiring to touch bare skin. With slow, tantalizing kisses, his mouth trailed down her body and sought her breast and its sensitive peak. As she squirmed, moving her hips against his thin trousers, he groaned.

Frustrated, he released her long enough to yank the flimsy piece of clothing off before tossing it to the wood planking. He pulled her to him, lying beside her on the cot, kissing each breast while his hand moved lower, slowly, exploring her belly, then between her legs.

She leaned into his caresses, sighing content as she clutched his shoulders.

He pushed his body against her, wanting skin against skin, heart against heart. His brain urged him to slow his lovemaking. Tamping down his desire, he took his time caressing her, pressing himself into her softness, charting the curves and angles of her body.

She slipped her arms down his back and just before he urged her to open to him, she pleaded breathlessly, "Tom, I have something I need to tell you."

"Yes, sweet," he answered, kissing her breast.

She reached for his head.

He kissed her lips again.

"Tom." She held his face in her hands, commanding him to listen.

What was it? A confession about how long since she'd made love? Or would she tell him from their very first meeting she wanted him too? He grinned, pulling her tighter to him.

"Tom. I never married. I've never been married."

That got his attention. Yet he kissed her again. "It's all right. Happened a lot during the war," he said as he nuzzled her neck.

"I didn't, I'm not…." She struggled against him.

"There was a girl in Oak Hollow who had a baby. Everyone knew she wasn't married, but no one let on. Her lover had gone to war before they could tie the knot." He leaned on his elbow, tracing the surface of her face, trying to make out her expressions in the dark.

"No, there is no baby. Tom, I never married. I was engaged. My fiancé died in the war. But we never, we never." She stopped. "We never made love."

"You're a virgin?"

"Yes."

Her answer was like pouring ice water on his body. He sat up. The cot wobbled. Memories of his time in the war flashed just as another lightning bolt pierced the sky.

For a fleeting moment, he was back at war. Insane carnage surrounded him. He was in a storeroom. Antiseptic filled the air. Rough bleached linens were strewn about, and a warm body pressed next to him. He and a nurse had found comfort, lust, peace, escaping the bloodshed, away from the war's ugliness, inhumanity, and stupidness, if only for a brief moment. Their coupling was one of redemption, healing, and elevation, all at the same time.

He shook his head in a vain attempt to clear it. Heavy, dark tarps closed in on him. The woman in his arms meant more to him. He refused to imprint a memory on her of an uncomfortable, hot, sweaty tent, either in her mind or his. A night that should be special and have meaning, beauty, sincerity, and even love. Releasing his hand from hers, he stood.

"I'm sorry," he said, throwing open the tarp flap.

The rain had stopped, and a cool breeze blew across the narrow inlet. Tom ambled to his collapsed lean-to and pulled the rain-soaked canvas off the wood planks. After rustling through his knapsack, he found a dry shirt and pulled it on. A quick look around revealed minor damage. Thank goodness, merely a heavy soaking. He walked to the edge and stared at the moon-reflected water.

Cammie joined him. She had slipped on her cotton dress and little shoes. He reached and clasped her hand.

"Because Headquarters listed me as a distiller on my draft papers, the doctor in charge of the field hospital requested me to work as his assistant. He wanted me to administer the morphine. They assigned me to a field hospital right on the front lines.

"During the war, every soldier lived for a quick 'toss on a cot.' What a generation earlier would call a 'roll in the hay.' If anyone had access to cots and nurses at that time, it was me. Not proud—but after twelve hours assisting surgeons at their operating tables—witnessing God awful insanity—making love with a nurse—those stolen minutes—well, I made it through to the next day."

Cammie squeezed his hand. "I thought I angered you."

He turned to her. "No. Surprised, yes. Never angry at you. Just didn't want tonight to be fused with recollections I'd rather leave behind. You deserve the sweetest memories. Not some... You mean..." *Damn.*

Hell, he would not say anything he'd regret. "And now I've made this whole blanking mess." He waved his hand over the raft and tarped barrels in frustration. "And I've put you right in the middle."

She raised her hand to her mouth, biting her fingers. "I…"

He turned and looked at her. Her face pinched. With her fingers, she tried to comb through her mussed hair. Faint traces of the morning sky filtered through the clouds.

"I'm sorry. I wasn't thinking. The day at the wharf, I figured I had to do something so they'd let me go. I took a look at the troops. There was the kid and you. And you being older and a widow was the less cruel target. So I took you."

He looked over the water again. Dawn was approaching. The magnitude of what he'd plunged her into hit him as hard as the water from the earlier storm. He had no right to wreck her life. When he arrived at his friend's house, he'd enlist his help and get Cammie back to Oak Hollow.

"Tom, I want you to know why I did what I did. Why I told people I was married." Cammie pulled at his arm. "When my mother died after succumbing to the flu, I continued living in the house with the woman we rented rooms from. She was a retired French teacher and supplemented her income by tutoring students from the neighborhood girl's school. While in school, I was an excellent French student too, and I started helping her tutor the younger students. Naturally, after she died, so did my prospect for income.

"A student's mother told me the neighboring boy's private school posted an opening for a French tutor. I found the advertisement. It stated female candidates applying must be married. At the same time, my former landlady's brother showed up, residing inside the house. He said I could continue living there, but my rent would be fifteen dollars a month.

"I considered the school's unreasonable marital status requirement. And I thought, why not? It was easy enough. I still wore my engagement ring and kept my mother's wedding band. So I became Mrs. Johnson and was hired for the next semester."

"Rather smart."

"No. No, it wasn't. You need to hear how I came to live with Aunt Beatrice."

"Go on."

"The night before I started my new job, the new landlord approached me with a proposition. He told me he knew I was not married, and he knew I'd applied for a job saying I was. He offered to keep it a secret and forgo my rent money if I became his mistress. Of course, I declined and said I would leave the next morning.

"He drank all that day, as was his habit. That night I locked myself in my bedroom, and I shoved a chest of drawers to block the door. It didn't work. He broke into my room in the middle of the night and attacked me."

Tom wrapped both arms around her and pulled her as close as he dared. *Just this once*, he told himself. *She's hurting.*

"I fought him as hard as I could. He was so intent on tearing off my clothes, he didn't see me reach for my flashlight. It was one of those heavy industrial types. I hit his head as hard as I could. He fell to the floor. I believed I'd killed him. I didn't stay to see if he was dead." She gulped back air.

"I gathered my possessions and took what little money I had saved and left in minutes. The only place I could think to go was the Women's Temperance Society building downtown. I knew Aunt Beatrice was active with their organization and hoped they could help me find her. As luck would have it, one woman working there remembered seeing her name in a recent newsletter. She found the announcement of my aunt's posting to Oak Hollow, Tennessee. They contacted her for me.

"I kept my marital status because I knew as a woman traveling alone it afforded me a little protection. The next day, I boarded a train for Nashville. My uncle was bringing me to their new Oak Hollow home at the time you found me at the mudslide."

"Did your aunt know you never married?"

"No. She was my father's sister. They were never close, so it was easy to pretend to be a war widow."

"Did she ever ask why you did not receive a pension?"

"Yes. I told her I applied and never heard back. I hinted his family might have received his benefits. That's when I offered to work for her. I couldn't live with them for free."

He laid his chin on the top of her head. He ran his hands up and down her arms to reassure her with more confidence than he felt at the moment. "I can't go back to Oak Hollow. At least for a while. It might be difficult for you as well, with your aunt and everyone else in her sphere, knowing we spent days and nights on this raft together.

"When prohibition was passed nationwide, I

debated going back to Scotland. I think I told you I worked for Sarah Templin at her distillery. I could do it again. Except my father's expecting me in Mexico, and Dillon…" He scraped his hand through his hair. "I'll figure something out."

He wouldn't tell her his cousin expected him back home to help take down the man who stole their whiskey and, more than likely was behind an attempt to take over their distillery. And without visiting it first, he could not imagine taking Cammie to Mexico.

His father wrote to his mother that there were very few English-speaking residents in the little town he was building his distillery. No mention if any residents were women.

Damn. What a mess. Would she be willing to uproot herself again and start another new life? With him?

He heaved a cleansing breath. "Let's try to shake out these tarps and give this raft a chance to dry out. If we're lucky, we will reach our destination by noon. We'll shove off at daybreak."

She gave him a ghost of a smile before turning to help him.

Chapter Thirteen

Tom

"We're here." Tom readied to throw their anchor ropes when they pulled port side to a large two-tiered dock. He and Cammie had pushed off from their mooring at dawn, encountering little river traffic along the way. Clear weather had followed them as they sailed the entire morning.

Tom turned and extended a helping hand to Cammie. Instead of happiness or relief on her face, she glanced at her faded cotton dress and then smoothed her tangled curls. Of all the provisions packed on a raft for five men, there wasn't a single comb or hairbrush. And mercifully, not a mirror either. Her hair resembled a briar patch, and her beautiful face was sunburned. She had an ugly scratch on her arm and one on her leg where a nasty blackberry bush pricked her when he helped her off the raft that morning.

The eager dock workers secured the raft, and Tom helped Cammie onto the dock. Grinning broadly, he waved as his friend approached the landing.

"We've been expecting you for days." His friend embraced Tom around his shoulders.

"Hugh, I want you to meet Cammie Johnson. She sailed with me the entire way down the river. Cammie, this is my friend I've been telling you about, Hugh

Thibodeaux."

"Nice to meet you." He removed his hat and gave her a welcoming smile, clasping her hand. "Thank Heaven you're here, Tom."

"Agreed." Tom kept his arm secured around Cammie's waist.

"Tom, head on up to the house. Jane is waiting. She's been on pins and needles, expecting you."

A flurry of activity surrounded the whitewashed brick house's back terrace as they approached. French doors swung open, and a very pregnant woman greeted them with a smile in the doorway. She looked at Cammie and without hesitation beckoned for her to come inside.

"I know there's a story here, but right now I'll take this young woman underhand. Tom, you go help Hugh." She grasped Cammie's hand and disappeared.

Before dinner, Tom shared a whiskey with Hugh Thibodeaux in his library. Tom had disclosed fragments of the reason behind Cammie's presence on their extraordinary trip down the Duck River. With the women cloistered upstairs the entire day, the two men mapped out a plan to complete their journey.

Feminine heels clicked on marble tiles outside the library door. In anticipation, Tom stood from the wingback chair to greet whoever came through the door. The vision stepping through the entry took his breath away. It was Cammie.

Hugh's wife must have not only delighted in having female company but relished in her late stage of pregnancy, playing dress-up with Cammie. Tom gawked at the stunning transition.

She was dressed in a gold silk sequined evening

gown with its daring deep V-shaped neckline and hip-hugging waistline. Her knee-length hemline glittered with rhinestones and fluttering fringe displaying her slender legs. A sparkling headband framed her face and little tendrils curled around her cheeks. As she moved, brunette waves cascaded down her shoulders. He stared stupefied as a slight flush crept up Cammie's neck.

So much for a relaxing evening. Tom tugged at the tie of Hugh's borrowed dinner attire, his hands shaking slightly. His fingers ached with the need to just touch Cammie. He took a second drink and observed Cammie, graciously accepting a glass of sherry. So she was not destined to be a teetotaler. He caught Cammie's eye over her glass's rim after he commented on last night's rainstorm. He hoped she'd agree to step out in the gardens with him after dessert. He urgently wanted to press his suit with her, afraid if she did not know his true feelings, he could lose her.

But that was unfair. What could he offer her? His whiskey shipment, the proceeds essential to financing their start-up distillery in Mexico, had not left US harbors. He was a wanted fugitive in his home state, and the ownership of Tom Tanner Tennessee Whiskey hung in the balance.

His gaze on her intensified. How could he rectify the situation he had placed her in? His choices were limited. Dillon had to make do without him. His father expected him in Mexico. He would leave Cammie with Hugh and Jane Thibodeaux. She would be safe with them. Determined, he dismissed negative thoughts.

As Jane rose at the dinner's conclusion, she quashed Tom's hopes of a lingering evening with Cammie when she spoke. "Tom, I know you are dying to take this sweet young woman to see my gardens, but I am retiring early tonight. So, if I can make a tiny request, could you send her back to me for company after you take a quick turn? I've been so deprived of female companionship during my confinement, I feel I can make a selfish request."

"No request from you, Jane, could ever be selfish. I'm the one who's abused your hospitality. I promise a quick walk, then I will send my enchanting companion back to you."

Jane's boxwood gardens were beautiful, but the strategic placement of her wrought iron benches left much in the way of privacy. After accompanying Cammie once around, Tom returned to the bench the furthest away from the house.

"Cammie, I've talked with Hugh, and he's agreed."

Cammie placed her fingers to Tom's lips, then shook her head. "I want to go with you to Mobile."

He took her hands in his. "I'm not staying in Mobile. I'm going to Mexico."

"I know. And I've talked with Jane. She is friends with the city's Female Academy mistress and has already written me a recommendation letter. I will apply to their faculty. She said I could live in their townhouse until I found a place of my own. One thing is for sure, I won't stay here. Jane's parents will be here in days. I do not want to be in the way. It's for the best. And Jane will be sure to visit."

She pulled her hands away from his. "They deserve their special time with family. And I don't want to depend on anyone else ever again."

He scraped his fingers across his forehead. *Damn.* If ever he felt hindered, clumsy, and pressured by his own doing, he didn't know when that was. "This is all my fault. I must have been insane to have dragged you onto the raft with me."

"No, Tom. Don't you see? You rescued me. What you look back on as a rash decision has been short of a miracle for me. Now I have a future."

Tom took her hand in his again and kissed her fingertips, meeting her expectant gaze. He looked into her violet eyes. She had lost her wariness, and a level of calmness found its way into her life. Even though she was among strangers, her spirits were uplifted.

"Cammie, I know I've given you zero reason to trust me, but I promise…"

The Thibodeauxs' house back door opened. Naomi, Jane's housekeeper, stepped out.

"I must go. Jane is, in all likelihood, ready for bed. I want to see her before she turns in."

Tom escorted Cammie back inside the house to the foyer's cascading staircase. He held her hand and looked deep into her eyes.

"I will dream about you all night." He kissed the back of her hand, then turned her hand over and kissed her wrist. "I would sacrifice five barrels of my finest just to spend one more night with you on that miserable raft."

Her tinkling, melodic laugh reached her eyes. "Why did I never fully appreciate your humor, Tom Kittrell?"

"Hopefully, we will have at least one day in the city together to talk about our futures, if you are still determined to go."

"I am. What time do you leave?"

"Six in the morning. It's an all-day trip. Are you

sure you want to go?"

"Positive."

"Cammie, there is so much I want to say to you."

"Tomorrow then."

Tom kissed her cheek. "Good night."

He reentered the library, slumping back in one of his host's wingback chairs. Hugh handed him a cut-glass tumbler of whiskey and offered him a cigar. "Well, I don't know if I'm much company, but I can commiserate with you about not having a woman's warm, passionate body lie next to me tonight."

****

Kit

Kit walked up Hillside Country Club's scrubbed stone steps. She smiled to herself, flattered Dillon entrusted her with such an important task. It had been easy to set up an appointment with the club's secretary. She smoothed her plaid pleated skirt and rearranged her Peter Pan blouse's collar. It was important to appear as collegiate as possible.

"Thank you, Miss Easterly, for meeting me on such short notice."

"I'm delighted to meet with and help in any way one of our local college girls. Although, as I told you over the telephone, I'm not sure how much help I'd be." Miss Easterly had left her bifocals on her desk as she stood to greet Kit. Her starched shirtwaist dress and prim hair bun were in sharp contrast to her red lacquered nail polish and freshly applied lipstick in the same color.

"As I explained over the phone, my journalism class assignment is to write a news article about community happenings. But the key to our task is to insert a different angle into our story. Our professor wants us to make ourselves more readable to the public. Did I tell you there are only two girls in my class? I want so much to do a good job."

"I thought once about becoming a reporter when stories about Nellie Bly were all the rage."

"Yes, I'd love to be a real reporter one day too."

"Won't you have a seat?"

"Miss Easterly, I know you are busy, so I won't take up much of your time. My article's premise is to not only feature what your founders have contributed to your community but to also highlight what their descendants are doing today. Are they still contributing to the community?"

"Your idea sounds interesting. I typed the list of founders for you." The secretary passed a list across her desk.

"I have already researched several. The secretary at the Black Mountain Quarry was most helpful. So many of your founders are connected to the town's quarry. One name I could not locate any children for was Lucas Stonecipher." Kit pointed to his name on the list. "However, I think I may have met his grandson at our homecoming. His name was Virgil or Vernon?"

"I know we still have some Stonecipher's here. I definitely know the name, but not a Vernon or Virgil."

"With the grandfather named Lucas, perhaps the person you recall is LV or VL?"

"VL has a familiar ring. All dues are paid to the treasurer, so I can't help you there. I'm sure Lucas Stonecipher's descendants would be invited to our upcoming anniversary."

Kit gave her most disappointed look but knew to

press further would make the woman suspicious. "You have been a tremendous help. I've learned that without these men, there would be no water, or trolly cars, or electricity in this town. All those wonderful things they brought to Lassiter will be what I write about, along with the excitement of celebrating your fiftieth anniversary."

"Since the war, so many of the families have spread out. I'm sorry I'm not more help. I'm sure the young man you met, Vernon or Virgil… was very nice. Hopefully, your college alumni person can help you locate him."

The secretary stood, bringing the interview to a close. "Invitations have already been mailed to our members for Founder's Day. Perhaps I'll see you at our dinner dance if you should be so lucky to find your young man." Mrs. Easterly winked.

Chapter Fourteen

Cammie

Tom left Cammie with Naomi at Hugh's two-story dwelling as soon as they reached the city's limits. Their trip to Mobile took the whole day. The Thibodeauxs' property had balconies in the front and a tiny courtyard in the rear. With instructions to both the housekeeper and Cammie to go shopping on Azalea Street, Tom kissed her cheek and departed. He hurried away to ensure Hugh's men loaded his whiskey on the boat and were safely headed to Galveston.

Wear something pretty. Tom had asked her to be ready to go to dinner with him at eight o'clock. "The hotel I stay in when I visit the city is away from the main business district. It's very private and in a secluded area. They have a wonderful restaurant. We will go out together for one of Mobile's fancy dining experiences and celebrate my whiskey's departure." He had told her.

Cammie and Naomi unpacked the small suitcase Jane had given her. Jane insisted she take three dresses from her closet, contending none of them was designed for a nursing mother.

Cammie looked at the dollar bills Tom gave her earlier. Was it right to take money from him? She had a brief list of needed items. How wonderful to have her own underclothes, stockings, a pair of shoes, and her own hairbrush, toothbrush, and soaps. A shopping expedition would make the afternoon fly. It would take her mind off Tom.

She glanced at the bills again. If Tom asked her to join him in Mexico, would she? He had not asked. She held her hand to her heart. For too long, she deliberately cut off any thoughts of happiness, much less love, returning to her life. Yet, from the moment her eyes met Tom Kittrell's, she was drawn to him.

Yes, he stood for everything she loathed and detested in life. He had been a womanizer and an outlaw, to boot. Still, he possessed a caring heart. She'd witnessed this firsthand with the Wilber Dobbs household and with Vern and his son as well. His loving family depended on him for support. And for some inexplicable reason, he gave her a feeling of security when she was around him.

Did he love her? He never spoke the words to her. Or she to him. How had she allowed herself to fall in love with him? And to discover it when it was too late. Their paths were leading them in opposite directions. She knew he felt a responsibility toward her. The thought of saddling him with another obligation filled her with dread.

When she arrived back from shopping, she bundled her receipts with her recommendation letter from Jane Thibodeaux and tucked them into the carpetbag. Her first task after Tom left for Mexico would be to contact her aunt. Getting charges dropped for kidnapping was the least she could do. Next, she would apply for the local teaching position.

Tom would be here within a couple of hours. Was this evening the last time she'd see him before he left?

Will there be a tomorrow?

From the dresses Jane gave her, she selected one and draped it across the enormous bed. The gown was a sleeveless tube silk in a deep rose color. It was a beautiful dress, one her modest upbringing would never allow her to select, yet any female under forty would love to own. She splurged on silk stockings and black patent leather heels and the fringe shawl Jane provided completed the outfit.

A knock sounded at eight o'clock. When Naomi answered the door, Tom stepped across the threshold dressed in evening attire. His eyes gleamed when he gazed at her. She smoothed her silk dress with her hands, so glad she had worn Jane's prettiest gown.

"I have mixed feelings about you." She searched his face, inching back from him.

"What do you mean?" Her forehead wrinkled. Was he second-guessing taking her out tonight? He was a handsome man. Would he prefer to be with another woman? Someone else he wished to spend his last hours with? She felt so unsophisticated next to such a dashing man. Was she becoming an albatross around his neck?

He chuckled at her confusion. "Whether I should take you out and show you off or keep you here all to myself, silly." Taking her hand, he twirled her underneath his arm in a dance move.

"You look gorgeous." Pulling her to him, he ran his thumb alongside her face, his eyes darkening as he traced her lips. She could not hold back a quiver as he kissed her full on her mouth. The shawl she'd draped about her shoulders floated to the floor. Drawing a breath, he released her. He stooped down to gather her shawl, then searched his pocket and handed her a long rectangular box. "This is for you."

A warm flush crept up her cheeks. She took the packet and opened it up. Inside was a long strand of pearls. "They're beautiful. But I can't. You've given me so much already."

"Yes, you can. They're not real," he confessed. "By the time I went to the bank and Western Union, the jewelry store was closed. But a local shopkeeper assured me these are just what every young flapper wants. I've been told it's all the rage."

"They would go beautifully with my dress." She peeked up at him. "Would you like me to wear them tonight?"

"Yes. We have lots to celebrate." He took the strand of beads from its box and draped them around her neck. He stepped back, surveying her. His smile let her know how pleased he was. "Ready?"

They left in the taxi Tom had waiting outside. Within minutes, they arrived at the downtown hotel and the restaurant's host escorted them to their waiting table.

"What are you in the mood for?" Tom asked.

She dragged her gaze from the palatial dining room's architecture and décor; she hadn't even glanced at her menu. "You decide," she said.

"I love seafood, but I expect it's nothing special to you."

Dining out and at such a lavish locale was a novel experience for her. She couldn't tell him the home she was from considered seafood a luxury.

"I'll order us steak and shrimp. I doubt it will live up to the cuisine highlight we had with Vern and his son's catfish haul," he said.

They laughed at the memory of that night. How simple and uncomplicated their lives seemed on their raft trip. She searched Tom's eyes and wondered if he was thinking the same thing.

The lady sitting at the table next to them glanced their way, then smiled. Did she imagine they were a betrothed couple celebrating upcoming nuptials? Far from the truth. She was glad Tom did not pressure her about her decision to stay in Mobile. Instead, he entertained her with stories during their candlelight dinner. He described catching frogs with his friend and eating them raw, then spoke about the time he tasted snails at a restaurant in Paris, leaving her laughing with tears in her eyes.

After dinner, they walked the short trip back to Hugh and Jane's house. They strolled hand in hand in silence except for the cricket's chirp, bullfrog's croaking, and other night sounds from the nearby pond. When they reached the Thibodeaux house and knocked on the door, no one answered. Tom turned the doorknob before noticing the parchment paper sticking out from the mailbox. Once inside, he opened the note addressed to them and read it out loud.

"Jane's labor started today. She wanted Naomi near her, so I've taken her back to River House with me. In celebration of my upcoming fatherhood, I've left you a bottle of champagne chilling in the butler's pantry sink. Enjoy!"

Tom fanned the letter in the air, blew her a kiss, and wandered down the hall. He returned from his search with the champagne bottle and two flute glasses.

"Thank you, Hugh. And congratulations!" He

waved the bottle in the air. "I did not know their baby was expected so soon, or I would never have asked Hugh to travel to Mobile with me. I hope everything is okay."

"Yes, I'm sure it is. You never know for sure with first babies when they'll come." She was happy for once to know something Tom did not.

"Let's go upstairs. It has to be cooler there with the balcony doors open. And I have from a reliable source there is a one-of-a-kind black marble mantle I must see," he said with a rakish grin.

He led her up the stairs to the spacious boudoir. The master bedroom suite, dominated by the black marble fireplace, also held a huge mahogany canopied bed and sitting area. A pink bubble glass lamp on the dressing table provided the only light. Tom draped a linen hand towel over the bottle after setting the flute glasses on the little vanity.

"Beautiful," he said, facing the fireplace. He turned and looked at her, his blue eyes gazing deep into hers in a way that left her breathless. "Yes, beautiful."

He reached down and took her hand in his and lifted it to his mouth. His lips were warm and soft, and her fingers trembled at his touch.

"Have you ever tasted champagne?" He released her hand and uncorked the bottle. Its bubbly contents exploded, flowing from the bottle and down his hand and arm. Laughing, he poured them each a glass.

"Your shirt is soaked." She giggled.

He loosened his tie while she undid his cuff link to roll up his wet sleeve.

"Let's toast. There's a lot to cheer about today. My whiskey sailed today and I'm here with you alone," his voice rasped in her ear. Tom kissed her neck, then shoulders as she tried to sip and balance her champagne glass at the same time.

"It tickles," she said as she took a drink.

"Uh-huh," he agreed. "Let's sit down." Sliding to a cushioned chair, he pulled her onto his lap. He leaned back, enabling him to see her entire face. "Along with the money transfer, I sent a telegram to my father today. I told him I would need my own house in Mexico. I'm sailing as a crew member on a freighter tomorrow. Once I get there and find us a place to live, I'll book your passage on the next liner."

"Tom, I—" She hesitated, a knot grew in her stomach.

"Cammie, I know I've given you little reason to trust me. Damn, little. But I want to be with you forever." He took her in his arms and looked into her eyes. "Please tell me you feel the same. I want to be with you forever. I want to marry you. We'll find a preacher tomorrow before I sail."

"No." She shook her head at her inability to have him understand her answer. "No, I won't marry you." Oh, how she loved him. But she would never allow herself to tie him down. One day he'd see the error of his way and resent her.

He slid her off his lap to his side. "What then?"

Her breath was unsteady. "I do not want to wait for you to come back to me. I don't want to wait to be married. I don't want to wait."

"My love." He pulled her to him and moved his mouth against her blushing cheeks and along the waves of her long brown hair.

She ducked her head into his shoulder. "I want

whatever we have now to happen." How could she make it clear to him that no matter when or if he ever returned from Mexico, she would always keep this memory of him? She dared not let this chance slip away.

"Sweet Heaven," he said as he crushed his body to hers. Cammie tried to hold her glass of champagne without spilling. Tom took the flute and set it away, then raised his head, fitting his mouth to hers in a coaxing kiss. She responded to his kiss, then he moved away and stared into her eyes. His hand moved down her back, unfastening the buttons on her dress as he went. He slid the garment from her upper body, pressing his mouth to her breasts through her camisole's thin silk.

Pulling her up, he discarded his tie and shirt. Kneeling, he removed her shoes and then one by one her stockings. She shuddered as he slid his hands up then down her legs. Taking her to the bed's edge, he pulled her camisole straps until the delicate step-in dropped to the floor. She stood draped in the pearls he had given her earlier in the night, her nakedness's only cover.

The luminosity of Cammie's naked skin and the strand of pearls matched. As his gaze traveled from her eyes to her breasts, her navel, her abdomen, the V between her legs, and down to her toes, his eyes glowed. When he pulled aside the coverlets and helped her to bed, her stomach fluttered. She sat atop the pillows, under the crocheted canopy, her gaze fixed on him as he undressed. When he joined her in bed, his hands journeyed sensually down her body. His palms cupped the swell of her breasts as his thumbs rubbed the tips of her vulnerable flesh, nudging them to peaks.

Light-headed and dizzy, Cammie clutched her fingers to Tom's shoulders. His magnificent physique gleamed in the faint light of the room. She stayed curled up on her knees, the pearls as radiant as she felt. He kissed her again on the mouth, his hands stroking her entire body. She wanted to explore him, too. Her hands trembled as she skimmed his muscular torso, his back, and shoulders, rippling with tightly correlated flesh.

"I've wanted you from the moment I first set eyes on you," he whispered, nipping the side of her mouth. "You have the softest lips I've ever kissed."

Waves of excitement and apprehension traveled through her. "Tom, I want to make you happy. I want to…"

"Shush, my sweet angel." He lifted her chin and met her gaze. His hands played with her hair, then swept down her body as he drew her to him. "I need you. I want you. I need to touch you everywhere," he insisted as he gathered her, half covering her body with his as he lay down with her.

Lingering at her breasts, kneading them, feasting on their fullness, he rubbed his hands down the beaded necklace. His fingers released the strand and moved to circle her belly, then dipped to caress her legs. He twisted above her, lowering his body, stringing kisses on her naked flesh lower and lower.

His kisses tickled her, making her self-conscious as he grazed the inside of her thigh. Lips pressed to the crevice where her hip joined her abdomen, making her quiver and arch toward him. Pushing her legs apart, his body slipped between them.

Cammie gasped as his tongue swept the most intimate part of her. Grasping at Tom's shoulders, she writhed, squirmed, and wriggled. A myriad of emotions assaulted her body and mind. Nothing prepared her for the world she was in now. Was she dreaming? Were stars bursting? Bright flashes of light sparked underneath her eyelids. She dared not open her eyes. Yet she could feel a man's powerful arms embracing her, feel kisses in unknown places.

The body wreaking such havoc rose above her. With care, he lifted the pearl strand from around her neck. A raspy voice murmured a mystifying message in her ear. "The next time we make love, I will bring you real pearls."

He smothered her with his body then and ravished her with deep kisses to her mouth. She was vaguely aware of the pressure. Her heart pounded against his, as inch by exquisite inch, he possessed her. Instinctively she moved with him, sharing the passionate moment. Every part of him designed to pleasure her. Was she pleasuring him?

She dared to open her eyes. Her surroundings were a blur, a white cloud floated overhead. Drunk on desire, their gazes fixated on each other. He kissed her again, every moment more intense than before. She closed her eyes again and let the wonder envelop her. Her emotions were coiling, curling ever more tightly. She was seeking something she knew nothing about but desperately desired. It came upon her, crashing like a giant wave. She cried out as he gasped his release, his body going tense above her as she swallowed his groan. He kissed her lips as if to capture her escaped ecstasies. Smiling, shivering once, comprehending, she lay nestled in his arms.

Pulling her tight against him, he whispered in her ear. "I love you, Cammie."

Basking in the moment, she realized the possibility of—up until this instant—elusive happiness. "I love you too."

****

Loud, insistent knocking woke Tom before dawn the next morning.

"Hurry, get dressed." He grabbed his trousers. "Stay here." Snatching his shirt, he headed down the stairs at the Thibodeauxs' townhouse.

Cammie could hear a man's urgent voice. "You can't stay here. Look what happened to your cousin!"

"You have to leave now," another voice cautioned. "Damn, don't be like Dillon and think they won't come after you."

"Give me a minute," Tom said from the bottom of the stairs.

Cammie backed away from the door, hearing Tom race up the stairs. She stood in the middle of the bedroom with both hands clutched to her mouth. Crossing the room, he grabbed her to him.

"I have to leave. Word must have gotten out I was here. They are stowing me away on a ship bound for Rio de Janeiro. If I don't leave now, I'll be arrested."

He found his jacket and pulled out a wad of bills. "Here's five hundred dollars. Get Hugh to help you. Don't stay here by yourself. Buy a ticket to Nashville. Call my mother when you get there. She'll come and get you. I don't know how long I'll be gone. With any luck, it'll be just a few weeks. But I will be back."

Cammie's heart hammered so hard she could

scarcely absorb what Tom said.

After shoving his feet into his shoes, he threw open Hugh's bedroom wardrobe. He snatched a long coat out and flung it on. Turning, he gathered her in his arms again. For one long moment, they looked at each other with longing and love, then he kissed her in a desperately long kiss. He took her hand and lifted it, turning its palm upward, kissed it lightly, and folded her fingers upon the kiss.

"I love you. I will always love you. Never forget."

And he was gone.

Chapter Fifteen

Dillon

Three weeks after Dillon learned Tom was on a boat to Rio, he drove underneath Hillside Country Club's front portico just as the sun set in the October sky. He saluted the gawking valet attendants as he motored past and into the club's parking lot.

"Felt better parking it myself," he told the two young men as he walked up.

One guy whistled, and the other gave him an unabashed grin. Dillon smiled. Perfect. He knew no one would question admitting someone driving a car costing four times the average salary of most working Americans. The auto was on loan from Alex, his cousin's best friend's automobile dealership.

The valet attendants moved aside as Dillon brushed his tuxedo's silk shawl collar his cousin Kit had ordered from that Nashville sleazebag. He mounted the steps of the building and entered the exclusive property, every inch designed to convey old-world appeal.

He stood in the grand entry hall. Exposed beams and giant ornamental mirrors flanked the room from its vaulted ceiling to the tile floor. His vantage point permitted him a view to the back of the club through French doors standing open to a veranda. The long sweeping patio stretched the entire length of the building into the hillside perched above the slow-moving river below.

"Yes! We Have No Bananas" played by the orchestra in the ballroom. He dodged patrons moving left and right and detoured to the barroom. Billiard balls breaking sounded close by. When Dillon entered, a man who looked as if he stepped out of a Gillette razor blade advertisement with his slicked-back black hair and white dinner jacket came up from a staircase niche between the billiard room and bar. He stopped at the bar to speak to the bartender. The man plucked a pink carnation from a flower vase and gave Dillon a cursory glance as he stuck it in his buttonhole. When someone called the name Reggie, he left. Dillon took a seat at a table, preferring the location to the bar where two other patrons stood. A server ambled over to take his order.

"Yes, sir?"

"I'll have a whiskey straight."

He glimpsed at Dillon's flickering diamond stick pin and returned with a cut-glass tumbler. Dillon motioned for him to remain as he took his first sip. The whiskey was first-rate.

"Have you seen VL tonight?" Dillon asked.

"'scuse me, sir?"

"Do you know VL?"

"I know a person called VL," the busboy stopping to clear a nearby table said. The young man seemed eager to help.

"Rudy." The bartender's command was discernible. The server returned to the bar, and the busboy disappeared back into the kitchen. After leaving a silver dollar for his tab, Dillon wove his way to the ballroom. A matron closing near fifty gave him a come hither eye as she passed, spilling her champagne glass against him.

"It's all right." Removing his handkerchief, he dabbed the liquid. From the ballroom's entrance arch, he stood watching the collection of dancers on the floor attempting a passable foxtrot.

When the song ended, a familiar drum and trumpet strain erupted from the here-to-now tranquil song list. A lazy saxophone and accompanying trombone joined the double bass. The piano player jumped in energetically as it burst into a popular ragtime tune. The band played two more chords before anyone attempted to dance.

From a group standing opposite Dillon, the Gillette advertisement guy in his white jacket, now with his boutonniere, led a petite strawberry blonde onto the empty dance floor. The young woman had a bobbed haircut and wore a champagne-colored dress with a beaded fringe which sparkled as he swung her around into his arms. The dance move showed off her shapely legs to perfection. With the next drum beat, the band transitioned into an evocative tango.

The couple began the dance with a suggestive embrace. They leaned against each other with their chests touching and one leg hooked around their partner's leg. Forward, backward, with a front cross and then back cross as they changed directions and swept across the dance floor. The oohs and ahhs of the crowd surrounding them generated clapping to the music. Excited faces of the young women and men made known their enjoyment. The couple, obviously used to being paired together, made several well-choreographed moves as one. Their appreciative audience's reactions even attracted folks from the outer rooms. Dillon stood apart and continued to watch, approving of the latest fashion trend of shortened hemlines, along with the young woman's elegant and expressive steps.

"Oh, my stars. Lucinda Dressler would die of mortification if she were here to see her granddaughter now." Two elderly ladies in lavender and diamonds squeezed in beside him.

Cheek to cheek, the pair traversed the dance floor's length, turning and instantly returning in the other direction. The couple completed a series of crescent-shaped steps and walked around each other. The band played its last alluring strain as the woman's partner twirled her into an ending pose with her draped across his knee.

"Oh, I think Lily looks marvelous," said the one closest to him, clapping her small hands.

"Yes. Well, there won't be a man in the country club who asks her to dance the rest of the evening after her cousin paraded her around like this."

An energetic round of applause followed the dance's conclusion. The strawberry blonde's dance partner took her to her friends at the bay windows, gave them a smirk, bowed, and left.

The band played another jazzy tune. Couples filtered out to the dance floor. The abandoned girl stood with two girlfriends and no dance partners anywhere close. Her enormous eyes scanned the dance floor. *Damn*. Dillon pressed between the two ladies and sauntered across to the girl.

"Would you like to dance?" He gave her his most engaging smile.

"My pleasure." She didn't know him and didn't care, but the relief on her face was clear. His cousin Kit made him learn to dance. First with formal dances, then as Kit came home from college breaks, always bringing the latest rage or dance steps, she forced him to learn those too. He danced another dance with the pretty flapper and once finished, he asked her if she'd like to get something to drink.

"No, I can't go into the bar. Bet you have a flask on you," she teased. Huge sky-blue eyes looked up at him. "If not, I have a 'hush-hush' hidden in a flowerpot on the back veranda."

"I prefer your idea. But let's give the pretense, anyway. I'll get two glasses of punch, then follow you."

Dillon grabbed two punch glasses, and the young woman retrieved her beaded purse. They walked outside to the unoccupied end of the expansive patio, where the woman dumped her drink over the balcony railing and then reached into a potted fern. She withdrew not a flask but two distinct bottles of Tom Tanner Tennessee Whiskey with the medicine license stamp pasted across.

"Where in the world…"

"Shush. Hand me your glass." After re-hiding one of her prize bottles, she poured Dillon a healthy amount, then one for herself. She raised her glass to him before guzzling down the contents. After refilling her cup, she asked, "What's your name?"

"Dillon. And you're Lily."

"How'd you know that?"

"I overheard it from a couple of dowagers dressed in diamonds standing next to me on the dance floor."

"I know everyone here, including those little ole biddies. "

"Glad to hear it."

"Got a match?" She fished into her purse, fumbling for a cigarette. Dillon pulled out a gold lighter.

"Let me ask you a question. I'm looking for…"

She turned into him and stood up on her tiptoes and kissed him full on the mouth. Not sure if it was the delicious feel of her lips on his mouth or the months of female deprivation and forced celibacy of the penitentiary, but he had no urge to stop. He dropped his glass in the same fern pot, freeing his arms to encircle the lithe body next to him.

Their tongues hurriedly danced of their own accord and within seconds, they found the canopy-striped settee with Lily positioned on his lap. His hands felt along her stockings, climbing her thigh to flesh uncovered by silk. His rasping for air was joined by her panting. She squirmed on his aroused body, causing him to groan. Confident she had done this before, no need to go slow, he hiked his hand up further, sliding underneath her drawers to cup her naked buttocks and pull her tighter to him.

Two overseas tours of duty and nine months in the slammer conditioned Dillon to identify every minute sound around him, but little Lily was playing mind games with him. He never heard the French doors open.

"Valerie Lucinda Stonecipher! What do you think you are doing?"

Dillon jerked up in full attention as if addressing a four-star general. He grabbed Lily to keep her from falling to the stone floor. Momentarily surprised, his face changed to wrath. He glared at the shocked face of a young woman giving him the eagle eye. She leaned in toward the couple and attempted to pull Lily from his arms.

Dillon pulled back, refusing to release Lily. He stared at her, then at Lily. "VL?"

"Yes," Lily answered him with a silly grin.

"Named after your father?" he asked.

"No," her companion answered him, laughing. She pulled Lily's arm again. "There's only one VL. And she's this little vamp right here. So say your apologies, mister—and, missy—you and I are going back inside right now."

"Sure, give us a sec." Dillon scraped his face, sizing up the situation.

"Go on, Judy. I'll get back... I promise," Lily uttered.

In a huff, Judy stomped off.

"Is there another way to the parking lot?" Dillon looked around.

"Sure."

"Show me."

"Are you trying to ditch me?"

"Not on your life, sweetheart. Let's take these with us." He retrieved the two Tom Tanner Tennessee Whiskey bottles. "Got me a fast car and a bottle of Penland Kittrell Rye under the front seat. Why don't we take us a little detour before we head back to the ballroom."

Chapter Sixteen

Dillon

Lily giggled, clinging tight to Dillon's arm as he navigated her through the parked cars. "Why didn't you have the valet boys park your car?"

"What and take a chance of them stripping my gears and or finding my hooch under the driver's seat?"

"Guess you're right." She slid her hand along the passenger door. "Wow. What a car."

Dillon helped her to her side and then reached under his seat after he jumped in. "Here's some really good stuff, sweetheart. Sorry, I didn't bring glasses."

She stretched, planting her upper body on his, and kissed him, grabbing the bottle at the same time. "I think we've shared enough of each other's spit already."

"Have we?" Dillon grabbed her for a quick kiss.

She scooted back in her seat and pulled out the cork of the precious bottle. "Cheers."

Dillon zoomed from the parking area to the open road. For the first five miles, Lily was happy to nurse the bottle Dillon relinquished and let the evening air blow her bobbed hair wildly about while singing.

"Every morning, every evening, ain't we got fun…Where are we going?" She held her hair back with her hand and studied the road.

"Does it matter?"

"Well…"

"So, VL. Is that what everyone calls you?"

"Pretty much."

"Ever help anyone get a load of hooch delivered to the country club storeroom?"

"What a question."

"Just happened to notice the man you were kicking up your heels with earlier on the dance floor was also hot-footing it from the basement stairs when I walked into the bar tonight. Seemed to know his way around pretty well and didn't particularly care for the fact I noticed him earlier."

"That guy is my cousin, Reggie. And I wouldn't be surprised at him being involved in anything."

"Where'd you get those two bottles of Tom Tanner Whiskey?"

"From Reggie."

"Happen to have an idea where Reggie got the whiskey?"

Lily glanced at Dillon again, then looked out her side of the car as they raced along the countryside. "I think you better take me back now."

"What?" Dillon gave her his friendliest grin. "Pass me the bottle. I haven't had a sip. Gonna turn around right here. There's a crest where we can look over the valley. Bet you've been up here before."

"No, I haven't." She frowned as she passed him the bottle.

"This cousin of yours, what's his name? Reggie Wyatt?" He remembered seeing that name on the Hillside Country Club Board of Directors' roster. "You have been helping him run whiskey?"

"I don't recall giving you his last name. Look,

you're very nice to take me for a ride in your fancy car and share your booze with me, but I think I'd better be getting back."

"Did you know they once trained troops here for the war? Turned it into a summer camp after the war ended. Has cabins and a lake."

"Dillon, what's your last name?"

"Dillon Tanner."

"As in Tom Tanner Tennessee Whiskey?" She emphasized each word as she asked.

"The same."

"Look, is this about the missing whiskey? I don't know anything about that."

"Oh, so you've heard?"

"Yeah, someone went to prison for it."

"Takes a big bankroll to pull off an act like that. Lots of palms greased and manpower muscle."

"To steal whiskey?"

"Not just steal it but deliver it to the other clubs you're supplying and pay to make sure the money gets to the right person in the end. Must be someone who has a lot of friends and connections."

"Could you take me back now?" She wet her lips, then bit the lower one.

Dillon made a sharp right turn onto a gravel road and drove beneath an overhanging arch. *Camp Red Oak* was carved into the wooden entrance sign. A full moon and hundreds of stars lit the night sky. Dillon drove toward a building with a solitary outdoor light glaring brightly. The instant he parked, Lily opened her door and bolted.

"No. Wait, Lily. Oh, shit." Dillon scrambled out of his car and raced down the road after her. She must have sensed him following her because she veered left and headed into the woods. "Lily, stop. I'm not going to hurt you," he shouted.

She ran another fifty yards, then a yelp sounded, and he lost sight of her. Once he reached where Lily had disappeared, he swore.

"Damn. You're in the compost and sewage drain spout for the whole camp." He attempted to pull her from the mud. She jerked back, and Dillon tumbled in over her. "Holy crap." Struggling to straighten, he pleaded, "Wait a second."

"I can't breathe." Lily lifted a mud-stained face, spitting sludge out from her mouth. Her beaded spaghetti strap broke and her dress bodice hung open. She unraveled thick strips of white cotton wrapped around her chest.

"What the hell!" Dillon stared in complete silence, mesmerized by the process.

After she pulled the end of the stripping off her body, the minute amount of moonlight revealed full white breasts. His heart pounded as a sudden flush of warmth spread from his groin.

She pulled her dress, covering herself.

"Don't pretend you don't know what women will do to look like flappers." She tossed the unraveled material in Dillon's face.

"Come on." He threw the fabric away and yanked her up, trudging up the hill, pulling her along. "Hopefully, there is enough hot water left in the tank for a shower."

Dillon half-drug, half-carried the slime-covered miscreant to one larger building near where he parked his car. He opened the front door of the structure, felt along the wall, then flipped the light switch.

"Inside."

Lily pulled from his grasp and entered the building on her own. Dillon strode to a row of five showerheads banked along the back wall. He turned the middle faucet on and motioned for her. He had powered up the hot water tank when he dressed earlier in the evening. "Better shower fast while there's still hot water."

Lily scrambled over and hastily unstrapped her shoes. She stood underneath the rushing water, allowing the stream to rinse away the muck.

"Strip down, everything off."

She wiped her face, staring at him. Dillon removed his diamond stickpin, gold cuff links, and wristwatch, placing them in a bowl. Next, he stripped off his muddy tuxedo jacket, trousers, shirt, and underclothes and threw them into a scrap pile, and stood under the first showerhead. "I'm not kidding. You do it or I will."

"Are you going to have your way with me?"

"'Fraid not, sweetheart," he said, spitting water.

Stubbornly, she started removing her clothes. Turning away from him, she threw her dress, stockings, and underwear into a wet pile. She peeked over her shoulder from the corner of her eye.

"Your fault." He stared back, certain she noticed his aroused state as he stood naked, showering. As the water temperature grew cooler by the minute, he became more stimulated. "I'm not taking my eyes off you the rest of the night."

If she was experienced with men, she'd try to make a play for him. He'd been around enough women who used their sexuality to trick a man into giving them what they wanted. Instead, she turned around and finished washing, then grabbed the towel he'd placed within her reach.

Dillon tied his towel around his waist, then strode to Lily's shower and collected her shoes. Instead of handing them to her, he picked her up and tossed her over his shoulder. "You can't walk. I'll clean your shoes later."

She pounded her hands against his bare back. "Let me down."

"Stop wiggling." He slapped her backside.

She stopped.

"I have clothes back at the cabin."

After opening the cabin door, he set her on the wood floor. The room held one chair, a narrow bed, a chest of drawers, and a lone table. "Get dressed. There's a bathroom over there." He tossed her a shirt and pants from a pile on a table. "Hurry up, I want to talk to you."

From his car, he'd brought in a duffle bag and had already changed into a clean pair of trousers and a long sleeve cotton shirt when Lily reentered.

She had rolled the men's trousers at the ankles and tied the plaid shirt tails at her waist. She reminded him of a ragged cloth doll with yarn hair his cousin used to drag around. Her strawberry blonde hair stuck up in peaks, and her eyes took on a smoldering look with the remnants of her black mascara encircling them.

"Look here. The time I planned this out, I figured I'd be bringing a man here. A man named VL. I was going to hold 'VL' here until he told me where they hid my whiskey or pay up if they'd already sold it."

"I have nothing to do with your missing whiskey."

"I think you did. And I'm going to find out just

how much you were involved. And my whiskey was stolen, not missing. Your first mistake was sharing medicinal whiskey with me. You don't get that from a country club—not with the government stamp glued on it, or at least the manager would have the sense to remove it."

Lily tiptoed barefoot to the bed and sat on the edge. "They'll be people looking for me."

"Maybe. And maybe someone won't care if you're found."

She continued to stare at him impassively.

"If you didn't tangibly help hijack my whiskey, then I think you helped bankroll the operation."

"You are crazy, without a doubt, very mistaken." She crossed her arms over her chest.

"Am I? I have from more than one source that V. L. Stonecipher signed a work order for the men who held up my truck." He pulled the chair over and faced her, straddled it, and placed his arms across the back.

"I have no idea who linked my name to your misfortune. It wasn't me."

"I think having to spend nine months in a federal prison would be considered more than a misfortune."

She let out an audible gasp.

"Yeah, prison. So see, little lady, I'm seeking more than just the return of my whiskey. And I'm sorry if you are the pawn who suffers in this—what did you call it? 'My misfortune.'"

Chapter Seventeen

Dillon

Dillon stood and crossed to the chest of drawers. From the top drawer, he removed a set of handcuffs, studying them as if seeing them for the first time. "Look here. As I said, I expected to be holding a man. But it makes no difference. Got to make sure you don't get away." He held up the handcuffs as if in explanation.

"No." Lily scooted off the bed and hurried across the room, pressing her body into the far wall.

Dillon stepped toward her, then stopped. He wouldn't let her vulnerable act change his mind. "I'll let you have the bed, but I'm going to handcuff you to the wrought iron headboard."

"No. I'll sleep on the floor, chair, anywhere. Don't handcuff me. I need to be free in case there is a fire."

"A fire?"

"Yes, a fire. It could happen." Her eyes dilated, and her body jerked as if in danger.

Dillon's brows furrowed. "Not going to happen here."

"My mother died in a fire. She couldn't escape the house. The firemen said her bedroom door was locked from the outside. They found her by the door." Her gaze darted around the room as if looking for an escape route. "Our neighbors rescued me. I was in another room."

Sweat dotted her forehead. She jammed her hands into her armpits. Dillon held her gaze for several seconds. Walking to the bed, he lifted the frame and turned its side flush against the wall. "I'll put you on that side. You can put pillows between us, but I'm sleeping on the other side of this bed. I warn you. I'm a light sleeper. Try to sneak off and I'll know."

"Are you serious?"

"Your only choice." He lifted the handcuffs.

"Fine." She crawled in and stuffed the two pillows in the bed's middle along with the top blanket.

Dillon sat in the chair and removed his shoes, stood, and took off his shirt before turning out the light. The bed sagged as he climbed in and tugged one pillow for himself. "Can't have both the pillows."

She huffed and then turned toward the wall.

"Don't go to sleep yet."

"Why? What are you going to do?" The edge in her voice was real.

"I just want you to talk."

"Talk?"

"Yeah, the eeriest time in prison was at night. The silence. Hated it. You couldn't sleep waiting for something bad to happen."

After a pause, she asked, "What do you want me to talk about?"

"Snow."

"Snow?"

"Yes, tell me about playing in the snow."

"I remember heavy snow. I think I was eleven. I lived with my aunt and grandmother. Don't you love waking up in the winter and looking out the window at all the white snow? White everywhere. So peaceful."

"Yes."

"So beautiful."

She had turned her head and closed her eyes. He listened for a minute to her steady breathing. He smiled for the first time in a long day before falling asleep beside her.

Before daylight, the next morning, Dillon felt a movement. In a half second, he twisted and pinned Lily beneath him, pressing a leg between her legs. He felt every inch of her. Her breasts were pressed against his bare chest. He raised her arms above his, pinioned between his hands. It would take only a movement before he was sexually assaulting her.

"I need to go to the bathroom," Lily squeaked, her eyes as big as saucers.

Dillon rolled off her. "Why didn't you say so?"

"I didn't want to wake you."

Not sure if she was being truthful, he grabbed his shirt and slipped on his socks and shoes. "I'll be back in a minute."

Dillon returned fifteen minutes later with two large apples and placed them on the small table. In his other hand were her shoes. "I cleaned them as best I could." He handed them to her. "I'm going to take you into town so you can call your grandmother. Do you have a school chum or someone she'd believe you'd slip away and visit?"

"Why?"

"Because I'm not ready to turn you loose. But I'd like you to telephone your grandmother and reassure her you're okay. It's up to you. Pretty certain folks of a certain age can easily have a stroke or a heart attack if they get overly upset."

"Why do you even care?"

"I need to play for some time. So let's go."

No frost had come in on the October night; only dew settled on the car's windows and mirrors.

"Want to give me a hand?" He tossed a rag to her as she stood on the other side of his car.

Lily shook her head, grabbed the cloth, and wiped the window on her side. "This is the last time I'm going to accept a dance from someone I don't know."

Dillon chuckled. He drove the car into the small town on the outskirts of the county. After spotting the bell sign hanging outside a local drugstore designating a public telephone inside, he pulled to the curb.

"Squeeze over. I'm coming in too. I want to hear what you are saying." He handed her a few coins before joining her in the cramped wooden telephone booth. She gave the operator the number and was put through.

"Granny, Granny. It's me, Lily. I'm with Sadie. We're almost at her parents' home in St. Augustine. We took the late train to Charlotte last night." She covered the phone receiver and nudged Dillon's ribs.

"Granny, listen. I told you yesterday. Right before I left for the dance at the country club. Don't you remember? Elsie helped me pack my bag." She pursed her lips. "What? Reggie came over? When? What did he want?" Lily looked at Dillon, frowning. "Looking for me? What do you mean he seemed upset?"

Dillon leaned in closer. "Granny, if Reggie comes back, tell him I went to St. Augustine with my school chum. Tell him it's none of his business where I am. Okay?" She paused. "Love you too." She hung up the phone and then pushed Dillon out of the booth. "My grandmother said my cousin Reggie came by our house this morning. She told me he was not too happy with her when she couldn't tell him where I spent the night."

"Does he make a habit of visiting your grandmother in the morning?"

"No. If he comes by, it's always in the afternoon."

"What's his relationship with her? With you, for that matter?"

"He's my pestering older cousin. He takes care of my grandmother's stuff. He has power of attorney for her estate. Guess that's why he's at our house so much."

"Is your grandmother incapacitated?"

"No. A little daft. But she's up to snuff."

"I don't understand. Unless she's frail or has dementia, why would she need a power of attorney? Bank and lawyer offices must line your city's streets."

"Well, she doesn't bank in Lassiter. She uses my grandfather's bank in Georgetown, South Carolina. That's why she gave him power of attorney. It's where my trust fund is, too."

A knot in Dillon's belly kicked in. He mentally weighed Lily's information. "Two questions. One, does Reggie have a trust fund too?"

"Oh, no. He's from the other side of my family. What was the other question?"

"How old are you?"

She paused. Her cheeks flushed as she avoided direct eye contact. "Twenty."

Still a minor. Could there be more than a coincidental connection between Cousin Reggie and access to a V. L. Stonecipher trust?

"Change of plans. We're going to follow the money."

"I don't understand."

"Look. I want my whiskey back. I have reason to believe it's still hidden. Word would get back to me faster than Tarzan zipping through the grapevines in the jungle if it were out. In either case—someone owes me big bucks."

"And you think that somebody is my cousin? I could see him doing an unsporting deed on the sly for money. Reggie's a big spender. Likes to strut around like a big movie star. But I don't see him getting mixed up with criminals. He wouldn't want to get his hands dirty."

"Sweetheart, you wouldn't believe the number of law-abiding citizens turning into full-fledged criminals these days."

"Do you think he was hiding your whiskey at Hillside Country Club?"

"Not sure. Those bottles you had at the dance. Where'd Reggie give them to you?"

"The club."

"Does he have other favorite spots where he'd hang out? Where whiskey crates could be stashed?"

She scrunched her nose, then looked at him. "The Playhouse."

"Say again?"

"He used to do summer stock plays at the Playhouse. He believed he was going to be the next—I don't know 'Rudolph Valentino.' "

"Let's go."

"Wait. You don't even know where it is."

"Excuse me. Lead the way." He stepped away, bowing.

She sent him a nasty look.

Dillon knew right where the Playhouse was located. It once was a giant auction house where local farmers from Middle Tennessee, including those from Oak Hollow, brought in their tobacco and corn to be auctioned off. With so many distilleries closed, the corn market had dried up. Once tobacco yields moved to other places, they sold the auction house. For New York investors looking for a place to try out their next Broadway play, it was the ideal locale. The setting was the reverse of traditional theaters, with the audience sitting on risers and the performers acting on a lower-level stage where the auctioneers once yammered, but the conversion worked.

It was a short drive from the city limits to the Playhouse. There were no cars or trucks anywhere around the premises as they drove up. The building appeared deserted. Dillon tried the front door. It was locked.

"Wait here a sec." Within minutes, the front doors opened. "Got in through the back." They walked into the small lobby and Dillon found the light switches. "I'll check downstairs if you want to look in the balcony."

Dillon searched the backstage dressing rooms, wardrobe closets, offices, and prop storage areas. Nothing. He walked onto the stage, studying the wood planking in more detail. If there was a trapdoor, underneath would be the perfect hiding place. He found a four-by-four square cutting different from the stage floor surface. Placing his fingers in the wood's small indentation, he lifted the plank.

Creaking spring hinges flung the trap door upward. Rickety stairs led below. It was so dark Dillon could not make out anything. Too late to wish for a flashlight. He cautiously stepped down three steps and swung his hand along the ceiling. A light switch wire dangled. He pulled.

Stunned. *Holy...* Random thoughts swirled through his brain. He imagined he'd been transported to the Bureau of Printing and Engraving in Washington, DC. He'd heard about setups like this but had never seen one. This was a first-class counterfeit operation.

He swallowed hard. *Who the hell?*

Cold invaded his body. His gaze swiveled from one wall to the next. Treading carefully down the stairs, he scanned the row of presses. Presses to print counterfeit Internal Revenue stamps, dyes, and plates. Hundreds of counterfeit liquor labels in all hues of the rainbow.

Dillon picked up a set of labels—American, foreign ones too. Everything needed for a big-time campaign to defraud the US government.

Taped along the walls were original playbills from earlier performances. Had Reggie discovered this underground room when he acted in plays and seen those posters? Had he seen the antiquated rollers which printed playbills? Were they what gave him the idea?

From above, a loud crash of metal hitting metal rang out like gunshots. Dillon vaulted through the trapdoor and flew across the stage. He bounded up the stairs leading to the balcony two at a time. He turned just as Lily ran into him. Grabbing her to keep her from falling, he looked over her shoulder. A stack of folding chairs had toppled and fallen like dominos, echoing throughout the empty theater.

He lifted Lily and carried her to the row of upholstered seats, propping her on the chair's back. Without releasing her, he leaned in and kissed the lips of her upturned face. His kiss, long, hungry, and passionate. Dillon explored her mouth with his tongue, daring her to do the same. Lily responded with equal enthusiasm. She held tight to his shoulders as he moved his body in to press her legs apart. His right hand skimmed over her breast before untying her shirt's knot at the waist. His hand slipped inside her shirt to caress her bare breast. Dillon pushed harder against her legs and the chair back. Afraid she'd fall backward, Dillon held her tighter.

A growl of frustration rumbled deep within his throat as his fingers shoved through buttons to open her shirt. Leaning her back, supporting her with his arms, he pressed his lips against her bare breast. She offered no resistance. Instead of pushing him away, she threaded her hands through his hair, caressing his head, pulling him close. He thrust against her, then stepped away.

"Guess you've done this before?" He unbuckled his belt.

"No."

He raised his eyebrows as he pulled his face up to meet hers. "Are you what the boys would call a tease?"

"No." She squirmed on the chair back, pulling her shirt together. "You men are all alike. Just because a girl cuts her hair and wears short dresses doesn't mean she's a slut."

Dillon extended his hand to help her down. She batted it away.

"I 'spec I've been out of circulation too long or a little out of practice." He rebuckled his belt. "Not sure which." He eyed her flushed face suspiciously. In general, when a girl returned kisses that intense, it meant she was okay for a good time. But Lily was a new phenomenon for him.

Before the war, there was a strict line between 'good girls' and 'bad girls.' After he returned from overseas, the tide was turning, albeit bit by bit. Kissing and heavy petting, once reserved for betrothed couples, were now the norm and acceptable to consenting couples everywhere. So where did Lily fit into the equation?

Was she so intent on putting up a big girl front she never thought about the consequences once she found herself with a man who wouldn't be scared off by her hovering cousin? Bet ole Reggie had scared away more than a few. No intention of letting another man dive into VL's inheritance cash pile. He'd sent more than a subtle message to men hanging around his little cousin. Not a bad hint for him to take, either.

"There's nothing here." He was not going to tell her about what he found underneath the stage floor of the Playhouse. He left her briefly to close the trap door. *Damn, what a mess.* And he did not need any reminders she had nothing on under her shirt and pants.

"I tell you what—let's go find you some decent clothes." He led her outside.

"It's Sunday. Nothing's open."

"I know a place."

Chapter Eighteen

Dillon

They returned to Dillon's car and drove a few miles before crossing railroad tracks and arriving at the town's train depot and warehouses district. One building among them was crowded with trucks and cars pulled up to its entrance, with patrons walking indoors.

The town's farmer's co-op posted reduced hours on Sundays but still opened. Farmers technically had no day of rest. If it was going to rain on Monday, they needed to get their hay baled on Sunday. If their tractor needed a vital part to start plowing, they couldn't wait another twenty-four hours.

Lily followed Dillon to a display of blue jeans. Lily hastily picked up a pair from the children's sizes. She looked around and grabbed a flannel shirt and a man's white undershirt and boy under britches. Dillon walked up, holding a pair of brown riding boots.

"These were the smallest I could find."

Lily grasped them as though he handed her a fabulous present. Her sparkling eyes gave him an electric jolt. His thoughts wanted to escape his brain rather than engage the present reality he had placed himself in. The sooner he had her out of the way, the better. He stood helplessly as she snatched up a pair of socks on the way to the checkout.

"I figure the drive will take nine hours to get to

Georgetown. Not sure exactly but think I'm in the ballpark. We'll go to the bank first thing. Do you have any identification inside that little purse you keep clutching?" he asked as they walked back to his car.

She placed her hands on her hips and scowled. "You're taking me to South Carolina? Across state lines. Have you thought this out? You are asking for serious trouble."

"Sweetheart, this isn't a game. This is not a grand adventure you can shock and entertain your friends with like a new dance move, showing off your pretty tutti. Over half a million dollars in whiskey was stolen from me, and I spent nine months in a hellhole prison because some son of a bitch set me up. So someone was looking for serious trouble long before I met you."

Lily looked at the clothing bundle Dillon had bought. She gave a slight shake of her head. "Yes, I have my driver's license. I got it the day I turned seventeen. Let's go. I need to find a place where I can put these on."

****

Lily

"Open my glove box. I have a map in there," Dillon said. "I'll pull over and let you change."

"Thanks."

He pulled his car to a roadside stop and took the map she handed him. He opened the leaflet and spread it across the concrete picnic table. As he studied the map, she finished dressing.

She needed time to think. At least with decent clothes that fit, she could clear her mind and figure out what she should do next. She rapped on her window.

"Probably take more than nine hours." He slid into

the car and then glanced her way. "Looks like everything fit pretty well. I was wondering. You took so long."

"Were you peeking?"

"Remember, sweetheart, you have nothing I haven't already seen."

She threw her bundled clothes at him. Refusing to respond, she stared out her window. They drove through the countryside, passing farms and pastures. Soon the landscape changed to rows and rows of pecan trees or vast stretches of peanut crops. She glimpsed sideways at Dillon.

Were things as serious as he let on? Never had she been so conflicted. Could he read her mind? Could he tell she was grappling with her decision to comply when he took long appraising looks at her? She was traveling cross-country with a perfect stranger. Well, I guess she couldn't call a person you almost fornicated with a stranger. Dillon Tanner was a strange man. And such a handsome one.

From the moment he approached her at the country club and asked her to dance, she was attracted to him. She loved how his chocolate-brown eyes bore into her, the way a smile lurked in his eyes, his dimpled chin, and his determined jaw. How the same lock of hair fell across his brow, no matter how many times he brushed it back. Her heart skipped when he embraced her with wholehearted passion this morning at the Playhouse. She would have done anything to have him continue kissing her. But he wanted to do more. Expected to do more. But that couldn't happen. And now this man was hell-bent on convincing her Reggie Wyatt, her only cousin, was a master criminal. And she was going along with him.

Her friend Sadie had gone all the way. She told her it wasn't so bad. The last words Lily'd use to describe what happened between them at the theater. She squirmed in the car seat. It wasn't her imagination. She could still feel his hands, his lips on her body. Swallowing hard, she tried to squelch the memory of kisses that shot fire through her body, exploding within her.

Well, she had no intention of letting that happen again. She looked at him once more. Anyway, as soon as he found his whiskey, he'd drop her like a hot potato.

A stop to buy gas and order sandwiches at a roadside diner reminded her why he was apt to think the way he did. As the cashier rang them up, she scanned the newspaper's front page stacked on the counter. The paper covered shocking and disgusting news stories and pictures of what was happening across America. Men were mowed down with bullets and killed in broad daylight for minor differences over bootlegged alcohol. If half the stories printed in the papers were true, it boded ill will for the country.

She picked up a Baby Ruth candy bar and the latest edition of *Movie Tone* magazine from a rack and flipped through the pages. Women's hemlines and haircuts were getting shorter and shorter. She glanced at her blue jeans and boots when an attractive girl close to her age walked into the store, escorted by a well-groomed young man. The young woman was dressed in the cutest green dress and matching cloche hat that Lily had seen in a while.

She made a quick guess, deciding the couple must have left church a short time ago. She sighed. *Have to get away.* She glanced around. Folks looking at her would think she was on the traveling rodeo circuit. *All I need now is a cowboy hat.*

****

Dillon

Lily replaced the magazine as Dillon paid for their purchases. "Go ahead and add that," he told the cashier and pulled the magazine back.

They took their sandwiches and sat at one of the inside booths. After finishing their lunch, Dillon slid from his seat. "Look, I need to call Oak Hollow and let them know I'll be gone another day. I'll just be a minute. Order another Coke if you want. You'll be okay? Want another magazine?"

He left Lily reading and crossed the store to the phone booth on the other side.

"Glad you called. Where are you?" his attorney, Wendell Deane, asked him as soon as his call went through.

"Long story. I should be back in a couple of days."

"We received a response from CBA, the folks who made that offer on Tom Tanner Whiskey, just like you said they would—but something I noticed is different."

"Spit it out."

"This time the letter is addressed to you, Tom, and Katherine Regina Kittrell."

Dillon's heart sank. "Holy crap."

"My thoughts exactly. They must have looked at state records and saw where Pen and Chloe put the distillery in all three of your names, yours, Tom's, and Kit's. They want a response by the first of the year."

"Do you have Kit's dorm number?"

"Yeah, give me a second."

"I'll give her a quick call. Make her aware." Deane gave him the number, and he hung up.

Dillon dialed and someone answered on the first ring. "I need to speak to Kit Kittrell," Dillon asked.

"Just a minute."

Dillon drummed his fingers on the glass door of the phone booth while he waited for the dorm monitor to locate Kit above the hubbub of girls' animated voices.

"Who is this?"

"Kit, it's Dillon. Why aren't you in class?"

"Really, Dillon."

A tap sounded on the glass door of the phone booth. Dillon turned; Lily stood on the outside, giving him a questioning look.

He opened the door a crack to her. "Is everything all right?"

"Yeah, just give me another minute."

"Who was that?" Kit asked.

"Never mind. Listen to me carefully."

"Okay."

"Kit"—he spoke with a steely edge to his voice— "promise me—don't go anywhere alone. Just to class and back. Hear me?"

"I promise."

"Kit, I'm serious. There's been an attempt to buy us out. With Tom gone, if they got you to sign over your one-third they'd control half the business."

"I wouldn't do that."

"You would if someone gave you a cock and bull story about Tom or me. Just warning."

"Okay. I'll do as you say."

Dillon slammed the receiver down once Kit hung up. His stomach felt rock hard. Was this proof that there was a connection between his missing whiskey and the attempt to buy out Tom Tanner?

He eyed Lily. She was engrossed in the tabloid pages. He rubbed his jaw. The memory of having his teeth rattle during a fight he had while in prison was a cold reminder of the people with whom he was dealing. He could fight back. Yet, neither Lily nor Kit would be a match against anyone as ruthless as whom he thought they were up against now.

****

"Look, I have two dollars in my purse. If you'll lend me the rest—I will go down to St. Augustine and visit my friend Sadie." Lily thrust the paper bills at Dillon. "I'll stay with her as long as you think I need to." Surely, he would let her go. She served him no purpose by staying with him any longer.

"I'll tell you what," he said as they walked out. "If you'll go with me to Georgetown and it doesn't turn out Reggie is involved with your and your grandmother's money—I'll buy you a first-class ticket to St. Augustine. And I'll throw in a handful of bills for some new duds too."

Lily sighed. "Do I have a choice?"

Dillon laughed. "That's what I'm starting to love about you, Lily—so pragmatic. Come on." He slung his arm around her.

"We always spent the night in Columbia on the drive down. Is that where you plan to stop?"

"No. Driving straight through. The roads are pretty decent to Spartanburg and Columbia. We'll drive to Sumter, then take the new highway down to Georgetown."

Dillon had not accounted for long delays as

construction crews completed the finishing touches of the United States' first highway system. Time after time they waited while blacktop road crews shut the road to one lane. The number of prison chain gangs asphalting the tarmac shelved his plan to pull off on the roadside and nap for a few hours.

As twilight settled in, he noticed a neon vacancy sign blinking ahead. He hit his steering wheel, then pulled into a modest motor lodge. He left her in the car and walked into the lodge office.

"Number ten. The manager apologized and said it only had twin beds." He laughed when he jumped back into his car and drove them to their unit.

"I'll give you as much privacy as possible. Just in case you didn't notice, chain gangs are working the roads throughout this area. If you hear dogs barking in the middle of the night, you'll know one's escaped and is no doubt close to us."

"Warning received."

Dillon nodded. "I'll go see if I can rustle up anything we can call dinner."

****

Lily

"Do you have a sweetheart back home wondering where you are?" Lily asked.

Dillon had locked the door, turned off the light, and climbed into his bed.

"Thinking of giving her a call?" he asked, tucking his pillow and turning toward her.

"I might be."

"Well, I don't have a sweetheart back home, Miss Curious."

She smiled at his response. "If you did, I bet you

wouldn't be driving her across state lines."

"I think you're right."

"I just wondered. That was a woman you were talking to earlier today."

"Yeah. My cousin. Warned her—too—about bad people being out there."

"You know, my family owns a beach house eleven miles from Georgetown. I left a couple of dresses there last summer and sandals too. I can't go to the bank in blue jeans. They will never believe who I say I am if I do." She wasn't sure why she divulged this information. Maybe because she did not want to spend another night in a single-room cabin with him.

"Good idea. Just give me directions in the morning. Night."

"Wait."

"What now?"

"What are we going to talk about tonight? You said…"

"Yeah, I remember. Tell me about your best girlfriend. The one who doesn't talk all the time."

****

They reached the Stonecipher summer beach cottage before dusk the next day. The small island's familiarity with its stretch of beach houses, even though shuttered or boarded up and abandoned until next summer, gave Lily a sense of security. A thick lump rose in her throat as she reminisced about happier times spent with her grandparents during summers.

She glanced at Dillon as she pointed out her family's house. No matter what kind of man he was, she was grateful he allowed her to call her grandmother. Lily grabbed the key kept in the downstairs washroom.

The two trudged with their small bundles up the street-side wooden steps.

The last of the evening's sunset tones filled the living area of the cottage. The view from the picture window was stunning. High tide was coming in and deep emerald waves crashed on the beach. Dillon turned from the view beyond the dunes to look around inside. Lily's family's rattan beach furniture with colorful cushions and pillows gave the room a relaxed and inviting atmosphere. Framed beach scene sketches hung on each of the walls.

Dillon walked to an ink drawing of seagrass blowing in the wind across sand dunes and a rickety fence with a beach cottage in the background. "V. L. Stonecipher?" He read out loud the signature at the bottom right. "You didn't tell me you were an artist?"

"You never asked. But I don't know if you could call me an artist. My grandmother signed me up for art classes after my mother died. My granny loved my pictures and had those framed. She even took a couple of my sketches to the printers and had postcards made."

Dillon ran his fingers across her signature. "Just out of curiosity, what plans did you have for your future? Don't tell me you intended on marrying one of those lounge lizards from the country club?"

"Really!"

"My mother raised me and worked at the distillery as a bookkeeper. She loved her job. And there's my aunt Chloe, who ran the distillery as far back as I can remember," he said before looking out the window. "Just saying you can have a career and have children too."

She pointed to the doorway to her left. "This is my

bedroom."

Two minutes later, she squealed and danced through the door of her room, waving her prize find in the air. "I never dreamed I'd be this excited to find old dresses. And underwear too."

Dillon let out an audible moan. "Wonderful. Let's be at the bank when it opens tomorrow. Wear something conservative and modest. You need to look upstanding."

"I am upstanding!" She slammed her hands on her hips.

"Sure."

Lily reached down to the couch and heaved a throw pillow at him.

"Guess you can sleep in your bedroom alone tonight, no reason to handcuff you," Dillon said. "Don't reckon you're going to try to escape and alert the county police in the middle of the night with dresses two years old." He snickered, ducking as she tossed another pillow.

She stomped back into her bedroom. Was he suggesting separate bedrooms tonight for her benefit or his? Silly question. Did he do anything for anyone's benefit other than himself? Thought she wasn't worth the trouble once he found out she wasn't "experienced."

But what happened in the theater earlier? She felt it. She knew he did too at the time. Did the attraction they have just evaporate? How could a man who kissed her so passionately, even for the briefest of moments, forget her? *Men.*

With a halfhearted shrug, she came back into the living area. She walked down the hall and opened a closet door. She pulled a game box from the hall closet.

"Let's play Chinese checkers." She was tempted to drag out the Ouija board but believed the irony of the suggestion would fall flat with him.

Chapter Nineteen

Dillon

Dillon and Lily walked into the First National Bank of Georgetown early the next morning. Lily tugged at the waistline of the cranberry-colored dress she found packed in a trunk that must have belonged to her mother. She had found a beret in the same search and slipped it on jauntily.

As they entered, eyes turned in their direction. They were an attractive couple. The bank manager, anticipating they would be there to open an account or apply for a home loan, eagerly greeted them.

"May I help you?" the middle-aged man asked, leading them to his private office. "Please have a seat. I'm Ralph Nelson, the bank's manager."

Lily and Dillon had agreed for her to start the conversation. "Yes. I'm Valerie Lucinda Stonecipher, and I am here to inquire about my trust fund." Lily pulled out her driver's license from her purse and presented it with the expectation the manager would ask for identification.

"This is most unusual." The man pulled at his tie, studied Lily's license, then looked at Dillon.

"Dillon Tanner. I am a family friend." He sat in the chair next to Lily and crossed his leg. "I agreed to accompany Miss Stonecipher at her grandmother's request, Mrs. Lucinda Dressler. As manager, I presume you are familiar with the V. L. Stonecipher trust?"

"Yes, I am." He cleared his throat. "I oversaw the account with my father when it was first established," he said with a slight jump in his cheek. "I'm afraid I have never met you before, Mr. Tanner. Are you Miss Stonecipher's attorney?"

"No, I am not. We are here today to determine if she needs an attorney."

The bank manager sat up straight. "Does there seem to be a problem?"

"That is what we are here to find out. We have reason to believe the person who was given power of attorney over Miss Stonecipher's trust has had illegitimate access to it."

"I'm afraid you are alleging very serious wrongdoing." The manager scooted back in his high-back leather chair. "Let me understand you. Are you accusing the bank of being negligent in managing Miss Stonecipher's funds?"

"Yes. Unless you can prove otherwise."

"I am sure you are who you claim to be…Miss Stonecipher and Mr. Tanner." Any pretense of warmth dissipated. He glanced at Lily's license once more. In an icy voice, he said, "However, it appears Miss Stonecipher is a minor and I am sure we have only made legitimate transactions here at First National with the appropriate designees. I wish I could divulge more."

"It is Miss Stonecipher's trust," Dillon said.

The bank manager swiveled in his high-back chair and pulled out a large leather ledger from the cabinet behind him. "I'm afraid V. L. Stonecipher no longer has an account with us. They dissolved the trust in June a year ago. By the trustee's power of attorney appointed by this woman's grandmother, I might add." He opened a page and turned it around for Lily to read.

He pointed to a line. As you can see, the money in the trust was transferred to a checking account in V. L. Stonecipher's name. A total of four checks were written from the account. It now has a zero balance."

Lily collapsed against the chair's back. Her face flushed a deep red. "No."

"Her grandmother, she has the same power of attorney, does she still hold an account with your bank?" Dillon asked.

"Yes. She still has an active account with us. For the mortgage of her home."

"Her home? She's lived there all her life." Lily stood, her face losing color. "That house was her grandparents' home. Willed to her after they passed. It's been in her family for years. Why would she need to mortgage her house?"

"Your family's attorney could best answer these questions," the manager said.

Dillon stood beside Lily. "Mr. Nelson, even though the information you have conveyed to us is very disturbing, it is without a doubt helpful. You may expect a return visit shortly by Miss Stonecipher's attorney."

Dillon clasped Lily's arm.

"One more question. Does Mrs. Lillian Dressler have a safety lock box here?"

"No."

Dillon dragged her from the manager's office and out the front door. Once back in their car, he steered it onto the state highway and did not stop until he spotted a short strip of land where locals were launching fishing boats.

Seagulls flew overhead. Gentle waves lapped the shore at low tide. A few cars rushed by on the highway, yet none entered the parking area. Dillon took one look at Lily's enraged face and placed his arm around her shoulders. "Are you okay?"

"I'm humiliated." She let out a forceful breath as she dug her fingernails into her palm.

Dillon took her hand.

"What am I to do? Reggie's taken everything. Was he just going to let people show up on my grandmother's porch one day with an eviction notice? I hate him. Hate him."

"First, your grandmother might have a safe somewhere where she keeps her jewels and maybe stocks and bonds, that's why I asked about the safe deposit box. Second, I don't mean to give your SOB cousin any benefit of the doubt, but I think he might have intended to reimburse your trust. Maybe intended to provide enough funds for you and your grandmother to live on once he made the money back. But like a lot of amateurs—and, I might say, professional criminals— he got in too deep."

"Too deep to who?"

"I don't know. I think this was Reggie's little red wagon from the get-go, but I'd say he had other connections. I'm sorry—but he's going to get what's coming to him and it might not be just from me."

Tears welled in Lily's eyes. "My grandmother. She trusted him. How could he do this to her?"

"Money. Power. They corrupt. Witnessed it even in the military."

Lily wiped her eyes with the back of her hand. "Is that why you were looking for a VL Stonecipher? Checks with my name on them must have paid for something bad?"

"Yeah. Looks like what happened." Dillon stretched his neck and looked out at the sea. He rubbed the back of his head, still remembering the plum size lump raised on it after being cold-cocked by Reggie's men. He gave a wry smile; guess they could have left him for dead after they hijacked him. Yeah, could have died and gone to Heaven rather than spend the next few months in hell for something he was wrongly accused of.

"I'm sorry. I guess I must seem selfish to you. When you told me you had lost your whiskey, I showed little sympathy. I apologize." Lily sniffed.

Dillon patted her hand and then reached inside his front pocket for a handkerchief.

"Here, take this." He switched gears, putting his car in reverse. "Today's news involves a change of plans—that's all."

Dillon wondered just how deep Reggie's debts ran. And what propelled him to take such drastic steps as depleting his own family's money. Did he have investments that soured? Did he get roped in by those Florida land scams? He wouldn't be the first person he'd heard about who lost his shirt with Florida land deals that ended up being swamps. People had lost millions on those swindles.

God forbid if it were drugs. Narcotics, opium, and heroin were making inroads into the US. It looked like that was going to be the new baby for the just-established Drug Enforcement Administration once prohibition was voted out. He took another look at Lily before swinging the car out on the highway. One thing was for sure, Reggie must be stopped.

****

When they arrived back at Lily's summer beach house, a scraggly pup scampered down the home's outdoor stairs. He wagged his tail, watching the two of them walk his way.

"Hey, little doggie. Are you lost?" Lily bent down to pet him.

"Lily, don't touch him. Most likely a stray."

Dillon searched the dog's neck. "No tag. Looks like a mix of terrier, Pekingese, or Spaniel. He's a mutt."

"He's just a little dirty. I bet hungry too," she said, holding the pup's front paws and looking into the dog's eyes.

"We'll throw out a few scraps, but he can't stay around here."

Lily picked up the dog, wrapping her arms around him. "Maybe we can find his home. You go in and scrape up a bit for him to eat. I'll hose him off down here."

Dillon rolled his eyes. After the shock she'd had at the bank earlier and everything he'd put her through in the past forty-eight hours, he did not have the heart to argue with her.

"What's your name, little fella?" She held the pup tight to her chest. Dillon exhaled and raised his eyes upward before trudging up the stairs to find the mutt scraps to eat.

She had already rinsed the dog's fur and was swabbing him with a ragged beach towel when he came back. Sandy paw prints and mud smeared her dress. The dog's tail wagged, and his ears perked, and he returned Lily's adoring gaze, only dragging it away once he set the food scraps under his nose.

"Maybe we could drive around with him up and down the beach and see if anyone is looking for him."

"Lily, in case you haven't noticed, there's no one else on the island. If there is, I haven't seen them. But if we're going to stay another night, we can take him with us to the corner store at the end of the causeway and ask the owner there if he recognizes him."

"That's a wonderful idea. Let me go change first." She raced off, leaving him with the dog.

"Well, buddy, what are we going to call you? Not Buddy, for certain." Dillon picked up a stick and threw it in the next-door neighbor's yard. The mutt did not attempt to retrieve it or even chase it. Damn. He was already jealous of the darn dog, remembering how Lily held him close to her heart a few minutes earlier.

Their brief trip to the local general store just off the causeway elicited no helpful information about the dog. Eager to help Lily and increase his sale, the store manager suggested a popular dog food brand.

"You must be the only folks left on the island if that's where you came from," the manager said.

"Yeah, we came down to make sure we winterized the cottage," Dillon answered as he shuffled through a postcard selection on a display shelf. He found what he was looking for and placed them on the counter.

"The pup could have wandered away from campsites around here or could be just a vacationer who let him out of their car and drove off." The clerk finished ringing them up and passed the bags over.

"Probably right. Thank you." Dillon placed the grocery items in the car's back seat when they walked out. "You didn't tell me your postcards were for sale? I bought both prints."

"Yes, something else Granny did. I'm sure she pressured the gift shop owners next door into stocking them, too."

"Don't you worry. I'm not going to desert you, Charlie." Lily pulled the excited dog into her lap for the drive back to the summerhouse.

"Where'd you come up with a name like that?" Dillon asked in an exasperated tone. Growing up with farm animals, he knew once you named them, it'd be hard to separate them.

"Don't you think he looks identical to the dog in Charlie Chaplin's movies?"

"Oh, so now he's a movie star." Dillon drove into the beach house's sand and shell parking area. "Wipe his paws if you're bringing him into the house."

The animated smile she gave him made his heart lurch. "Yes," was all she said. It was impossible not to fantasize for a second about her saying yes to something totally different. He grabbed their bags and followed them upstairs.

They ate their grilled cheese sandwiches barely talking. While Dillon rinsed an old coffee thermos for their road trip back, Lily walked out on the porch with her dog.

She stood on the deck watching the sunset. The white cotton dress she had changed into blew in the late afternoon breeze. She shook her short locks of hair and laughed out loud as the wretched dog raced down the deck steps to chase fiddler crabs on the beach.

Dillon scrubbed his chin. It was discomfiting to find himself trapped at last by an emotion he had purposely avoided for years. And by Lily Stonecipher, of all people. A young woman who adopted all the rebellious trappings of flapperdom with its bobbed hair, short dresses, makeup, slang, and cigarettes. Absolutely the last type of woman he'd thought would appeal to him. Which was why he was taken in so unaware.

When he pushed open the screen door, it screeched. She turned, and both stared at the other for a long moment. How had she come to mean so much to him so quickly? A feeling of powerlessness concerning the present or the future disturbed him. The last thing he wanted was to take advantage of her vulnerability at this time. It took every ounce of self-control not to pull her into his arms when he stopped on the roadside after they left the bank. Her crying had stopped on the way back from town, but he'd be a stupid man not to realize how hurt she still was. And how much more he was going to have to do to gain her trust?

"I feel so manipulated, so used," she said. Was she having as much trouble forgetting about the day as he was? "But, Dillon, Reggie, taking my money doesn't prove he was the one who stole your whiskey." She plucked a black-eyed Susan from a branch twisted in the deck railing and began pulling off the petals.

"Still unconvinced your cousin's not an innocent party?"

She threw the last of the flower stems over the rail. "It's just so outlandish."

"I didn't tell you, but at the Playhouse, I discovered a sizable counterfeit operation underneath the stage. I'm afraid your cousin is in a lot deeper than I even imagined. He's definitely not a fly-by-night operator. It explains why my stolen whiskey hasn't hit the black market yet. From the stash of empty bottles stacked in the basement, it looks as if plans are to dilute the Tom Tanner stolen whiskey with something. Double his batch easily, stick a government sticker on it, and he's good to go. Makes my half a million in whiskey worth a million." He whistled.

"What will you do next?"

"I can't take you back to your grandmother's. Too risky. Reggie would figure something was up. Maybe we can find a place your grandmother can join you." *Or I could take you back to Oak Hollow. You'd be safe there.*

"You think I should get Granny to come here?"

"Have you stay down here on the beach? No, not first on my list, with winter closing in and no inhabitants on this island."

It would be difficult to take Lily back to Oak Hollow after spending days and nights with him. He lived under the cloud of illegitimacy his entire life. His father left his mother pregnant and right away disappeared and drowned in a shipwreck before marrying her. If it hadn't been for his own grandmother's insistence, he would not have the legal last name of Tanner.

Once neighbors found out who she was—talk would be about not only her inheritance being in tatters but her reputation as well. Better for both of them to go their separate ways. The sooner he found his whiskey, the better. He frowned. One thing he wasn't used to was second-guessing himself. Getting saddled with a beautiful woman had never entered into his plans.

"Look, do you honestly have a school chum in Saint Augustine?" he asked.

"Yes. Why?"

"Well, the way I see it, you have two choices. You can visit her, or you can come back to Oak Hollow with me. The problem is, eventually, Reggie is going to look for you more intensely."

He walked to the railing. Charlie scampered back and forth with the waves as the tide came in. Was she going to feel trapped? Like she had no options? His stomach was one tight knot. Reggie was going to get desperate if he hadn't already. And if he determined Lily was a spoke in his wheel, no telling what he'd do to get rid of her. The SOB certainly had no compunction about draining her trust fund account.

"I'll stay with you." She nodded her chin forcefully. "When do we leave?"

Chapter Twenty

Dillon

"I called my aunt, didn't want to show up on her doorstep without notice. She'd love to have you." Dillon exited the roadside restaurant's phone booth. The two had stopped on their way back to Tennessee to grab a bite to eat and let the dog run around. He'd called his aunt Chloe while Lily was in the lady's room. "She's excited to meet you. Come on. We're only a couple of hours away from Oak Hollow."

"Are you telling the truth, Dillon? If she'd rather not take me in, you could check me into a hotel." Lily tugged her outfit's skirt once she climbed back into their car. She retied the cream-knit sweater around her shoulders and peeked back at her dog. He was now napping comfortably on a blanket in the back seat.

Dillon laughed at the idea of checking Lily into the Star Inn. "Fifteen minutes would be all it took before gossip flew through the entire town that I checked some pretty flapper into our town's only hotel."

Reaching across the seat, he patted her knee. She was a trooper. Of all the dealings he'd put her through the past few days, she had not once threatened to throw in the towel. Charlie barked from the back seat. He chuckled. *Now I have a dang dog to compete with.*

The flattened countryside gradually changed to hilly terrain. Giant cedars, white pine, and other evergreens dotted the landscape against the backdrop of hardwood trees rapidly losing their leaves. Straggly goats and a few cows clung to naked hillsides of plowed corn and hayfields. They crossed the fast-moving river at dusk as orange and purple streaks rippled the sky.

"We're here." Dillon shifted gears turning off the main road. He drove the long driveway toward Tanner House, where his family's Victorian mansion stood with its electric lights illuminating the interior. First, he'd take her inside and let her get settled. He would love to take her on a tour of the distillery; however, the visit would have to wait.

Chloe Kittrell waited on her family's porch as Dillon escorted his companion up the steps. He caught his aunt's smile, knowing precisely what she was thinking. Never in a million years would she picture Lily as the woman he would bring home to meet her.

"Come in. It's cold out here."

"Aunt Chloe, I'm going to put Lily in your hands. I need to get down to the distillery. And this is Charlie." The little dog scampered from the car and dashed up the front porch like he owned the place.

Dillon left them and did not return until after dark. He scraped his boots on the kitchen's doormat. "Everything all right?" he asked.

"Yes. I've fed her," Chloe said. "She's had a bath, and I peeked in not five minutes ago. She's sound asleep. I put her in the guest bedroom."

Dillon kissed her cheek. "Thanks, Aunt Chloe. If you have some dinner left, I'm starving."

His aunt filled a plate with roast beef and potatoes. She set it on the table as he drew up a chair. After placing a hot biscuit on his plate, she reached into her skirt pocket and pulled out a letter.

"Aunt Maggie received this letter from Pen two days ago." She handed the letter to Dillon as she sat down at the table to join him. "I believe he mailed it to her because he was not sure once someone noted the Mexican postmark, it would ever have made it into my hands. Look at his line, '*I'm about to receive a package from South America any day now.*' I think he's telling me Tom is on his way to him."

Dillon read the letter, then looked up, smiling. "I think you're right. Darn good news."

Chloe stood and retrieved the coffeepot and refilled Dillon's cup. "Has it crossed your mind, Dillon, that stealing our whiskey might not be the only intention those crooks have?"

"You're talking about our medicinal contract, aren't you?"

"Yes."

"Tom and I talked about it. We're afraid of exceeding our limit, but someone else with the right connections might not be. And some unknown folks have made an offer already. We figured a criminal element wants control of our distillery to run a third shift right under the government's nose. Damn, 'scuse me. What a world we live in."

"One thing's for sure, the government will not award any more medicinal contracts. If whoever this 'someone' is can't get you to agree to sell, they might force you." Chloe poured herself a cup of coffee.

"Yeah, I'm afraid it's where we are right now." He scrubbed his face. "Ever heard of CBA and Associates?"

"No. Is that whom you suspect?"

"They've offered to buy controlling interest. Our attorney knows. We're taking a wait-and-see." He took another coffee sip. "Aunt Chloe, the main reason I brought Lily here is I can't have her cousin, Reggie Wyatt, finding her. Got to keep it quiet. If he learns she's here, the plan I cooked up won't work. He's the man who I believe is behind my whiskey theft and maybe more." He stood to leave. "When's the last time you talked to Kit?"

"She called the other day. Why? Is anything wrong?"

"No. Just asking. I'll stay at the manager's house tonight. I'll see you in the morning." The last thing he wanted to do was worry his aunt about Kit.

****

Dillon cursed, clambering out of bed when his foot banged the chair leg. Disoriented, he had forgotten he was back in his manager's cottage. He glanced at the bedside clock. It was two in the morning. The phone continued to ring from the hall.

"Hello?"

"Dillon, thank God you answered," the voice on the other end said. "We received a tip minutes ago, hell more than a tip. They're here now. Just got off the train."

"Feds?"

"Yeah. It's a surprise raid. Someone's accused you of producing excess whiskey."

"Hell, you know we don't do that. Too risky. Can't lose our license."

"Maybe poking around. Looking for something else. They're loading up. Counted at least fifteen.

177

Going to shut you down while they search."

"Damn. How'd you find out about the raid?"

"That's what's odd. The call came from my attorney friend in Lassiter, of all places. Said it's where the charge originated from. A 'concerned citizen' there accused you of overstepping your allotment."

A cold rush invaded Dillon's body. His muscles went numb. "Hell. Call the main house for me. Wake up, my aunt. Got it from here, thanks."

He hobbled back to his bedroom, scrambled into his clothes, and grabbed his jacket and pistol. He raced up the path to Tanner House and hammered on the washhouse door.

"Marcos, can Tena drive?"

"Yes."

"Feds are coming. I don't want them to know Lily is here. Or you, either. Get Tena in my car. Throw in a bunch of curtains; yank them down from my aunt's windows. Toss them into a bundle in the back seat. Make a big pile as if something is under them and get her going down the road to town. They'll stop her to search the car. That will buy us time."

Marcos called for Tena as he threw on his clothes. "Get dressed, then go into the house. Pull down the dining room curtains."

"Marcos, grab the saddles hanging by the wash tubs, get our two horses from the pasture—the reins are hidden in the birdhouse by the paddock gate. Take Lily and ride to the path I showed you. The back way to the highway, heading east. Tena can meet you there after she goes through town. Tell her there's a little general store. Can't miss it. From there, head to the hunting lodge."

He reached into his back waistband and pulled out his gun. "Use it if you have to."

Dillon scampered up the house's back steps. The kitchen light was already on.

"Aunt Chloe. Let Tena tear down the dining room curtains. Go wake up Lily. Tell her to meet Marcos in the back and dress warmly. We only have a few minutes. Don't want anyone knowing Lily's staying here."

He went to help Tena, who was already in the dining room. "The police will flag you down," he told her as he jerked down another curtain panel. "The feds will see this pile in the back of the car. They'll think you're hiding whiskey. Stop in the middle of the road. Turn sideways. Try to block them. Let them search. Just cry and tell them your mistress has you taking them to the big hotel laundry in town. Tell them you needed to go now while they're not using the washing machines for the hotel linens. They'll let you go once they figure you have nothing. But that'll buy us some time."

He loaded the heavy curtains in her arms. "All right? The key is in the car. Time to go."

Lily hurried down the stairs with Chloe. She was dressed in pants and a heavy jacket his aunt must have lent her. "Your aunt told me I needed to leave."

"I'll explain later. Marcos is taking you on horseback to our cabin. Ride fast till you reach the woods. By then you'll have cover. Can't afford for anyone to come in and see you, or Marcos, for that matter. It will ruin the plan. It's cold. Have you any gloves?"

"Here." His aunt handed her a pair.

"Turn off the lights. Don't want them to think we

were forewarned. Let's go." He hurried with Lily to the pasture's opening behind the washhouse. Dillon whistled for the two horses. Marco was up ahead. The big man was carrying the two saddles like they were bags of candy.

He pulled the reins from the nearby birdhouse. "Lily, Marcos will take you to a little hunting cabin we have down there on the lake. Might be a day or two before these feds decide they're not going to find anything."

In the moonlight, Dillon made out Lily's white face. Her teeth chattered. Impulsively, he squeezed her hand; she was trembling. Not sure if she was cold or afraid, he wrapped her in his arms for a brief second. "You can do this. Just getting you and Marcos out of the way relieves me."

Dillon kissed her on the top of her head, then led her to the horse Marcos had saddled. He hoisted her up, then thought to ask. "Have you ever ridden before?"

"What a time to ask." She tucked her boots into the spurs and turned her horse around with skill. With a swift kick to the pinto's sides, she rode away with Marcos.

****

Dillon took his time answering the clamor at his door.

"Coming, coming," he shouted. "What the hell?" Five government agents stood poised on his doorstep.

"Don't act surprised, Tanner. Your big deflection—sending that woman. Must admit, it worked. God, she was screaming like a banshee. Never heard such going on about laundry. Gave you at least an extra fifteen minutes."

The man in front slapped a folded paper into Dillon's hand. "What 'cha hiding? Guess we'll find out. Here's the search warrant to inspect the entire premises."

"Can't search private homes."

"Maybe so, but we can interview everyone on the property. So let's say you go rouse everyone at the big house before we head to the distillery."

"Just letting you know ahead of time, you ain't liable to find anything. You have been down here too much already for us to slip up."

"We'll be the judge of that." Their leader snickered.

It was a running joke initially with distillers to aggravate and stymie government agents when they made their unannounced raids. However, it soon became apparent that when the men purporting to look for lawbreaking couldn't find anything, they'd plant their incriminating evidence or make purposeful errors in counting.

"We will, of course, have our employees accompany each of your agents as they count our inventory," Dillon said as he pulled his jacket on.

"Certainly." The officer gave Dillon a penetrating look. "And I will require a complete list of your distillery's employees."

Dillon and his aunt entered the distillery. His two guards stood aside and allowed the federal troops to enter behind them. They passed the inventory sheets of their allowed medicinal whiskey barrels to the officer in charge. Dillon knew they would take their time. Based on the conversations he overheard, they had plans to remain on the property until the weekend.

Early the next morning, a horse whinnied as he walked down to the distillery. Tena had never returned with his car. His hope was she had made it to Marcos and Lily. The pinto was tied by herself to the paddock gate.

"Hey, girl." He carried a bucket of oats to the horse and placed it behind the gatepost. "Looks like Marcos rode you back last night." Patting the brown and white filly, he looked at the tracks in the mud. Dillon could tell Marcos rode back on the second horse. A clear sign they were safe and hunkered down at the hunting lodge.

After two nerve-racking days, the federal troops left. Dillon mounted the pinto and cantered off to the hunting lodge. He would have preferred to take his aunt's car but was still unsure if their distillery was being watched. Disturbing thoughts nagged Dillon. Just who was behind this last raid?

Why had the accusation originated from Lassiter? Was it a coincidence that it was Reggie and Lily's hometown? With their deep pockets from rock and marble quarries, Lassiter's leaders always had political pull. Had someone tapped into those influences? Was it merely to aggravate or was it something more sinister? Like gaining ultimate control of Tom Tanner Tennessee Whiskey? He swore to himself, giving his horse a quick kick.

****

Dillon shook his head. He'd never thought of using the cabin as a hideaway. His family's hunting lodge had at one time been an original settler's log home. The structure was located next to the shallow stream which ran through the Tanner property. His grandfather had staked it out years ago as the idyllic hunting and fishing cottage. He and Tom had used it through the years. They had kept the pantry stocked with provisions that wouldn't spoil, stored linens and blankets in the cedar chests, and kept chopped firewood for the cast-iron stove and fireplace. Up until now, they had used it as the ultimate getaway spot.

Marcos met him outside when he rode up. "Are they gone?"

"Yes, they left this morning. Hell, don't want to go through that again." Dillon dismounted and handed Marcos the reins. "Usually, they are paid off under the table somewhere. But this time, I had to pretend I didn't see them sneak two crates of whiskey out to their cars before they left."

"Don't they try the other tactic? Add to your inventory?"

"Yeah, they do. Gives them a reason to start smashing barrels. This group must have determined their payment needed to be in liquid gold form. They had no interest in busting our barrels of whiskey."

Marcos was still chortling at Dillon's comment when they entered the cabin. Lily sat at the room's big oak table, surrounded by black dust and pieces of crinkled paper. A hyper-awareness of her struck Dillon. His heart hammered as she beamed at him with that silly grin. She swiped a black smudge on her cheek.

"Looks like you've been busy," he said, removing his hat.

Lily stood, dusting her hands. "Marcos found these old floor plans in the drawers. I used the backs of them to draw on. Hope you don't mind. Got the charcoal from the fireplace."

Dillon walked over to study the charcoal sketches.

Joy Allyson

"I set her up an easel outside, right by the bank," Marcos bragged.

The charcoal prints captured the lazy creek and bare limbs of the shoreline trees to perfection. The detail of the rock and crevices with her shading and crisscross would impress even a trained eye.

"These are beautiful." Dillon leafed through the half a dozen prints. She had visibly taken advantage of her isolation time at the cabin.

"She's really good." Marcos helped to clear the sketches from the tabletop.

"I can tell," Dillon said as he perused the artwork.

Lily beamed. "Well, I needed to do something. Marcos has been fishing and Tena cooking." She lowered her gaze from Dillon's stare, pinning her arms to her stomach.

"And I was worried about you all." Dillon chuckled.

"Is my pup missing me?" Lily asked.

"That's kinda why I figured I better come get you. He's getting pretty partial to my aunt Chloe."

"No." Lily looked genuinely alarmed.

"Miss Lily, can you finish clearing the table and set out plates? This fish is ready, and it's best eaten hot." Tena lifted the remaining fillets from the skillet.

"Tena"—Dillon turned to face her for the first time upon entering—"I meant to tell you the feds will remember you for a long, long time. Don't know what you did to hold them up the other night, but it worked like a charm."

He helped Lily make room at the table by placing her work on the top of a bureau. They laughed as Marcos pulled up another chair, and they sat down to fried catfish and hush puppies for lunch.

****

After they finished eating and cleaning, Marcos and Tena headed back to Tanner House and Lily remained with him and the horses. As the two of them walked into the cabin, Dillon studied Lily's artwork in more detail. He pulled another drawing from the chest and held it up to the light.

"You know, you could sell these. They are amazing."

She came to stand beside him. Blushing, her blue eyes flickered. "Are you trying to help me earn a living now that you know I'm broke?"

He winced. He needed no reminders of the position she was now in. "No, really, you could sell these." His suggestion held weight. She had serious talent.

"And sell them how? Aren't I supposed to stay hidden?" She sat back in the wooden chair, her voice devoid of emotion.

He ran his hand through his hair, then rubbed his neck. "Just until I get my whiskey back. Won't be long. Come on, let's go to Tanner House." He looked around the cabin. "Leave your drawings here. We can come back tomorrow. Set you up a sort of art studio."

The appreciative look on her face made his heart wobble. He released a deep breath, feeling the tension leave his body for the first time in days. Here at the cabin, he could forget for a while his frustrated efforts to find his stolen spirits, his wasted time spent dealing with prohibition, and his complicated feelings for her. If only he could stay.

"I'll go get the horses." A long horseback ride might be the next best thing.

"What are their names? Marcos didn't tell me."

Dillon lifted Lily onto the pinto.

"Her name is Julie, don't ask me why. Tom named her. This is Prince," he said when he mounted the black stallion. "So—you ride extremely well, Miss Lily, and are quite an artist. What else do I not know about you?"

Her laughter was a warm caress. "Well, I know you know I'm an only child. And you are too. Did you ever want brothers and sisters? I did."

"Me. Not really, I have two cousins. Sorry, didn't mean to remind you of Reggie."

"That's all right. Boys or girls?"

"One of each. Love it if you could meet them. But Tom's in South America right now. And Kit's at college. You'd like her. She's your age."

"I'm not a college girl, Dillon."

"Hey, don't go thinking she's a snob or anything. Far from it." He laughed, then kicked his horse into a canter. "Come on, it's going to get cold once the sun goes down. We better make up some time."

****

The next morning, Dillon took Lily on her first tour of the distillery. They crossed to the footbridge, spanning the gurgling stream.

"This water is the lifeblood of our whiskey. The limestone bedrock below is a natural filter." Dillon stopped while Lily leaned across the railing. "Been more than one fight against our family about who controls the water. Some say it's the source of the finest distilled whiskey in all the Americas. I have to agree." *And I don't plan to sell out to a criminal syndicate in the end.*

Dillon saluted the two armed guards as they

walked past the fenced compound's gated entrance. He led her inside the two-story structure with its massive cedar and oak beams, past the drying rooms and giant mash turns, then to their gleaming pot still.

"This place once bustled with scores of workers. Now we operate on a scaled-down schedule. The medicinal contracts we signed allowed Tom Tanner Tennessee Whiskey to survive, but the revenues barely keep us above water." He didn't add that another dagger to their bottom line was the loss of military contracts once the war ended.

When they finished the walk-through, he took her upstairs to the offices. They walked past a closed door with *Finance* etched on the glass panel. The next door was half glass as well, with *Tasting* imprinted on it.

"If there's tasting going on, do not interrupt. Aunt Chloe's hard and fast orders." Dillon opened the door to the empty room. "The most important decisions the company makes are in this room."

A large walnut table centered the square ten feet by ten feet room. Individual ladder-back chairs surrounded the tabletop.

"These don't look very comfortable."

"No, they're not supposed to be. Tasters are to only concentrate on the whiskey." Dillon walked to the wall full of shot glasses. "Come here. Taste this."

He poured her a thimble of amber liquid. She nosed the whiskey, then sipped it.

"What do you think?"

"I like it. I detect fruit and spice."

"My aunt thought with more women drinking now, we'd try some new recipes."

"Cheers." She held up her shot glass. "I like that

idea too."

From the tasting room, Dillon led her into an open area with four giant desks facing each other. "We dismantled the individual walls of our manager's offices after Tom and I came back from the war. My uncle, aunt, Tom, and I run our business together from this room now."

"And didn't you say you had a girl cousin? What about her? Where will she put her desk?"

"Anywhere she wants it." Dillon laughed.

Lily strolled to the paned glass windows and looked out. The view included the giant rick house where the barrels of whiskey were aged and stored to the open space where charcoal was burned. A giant nine-foot wall surrounded the whole compound.

Dillon joined her. "Over there is our newest building. We built it right before prohibition; it's where we do our bottling now and attach the medicinal stamps. We have the biggest safe in the county, keeping those labels secured. I'll show you later."

He opened a door at the rear of the offices. "Come look in here. There's something I want you to see. This is our old storeroom, a ton of neat things in here. We have good parchment paper in here somewhere. If we can find it, you could use it for drawing."

Lily entered and stared at old posters hanging on the walls, along with assorted medals and trophies stacked haphazardly on shelves. An enormous pile of broadsheets and posters was heaped on a table in the corner. Dust-covered artwork was stacked in another pile. She leafed through a mound of old lithographs. They had to be thirty or forty years old. She'd seen examples before of these temping nymphs with their cherubic smiles and chubby cheeks, arms, and ample bosoms, all promoting whiskey. Among the samples, the Tom Tanner and Penland Kittrell Whiskey brands were front and center. A bygone era.

"These are works of art. You should frame them." Lily lifted a few for closer inspection, measuring each one for its appeal. "Where do you meet your customers? You could hang them in your reception room."

"Haven't you heard, sweetheart, prohibition is the law of the land now. There's no reception area. Don't have customers knocking on our doors anymore." He pressed his palm against the doorframe, fisting his hand. No point dwelling on things he couldn't control.

"Well, prohibition can't last forever."

"Yeah, that's what everyone says. Here, let's find you a bit of plain paper." He reached over and opened an antique rolltop desk. Inside lay rolls of newsprint quality paper and assorted pens and different colors of ink.

Lily shuffled through the pens and ink after Dillon removed the paper. "Most of this ink has dried. But I might salvage it. Do you have something I can put these in?"

"Let's use this basket. After lunch, I'll drive you to the hunting lodge. I'll set you up with the easel Marcos made. I think you'll be safe there while I run into town to finish a couple of errands."

****

Once back at the hunting cottage, Dillon dragged Lily's easel to the water's edge. It was a warm day in October. The sunshine played hide-and-seek with a few puffy clouds.

"This spot is perfect." Lily attached the blank newsprint and then stood back to take in her view. "Providing the sun stays out long enough, I can catch the shadows on the rocks just right."

"If you think you're all fixed up and will be okay for a while, I'm going to take off. I shouldn't be gone more than a couple of hours."

Charlie had come with them. The dog scampered around the cabin and then returned to explore a steep area leading to the stream. Dillon double-checked the perimeter. The hunting refuge offered the perfect sanctuary; its seclusion reassured him. "I'm leaving you with this here guard dog. I'm confident he'll yap any intruder to death."

Lily wore the little beret she had worn to the bank. With his aunt's oversized jacket, she looked like a genuine artist. He wanted to kiss her but stepped away before the temptation grew stronger.

By the time Dillon returned from his errands, a stiff breeze had blown in more clouds. Lily had kept her easel in the same spot. She waved when he drove up. He ambled toward her, holding out a paper bag.

"What's this?"

"Something I found."

Lily dug into the bag. Inside were paints, paintbrushes of different sizes, and a dozen colored art pencils. "Dillon, you shouldn't have." She gave him a huge smile.

He cleared his throat. "Show me what you've drawn today."

They stood together as she presented him with her etchings. While explaining her efforts, he became acutely aware of her lilac scent, the warmth of her body, and how the strawberry blonde of her hair glistened when the sun peeked through. When their sides touched, she did not move away.

Dillon's pulse raced, and he pulled at his shirt collar. "I think I'll carry this old wood chair over by the tree and just watch you paint." He carried more packages from his car inside the cabin. He returned carrying cushions and dragging a high-back chair from the porch.

"I see a piece of driftwood that looks interesting."

"Do you want me to bring it to you?"

"No. Just relax. I'll show you what I'm trying to capture when I am finished."

Dillon positioned the pillows and laid his head back where he could watch Lily work. Within minutes, his eyes grew heavy, and he drifted off to sleep. When two heavy raindrops fell on his face, he shook himself awake. Dark clouds had moved in from the west and more drops of rain fell.

Lily was no longer in front of her easel.

Chapter Twenty-One

Dillon

"Lily."

He jumped from the chair, canvasing the area. She was nowhere to be seen. Hair lifted from his arms and the nape of his neck. Threatening gray clouds crowded the skies.

"Lily," he called again.

Charlie's bark sounded from the river stream's bank.

"Down here." He heard her voice in the distance.

He ran to the water's edge. Lily had hopped across a section of rocks and held a large driftwood branch she'd pulled from the creek and that darn dog was with her. Had she chased after him, or had he followed her?

"Leave it. Storm's coming." Dillon jumped off the embankment. His leg muscles tightened as he hurdled a tide pool and then jumped on a flat rock, avoiding the jagged and uneven ones. She dropped her find and leaped from rock to rock, lunging for Dillon's hand. He grabbed hold of her, gathering her in his arms, and lifted her to the top of the bank. When her feet touched the ground, her drawing fluttered in the wind as the easel toppled to the ground. Her artwork floated by in the air.

"My drawing!" Rain pelted them as they scrambled

to save her print.

Charlie barked and raced around them.

"Got it." Dillon grabbed Lily, tucking the drawing under his arm, and dashed with her toward the cottage. Once inside, he placed her sketch on the big table and removed his wet jacket while Lily did the same. Charlie stood in the middle of the room and shook his coat.

"The cushions," they said in unison. Dillon raced out to retrieve them.

Outside, the rain turned into a downpour as if huge buckets of water poured from the sky. Dillon reentered the lodge soaking wet. He threw the damp cushions in a cane chair and wiped the water from his face. A rhythmic deluge on the cabin's tin roof lent an intimate feel to the room.

"I'll start a fire." Dillon threw a couple of pieces of wood on top of the kindling stacked in the fireplace and lit it with a wooden match from the mantle. He bent down to stack another piece of firewood on the flames, then stabbed the logs with an iron poker. "That should do it."

Charlie shook his little body again, then scratched out a place on the hearthrug in front of the fire.

Lily stood in front of the hearth, rubbing her hands up and down her arms, warding off the chill.

"Your shirt." She reached with her hand and then withdrew it as smoke billowed from the fire. "You're soaked."

He rose from the hearth and removed his wet shirt.

She inched closer to him, studying his naked torso. Her eyes widened and turned a dark blue. This was not good. He had counted the seconds, the minutes, the hours, the days he had kept himself away from her physically. Knowing if he held her again like the day in the Playhouse, he could not let her go.

All the memories of those brief moments—the taste of her sweet mouth and the response of her body to his flooded back. Throwing away caution, he pulled her close and pressed his lips to her mouth, urging her to open to him. His hands swept down her body and then lifted her. He carried her into the bedroom, holding his breath as he lowered her. If she was going to deny him, this was the time.

Instead, she lifted her hands to his chest, smoothing her fingers along the plane of his muscles. She started unfastening her shirt, releasing each button at a tortuously slow rate. He shoved her hands away and pushed the buttons through at a rapid pace. She had worn the same blue jeans and flannel shirt bought the day at the farmer's co-op, and he grinned at the memory. Once he'd removed her shirt, he sat her at the bedside and tugged at her tight jeans, causing them both to fall into the bed. Covering her body with his, he kissed her as she dug her fingers into his hair and shoulders. In a tangled fight with quilts and sheets, they removed the rest of their clothing within seconds.

Once naked, they held each other tight. Relishing the fact there was nothing between them, he embraced her, whispering words of love in her ear. No barriers, no constraints, and no obstacles. Each needed the other for inexplicable reasons. Dillon schooled himself to be patient, but his effort gave way, as his heart pounded in his chest. His control slipping, he pulled her once more into a passionate kiss and let all logic dissipate.

****

Lily

Lily never imagined kisses so softly sensitive, yet forceful at the same time, as his lips crisscrossed her body. Dillon loomed over her, his eyes dark pools of passion. The feelings of warmth and connection were not an illusion. Pleasure resonated through her at this revelation. She trembled, pulling his body tighter, yet he ignored her urgings, taking his time.

She swallowed hard, realizing he no longer cared that she was inexperienced. His mouth and tongue blazed a trail down her entire body. The mood was no longer playful but intense and purposeful. Leading her into a world she had never traveled. Not ever had she imagined lovemaking so raw, so transforming.

She sighed with the pleasure of it, pleased her response was shared with him. She gave herself over as he took her completely, plunging her into an abyss, then capturing her to him again as he ravished and plundered her body once more. His name escaped her throat as she arched against him.

He took her low cry in his mouth and kissed her long and hard.

Her brain shattered like crystal, sending broken pieces of glass outward as his shuddering weight fell full force on her. Breathing hard, they clung to each other as they slumped back into the bedding, stunned. With an effort, she tried lifting her hand but couldn't.

Once her breathing quietened, he brought his lips to her and kissed her sweetly. He held her, cradling her against him.

"I just never imagined..." Her voice trailed off.

"I did," he whispered as the two of them drifted off to sleep.

****

Dillon

Dillon woke in the middle of the night and reached for Lily. They made love again. The rain had stopped. The only sound was the drip, drip from an overflowing gutter. Content to lie among the tussled linens, Dillon repositioned his head on Lily's stomach. He playfully intertwined their fingers as Lily ran her hand through his curls with her free hand.

"If the only way I could ever meet you, Lily, was to be sent to prison, I want you to know it was worth it." Dillon lifted his face to hers.

She shook her head in response before being gathered in his embrace. "I love you, Lily Stonecipher."

She smiled. "There is no need. They are just words. What happened between us will be enough. You must—"

He drew her tighter. "It is not enough." He knew loneliness and understood how her outlandish behavior when he first met her was a front for her vulnerability. She had sacrificed too much already. She had lost her inheritance and now was helping him. It was a late realization that what happened between them, he wanted to happen. And in the days ahead, he wanted her to remain a part of his life. They made love once more with no desperation, no sense of time passing too fast, only unshakable, enduring pleasure at their closeness to one another.

Before dawn, Dillon left their bed, grabbed his trousers, and walked into the living room. At some time in the night, he'd hung his shirt in front of the fire to dry. Charlie scratched at the front door. He opened it and let the little dog out. After he slipped on his shirt and let the pup back in, he went back into the bedroom. Lily was dressing. He took her in his arms again and gave her a deep kiss.

"We better head back home. I don't want Aunt Chloe thinking something bad happened to us."

Their worries were for naught. When they arrived at Tanner House, a note lay on the kitchen table from his aunt. She had left for Huntsville to help with a baby shower for her cousin, Maggie's daughter, whom everyone suspected of carrying twins.

****

"Dillon, since our accountant is no longer with us, perhaps it would be better if Lily and her grandmother used a person they knew, a trusted attorney, to untangle the financial situation concerning her trust."

"Thank you, Aunt Chloe."

She handed him the cup of coffee she had carried up to his office in the distillery. After her trip to Huntsville, she sought him out. She broached the subject of Lily's situation.

"Her grandmother needs her. For both her company and support to help her navigate through the awful mess her nephew has thrown her in."

He scrubbed his face. "Can't let her go back to her hometown. Her cousin, Reggie, would be on to her at once. I hope he thinks she's in Florida visiting with a school chum."

"Dillon, that might be the soundest solution right now. I mean, sending her to Florida. Her grandmother could meet her down there. I could arrange it. I'll help."

"Maybe it would be for the best." Dillon scraped his hands through his hair. Any debate he was going to have with his aunt about the matter he knew he would lose.

"You know it is. You are intent on finding out what happened to our whiskey and until you do, you won't be able to help Lily."

"Give me a few days? I'll get her situated in St. Augustine, then you can help me get her grandmother down there to her."

"Dillon, you'll be relieved if you can get her settled. And I can't think of a lovelier place to spend the winter. She'll be fine and it won't be long before she'll be able to come back here. I'm positive."

****

"Your aunt's right. You're right. I understand. I need to be out of your way. And I should be with Granny when I break the news about my cousin."

Dillon propped himself up on his elbow with his arm under a pillow. The late autumn afternoon sun's afterglow filtered through the hunting lodge windows. The brief escape for a tryst before Lily left him was his doing.

He traced the arch of her brow, the delicate line of her nose, and her lip's sweet curve. It might be weeks before he saw her again.

"Dillon, did it ever occur to you, maybe Reggie didn't steal your whiskey, maybe he just stole my money? I don't want you to get hurt."

His Lily, always concerned about practical consequences. He took her hand and kissed it.

"I mean Reggie comes from bad stock. But…" She pulled her hand back.

"I wish what you suggest were true. It would be a lot easier on your grandmother, once you break the news. It's going to be hard to take," Dillon said.

198

"Oh, my granny's pretty tough. She put up with Reggie's grandfather, her brother-in-law, for years. He was a real case. He resented the fact that all his money came from my side of the family, and they wouldn't let him control it. But it didn't stop him from putting on a big show of being 'the man about town.' Curtis Bart Asshole. That's what everyone called him. CBA."

Dillon's posture stiffened.

Lily dragged her hand through her hair, rolling her eyes. "Don't look at me like you've never heard a gal curse before." She scooted away, grabbing the covers.

Drawing a breath, then releasing it before speaking, he asked, "What was his grandfather's name again?"

"Curtis Bartholomew Axelrod. CBA."

"Lily, you are magnificent!" He encircled her waist with his hands, lifting her high in his arms; he kissed her, not releasing her as he let her down.

****

Three days later, Lily boarded the train with Dillon as her escort after repeated assurance her dog would travel in luxury in the livestock train car adjoining theirs. Lily clutched Dillon's arm. She had bundled up in a heavy winter wrap with autumn temperatures dropping to record lows.

Dillon laughed at the thought of Lily tossing away the stylish raccoon coat she relished now the moment she reached Florida's shores. Not more than a sweater would be needed where she was going. He found a nice apartment on the beach, and her grandmother would join her there.

He swung his arm about Lily, hugging her tightly. With a bit of luck, Christmas would see the end of their ordeal. Tom, hopefully, was making his way to Mexico from Rio and joining his father. Their specially designed truck, like a Trojan horse, was almost ready and would serve as the shiny object to ensnare the crooks. And the mastermind's connection to CBA would be revealed. Dillon wished Lily could stay with him, but her safety was uppermost on his mind. He and Lily waved goodbye to his aunt and settled in their cabin for the long train trek to Florida, determined to enjoy these last few days together.

****

All November and December, Dillon and Chloe waited anxiously for word about Tom. No letters arrived with news he had made it to Mexico. On Christmas Day, Dillon took Kit to the train station to board a train back to school for her last semester. The *Farmer's Almanac* had predicted an extremely harsh winter and early reports from west of the Mississippi indicated that bad weather was already on its way.

"I hate to have you leave us this early, but your mother is right. If you got stuck back here with us in Oak Hollow, you'd be in danger of not finishing school."

Dillon kissed his cousin's cheek goodbye and left to mail a letter to Lily. He smiled wistfully. Her last letter to him indicated she and her grandmother were settling into Florida's peaceful routine but that she and Charlie were missing him terribly.

That night at the distillery, Dillon had the armed guards assist him with unloading his last coal order shipped in on the trunk line. He was not taking any chances of having his coal reserves diminish. He then sent them home to spend the rest of their Christmas with their families.

As soon as he locked the distillery's gates, Dillon felt the weather change. The white Christmas so many had cheerfully wished for twenty-four hours earlier turned into a blizzard by midnight. The new year did not come in as a lamb. Snow squalls with strong gusty winds reduced the visibility to only a foot in front of one's face for the next week. The mid-state region was gripped in a record ice storm. First freezing rain, followed by blinding snow, then more ice smothered them. Heavy ice crystals suspended on electric wires weighed them down, dangerously downing power lines for miles. Glazed trees became uprooted, making any effort to travel or hunt a deadly act.

In mid-January, Tena went down first with a sharp attack of fever, and Chloe followed, succumbing to the bitter flu. While they nursed each other, he and Marcos took up residence in the distillery. Their guards and workers would not be returning. Between the two of them, they were able to keep the distillery running at minimum capacity.

Dillon swore as he pulled the distillery door shut as another fierce wind attempted to take the door off its hinges. He walked the breadth of his distillery. His pot still blazed with an intense fire. He rubbed his neck and glanced at his coal bins and their dwindling piles.

"How long will the coal reserves last?" he asked Marcos.

"Not much longer."

Dillon smiled grimly. "One thing's for sure, I'm giving up sleeping with my shotgun at night. If anyone dares to show up to rob us, let them have the place."

Dillon's frustration grew as his plan to lure Reggie Wyatt into another whiskey heist was put on hold. The government pharmacies weren't placing any new orders, so there would be no transporting of spirits, even if he could get a delivery out. The record ice storm tightened its hold on the region, accumulating huge economic costs in its wake. Business was non-existent.

Added to Dillon's concern for the distillery was his attempt to find out about CBA and Associates. A solid half-inch of ice continued to paralyze most of the state. Nashville was shut down. And when the lieutenant governor slipped on a sidewalk and broke his kneecap, the capital became a ghost town. His effort to have the state's commerce department reveal who was behind the corporation was the only thing he knew of melting away. With no means of communication or transportation, the state was at a virtual standstill. For the first time since Lily left for Florida, he was glad she was away.

Chapter Twenty-Two

Kit

Kit Kittrell stepped on Oak Hollow's celebrated Victorian train station platform as a brisk March wind blew her hair. The townspeople still reveled in pride over their station's wide verandas, intricate filigree iron banisters, imported tile work floors, and stained glass windows. Remnants of the winter's harsh ice storm still survived in shady spots. Unsure who, or if anyone, would meet her, she looked around. Aunt Maggie's maid's garbled message led her to believe both her mother and aunt would be in Huntsville attending her cousin's birth of twins. Her father was still setting up his business in Mexico, her brother was nowhere to be found, and she didn't want to bother Dillon, so she might have to hire a taxicab.

She smoothed her rose-colored traveling suit, wishing she had dressed in a cotton frock and sweater for the three-hour train ride from her college town. She brushed back her hair from her shoulders, debating for the twelfth time whether to leave it long or have her locks cut into a bob like a ton of her friends. She put on hold any haircut, feeling certain her golden brown wavy hair wouldn't achieve the same effect as Clara Bow's vamp look.

She scanned the parking lot once more before

noticing the tall figure leaning against a cherry-apple-red convertible coupe facing her way. He tipped his hat off his brow.

"Alex Stooksbury!" She laughed and raced down the stairs and fell into his strong arms, giving him a welcoming hug. She stepped back to see his reaction. He was the most handsome man in town, second only to her brother. The man she imagined she was in love with since she was old enough to ride a bike. "Are you here to pick me up? I hope so because there is no one else here."

"My secretary got a message from your aunt's maid, who said your aunt would give your mother the message you were being picked up by me. So could I please pick you up? I must have gotten something right. You're here. Not much of a welcome back, I guess?"

"No, this is perfect. A lot less complicated."

"That can't be your only bag?" He looked up at the platform where she abandoned her small suitcase.

"No, I told the train manager I'd come back for my trunk."

"Look here. I'm not a college boy, but I'd say it's a good two months before any semester ends."

She breathed in. "Yes, it's a long story. Are you in a hurry? I need to go back inside to get train departure information from the depot." After she came out, she asked if he would take her to the bank before driving her home.

"Bank is already closed. Are you going somewhere? You were talking to the ticket master for a pretty long time."

"If you must know, I'm meeting my father in Mexico."

"None of my business, but does he know this?" Amused doubt filled his expression.

"No. It's going to be a surprise."

Alex secured her suitcase in his car's trunk. "Well, let me get you back to your aunt's."

"No. I'm going home to grab more clothes. I'll stay there."

"Okay, got to swing by my office first."

On the short drive to his office, she studied Alex. How long since she last saw him? The Christmas before last. He was wearing a smart, well-cut suit that fit his tall, muscular body to a T. And wow, he smelled great. She had whiffed the saddle soap and pine scent on his neck when she hugged him. So different from the oil and grease, which perpetually covered him every time she was around him growing up. With his dark hair mussed up, covered in goop, and playing tricks by jumping out to scare her, she called him affectionately, "my grease monkey."

Had he dressed so nice to meet her? His smile reached his soft chestnut-colored eyes, and the breeze ruffled his brown hair. Her pulse quickened when he patted her hand. She was positive he did not remember that Christmas Day. She had just come home from college. They were supposed to help collect firewood for the night's bonfire. Alex suggested the two of them play hooky from the preparations and take off for a long walk along the creek.

Oh, the things they talked about. The jokes they shared, the stories they reminisced. Her hands tingled, remembering his grasp. The same feeling of warmth radiated through her body, recalling the day. But he never followed up with a phone call or a letter. Reality set in. He was serious about wanting to avoid Dixie Margrave, his reason for needing her near him the entire day. And, of course, everyone forgot everything else when the government agents showed up.

Alex raced through town before shifting gears to turn into his dealership's parking lot. Her brother told her Alex had served under a general during the war and saved the general's life. After they returned to the States, he awarded Alex with one of the first car company dealerships of his family in the mid-south. Folks from Nashville drove to Oak Hollow to make purchases.

At long last, something good happened to her brother's best friend. Alex, whose brutal father only cared about the plows and tractors he built and sold from the family's old blacksmith barn. A barn where his father's tractor fell on him and crushed him to death, leaving Alex and his mom to survive, trying their best to keep the business afloat. Everyone knew if that hadn't happened, Alex would have accepted the engineering scholarship Georgia Tech offered him. Instead, he was forced to drop out of high school and work for a living to help both his mother and him survive.

Rows of shiny new automobiles gleamed in the late afternoon sun as they turned into the sales lot. His dealership must have doubled in size since she was last home. She looked overhead. A gigantic billboard proclaiming "Stooksbury Automotive" sat on the rooftop's main building. Next door was Alex's other business, Stooksbury's Farm and Tractor Supply. Its showroom displayed the latest equipment any farmer would need in the surrounding three counties.

"I'll be back in a minute if you want to wait in the car."

A salesman waylaid Alex as he exited the car showroom. They laughed at a joke. Alex gave a good-hearted slap on the man's back and then sauntered her way. *Gosh, if I can't get to the bank tomorrow, I could borrow the money from Alex.*

"Nice car," she commented when he climbed in.

He squinted sideways. "You in the market?"

"No, I don't think I'll be buying a car anytime soon."

"You know I understand your aunt Maggie going to Huntsville, but if your mother knew you were coming home today, seems like she could have waited."

"She didn't know I was coming home today."

"Okay." He didn't ask the obvious. Just waited her out.

"Well, I guess you're bound to find out sooner or later," she said a minute later. "I was kicked out of school."

He pressed his lips together to keep from smiling.

"I don't think Dad would care. Mother's a different story."

"What 'cha do? I know you're too smart to need to cheat on a test. Bet you snuck some fellow up to your dormitory room."

She crossed her arms, pursing her lips. "Honestly."

"My Lord, you didn't have an affair with one of your professors, did you?"

"No, I didn't." She scowled, squirming in her seat. She gave him the closest version of what she thought he'd believe. "I smuggled bootleg whiskey into my dorm, if you must know."

"And that got you canned?"

"Apparently, the drys outnumber the wets in alumni donations this year."

"Even with…didn't your family donate money to build an auditorium or something?"

"Well, the Kittrells might as well be Chicago gangsters now—our name on a building is worthless." She sighed dejectedly. "Everyone wanted my mother's help when they were trying to get 'votes for women' passed. They wanted the perfect role model, a beautiful, intelligent, real mother, to work for their cause. Can't use her now because she's a Tanner and married to a Kittrell."

"Prohibition can't last forever."

"I'm beginning to wonder. My father is too. That's why he's in Mexico. He's trying to revive Kittrell's Rye Whiskey there. He's already built a still. I've made up my mind to go down there and help him. Tom can't go. We don't know where he is. And it's about time I started working for a living."

****

Alex

Alex pulled up to Kittrell's red brick Greek Revival mansion, parking his coupe in the front circle drive. He scanned the columned porch and the overhead balcony. For years, he had visited the iconic property. He couldn't recall a time when family members or distillery employees were not running in and out. This evening, the house seemed deserted. Since prohibition and the Kittrell distillery shutdown, the score of workers, who for decades produced the finest rye whiskey around, had long since left. He took a quick look over his shoulder beyond the split-rail fence. The family had sold their prized horses and converted their barn into a garage.

"Hello. Hello, anyone home?" Kit shouted as she walked through the house. A figure appeared in the kitchen doorway. "Sicily. I am so glad to see you, " she squealed.

Alex followed her through the front door. He returned to his car to retrieve her suitcase. "I'll take this upstairs."

"Where's Sicily?" he asked after coming downstairs and finding Kit alone in the kitchen.

"She wanted to get back home before dark. She left on horseback."

"You can't stay here by yourself. Is she or her Mother coming back?"

"I don't think so. Look. She's cooked an awesome stew. Kept it warm on the stove." Kit lifted the lid from the pot. Home-cooked vegetables and beef permeated the air.

"Smells great. Wonder for whom she was cooking?"

"She must have thought Aunt Maggie's housekeeper told her I was coming home. Let's eat. I'm starved."

"Okay, but after we eat, I'm taking you back to your aunt's house."

"No. Can't do it. You can't leave me alone in her house with her boarder, Mr. Jamison. He pinched my derriere at Nancy's wedding."

"Your what?"

"My butt, silly."

"I know what it means. You slapped him hard, I hope."

She huffed impatiently.

"Well, you can stay with one of your chums in town, then. Stay with Jenny Barber. Wasn't she your best friend?"

"You know she's married now."

"So?"

"She married Jack Jarrett. Don't think Jenny would care for me staying overnight in the same house as her husband—my old beau."

"Yeah. Guess that could be a little awkward. How about Carol Patterson?"

"Nah, she's still mad about my brother dropping her. There's your old girlfriend," she teased, "Patty Sawyer or Dixie…"

"No." He looked out the window. "I don't think so. Let's eat. We'll figure something out. Can't stay here by yourself. Too many people roaming the countryside, in particular around here, where they know there once was a working distillery. Hell, it's why your dad burned down the place."

She took a deep breath. "Let's make cornbread."

Alex rolled his eyes at her change of subject. "Okay, I'll help. That's one thing I can cook."

"Look in the pantry for cornmeal and flour."

Kit pulled out a mixing bowl, then looked next to the stove and lifted the cast-iron skillet from the cabinet. Alex found the measuring cups and poured in the dry ingredients while she pulled the eggs and milk from the icebox.

"Let's put in a spoonful of sugar."

"You put sugar in your cornbread?" Alex asked, dumbfounded.

"Of course," she said, smiling, then raised her hand

to wipe a spot of flour from his nose. Alex took her hand in his before he realized what she was doing. He looked into her eyes, still holding her hand.

"You got it from here. I'll go check the barn. Guess it's a garage now," he said, passing off what happened between them. Twilight approached. He glanced at his watch and then looked out the kitchen window. "I'll walk down and get a look around the place—just to check things out. You have a flashlight around or an old lantern?"

A lightning flash lit in the distance, forewarning an approaching storm. Kit pulled a flashlight from the top pantry shelf. "Hurry back."

When he returned, Kit spooned two generous helpings of stew into bowls and cut cornbread from the skillet.

Alex searched for glasses, pouring them milk.

"This is delicious. I haven't had a home-cooked meal in a while," Alex said after taking a bite.

"Don't you have someone cook for you?"

"Nah. Like having a bachelor apartment all to myself."

"Sorry about your ma, Alex. Mother wouldn't let me come home. The flu came through here badly, Dillon's mother, Aunt Raelynn, died from it."

"Lost my uncle too, right after my mother died. Gosh, almost five years ago. I was overseas. Couldn't come home for either funeral."

"Alex, stay here tonight."

"What?" He finished a gulp of milk, wiping his mouth with the back of his hand.

"Stay here with me. That'd be the best. We'll wake early, then you can take me to the bank and then to the train depot."

Alex scooted back in his chair, placing his napkin on the table. "Can't do it. Word got out—your reputation would be ruined."

"Alex, who's going to talk? There's no one here. Besides, once stories start swirling about me getting kicked out of school—especially after my embarrassing speakeasy fiasco, I won't have a reputation left."

His face lit up, the corners of his eyes crinkling. He stood, taking his plate and bowl to the sink, then peered through the window into the darkness. "Tom used to have a bunkroom at the distillery. Nothing there now. Just burned timbers. Can still smell it. Damn shame. I walked around the perimeter when I checked it out."

"They took everything of value out before the fire. The pot still, the fermentation tanks, all the office stuff. Took it all to Tom Tanner Distillery or sold it after they were awarded the medicinal license." She sniffed, then wiped her nose with the back of her hand. "Just sleep in Tom's old room upstairs. You know where it is. Down the hall from mine. I'll get the dishes, then get Tom's room ready."

****

In the middle of the night, the threatening storm had crawled in at a snail's pace over the county's pastures and cornfields. Alex was sound asleep in Tom's bedroom when a fierce lightning bolt struck nearby. Within seconds, a white apparition rushed into his room. He lurched upright and rubbed his eyes before recognizing Kit. The wind from the open window blew her long hair off her shoulders and wrapped her thin cotton nightgown around her slender form. She climbed from the foot of his bed up beside him, dragging a patchwork quilt.

"I'm afraid of storms." She wrapped herself in her blanket and, in an instant, went back to sleep.

Alex remained motionless, his back propped against the headboard. Would she honestly think he could go back to sleep? *Kit Kittrell is in bed with me.*

Damn. It was bad enough seeing her at the train station. A year and a half passed since he'd last seen her. Had it been that long? It was Christmas. She had grown into a beauty. Hell, she was a doll when she was a baby girl. But that Christmas, she was nineteen and a full-fledged woman. Twice they had kissed. The one he relished the most was under the mistletoe. He knew, and she knew, there was something between them. They talked, took long walks, drank, laughed, and held hands. They wedged themselves on her family's back staircase steps and talked until two in the morning. Even Tom noticed.

Then the next day, the ruckus started, and all hell broke loose. Federal authorities, who until then pretty much left Oak Hollow off their check sheets, showed up and made an all-out "Christmas Surprise" inspection of Tom Tanner Tennessee Whiskey Distillery. Old-timers said they hadn't seen that many federal troops in the county since the war sixty years earlier. They sent Kit back to school without delay, and the remaining Tanners and Kittrell clan closed ranks.

And now she's in bed with me. In her sleep, she touched his leg. He was afraid to move; he silently counted the spare car parts inventory he stocked in his warehouse. Finally, he fell asleep, sleeping sitting up. As dawn broke, Kit slipped from the bed and left the room. He lifted his head off the hard wooden backboard and stretched his stiff neck. A moment later, she returned.

"I forgot my quilt." She gave him one last view of her shapely body as she disappeared again.

Damn. He threw the covers off his bed. *I need one cold shower.*

Chapter Twenty-Three

Kit

Kit waited in the car while Alex strode into his dealership showroom. He returned in less than twenty minutes, carrying four Cokes and a bag of snacks in his arms. He'd promised he'd be quick after saying he needed to swing by the dealership before taking her to the bank.

She'd been ready to leave her house early. Before breakfast, she had packed her small suitcase and placed it by the door. She agreed with Alex's plan. He would take her to her aunt Maggie's house, and if her housekeeper was back, she would stay there. If not, she would ask her old girlfriend if she could stay with her overnight.

"Who are these for?" she asked as he walked up to his car.

"Anyone who wants them." He leaned over and tucked the colas behind the driver's seat. After passing the snacks to her, he climbed in. He took a left out of the parking lot and drove north until he pulled onto the main highway. They passed familiar farms and pastures Kit had driven or rode by her entire life.

"Where are you going? I have to go to the bank?" She sent Alex an alarmed look.

Alex increased the car's speed and passed a trailer

carrying horses.

"You promised to take me to the bank. Where are you taking me?" she pleaded.

"Cincinnati."

Kit looked at Alex's passive face, then turned her head, counting mile markers as they distanced themselves from Oak Hollow. Too enraged to say anything unless it sounded like a rant, she remained silent.

"Look, you want to show you can help your father. When you call him next, tell him how you almost single-handedly brought his custom-designed truck down from Cincinnati overnight."

"Are you kidnapping me?"

"In a way, yes. You will be a lot safer with me than on a train headed to Mexico."

"I wasn't going to go. This morning, I said I changed my mind. I told you I'd go ask Debbie to spend the night until my aunt came back."

"Remember when Tom and I tried to teach you to play poker? I told you every time I dealt the cards, I could read your face like a book. I could tell that brain of yours was clicking on all cylinders this morning, planning to convince someone to go to Mexico with you as soon as you bought tickets."

She fumed, stamping her foot against the floorboard.

"I hope it wasn't poor Sicily—just the thought of you dragging that sweet girl down there…"

"You have no idea how inconsiderate you have been and still are? You have been an absolute grouch the entire day. So cranky—not to take me to the bank to get out my money…"

"Damn right, I'm cranky. I've been carting you around and babysitting you since three p.m. yesterday. And lucky to get two hours of sleep on top of that."

"What? Now you're blaming me for the thunderstorm last night."

"Hell, no, and you know what kept me up all night. You crawling into bed with me and not so much as…" He slammed his hand on the steering wheel.

"It was me, Alex."

"Damn right, it was you. Can't go climbing into bed with any man."

"I don't go climbing into bed with any man."

"What if I woke up, still half asleep, and rolled over to find a woman in my bed?"

"It was, I'd…" She became flustered.

"You'd what? I'd show you what's what before you could even say your name." He scraped his hand through his hair and gave her an annoyed look.

A shy smile crossed her face. She brushed a strand of hair blowing across her face behind her ear.

Frustrated, Alex studied the road. "Let's concentrate on getting your dad's truck."

"Can I have one of those RC colas?"

"Yeah, open one for me too," he asked in an exasperated tone. "And hand me a Moon Pie.

"Look here, Kit. I don't know how much you know about Dillon's plan to catch the scumbag who set him up." Alex sent Kit a penetrating look.

"I know it involved some smarmy country club swell. I ordered him fancy tailored clothes, so he could fit in with the members. He's determined on revenge." Kit unwrapped a cracker package.

"Do you blame him?"

"Not on your life." She stuffed two crackers into her mouth.

"Well, the takedown involves this new truck we're picking up. It must look like a legit whiskey delivery is being made in this souped-up vehicle. That's part of the lure. Hell, every bootlegger in five states would want this truck. It has a five hundred horsepower engine and armored doors and double thick windshields, and industrialized springs.

"Cost a pretty penny, I bet."

"And then some. But my friends in Detroit have given us the bare bones. They're adding the final touches in Cincinnati. We'll go there first. If it's ready, we'll leave my car there and you can ride back with me. I'll get my car back later."

****

"Well, hello, little lady. I'll need excuses for Stooksbury to visit me more often if he's going to bring the likes of you with him." Alex had pulled into a large car and truck dealership on the outskirts of the main downtown Cincinnati late that afternoon.

Kit blushed and pretended to study the other cars in the showroom as Alex ambled back into the dealership's garage area with the owner. A few minutes later, Alex returned.

"They have to resolder a part that's come loose. He said to give him an hour, and he'd know if it took."

"This advertisement is all wrong." Kit stood studying a poster mounted on a wall above two shiny sports cars.

"How's that?" Alex considered the poster.

Kit waved her hand over the gleaming new cars in the showroom. "If I was selling fun cars like these—I wouldn't show how to change a flat tire on the side of a highway. I'd show a family out for a Sunday drive or a couple driving up into the mountains or to the shore in their snazzy new automobile."

"Um, yeah."

Kit slid her hand across a baby-blue Studebaker coupe's sleek fender, then leaned over the front door to check the interior.

"Hey, hop in. You must feel what it's like if you're ever going to buy."

She smiled and opened the passenger door and slipped in. Alex went to the driver's side. He slid across the huge bench seat and threw his arm across the leather-upholstered back.

"Do you know people make love in their cars second only to bedrooms?"

"How could you know such a thing?"

"I know everything about cars." His hand reached over and stroked a strand of her hair. "Don't you believe me?"

"There's not much room." She stretched her legs. "I mean, this car is big, but…" She flustered. "I mean, I know people do it in haylofts and other places."

"Do what in haylofts?" Alex slid closer as his right arm curled around her. "Tell me more about these hayloft encounters." He brushed her hair off her shoulder and leaned down to kiss her exposed collarbone. When he raised his head, his lips were inches from hers.

A heavy bang slapped the trunk of the Desoto. Kit jumped. "Hey, you two lovebirds, got disappointing news."

Alex moved away from Kit, and she looked toward

the showroom.

"What's up?" Alex asked.

"Solder not taking. With a bit of luck, it's going to before we close today. Figured you two might want to get a late lunch, dinner, or something rather than hang out here for hours. We close at six. But I'm staying to keep working on it. Hopefully, won't take overnight."

****

Alex

"We could have taken in a movie," Alex said as he opened their hotel room door. The two agreed to rent a room with a long wait in front of them.

Kit rubbed her backside. The last thing she wanted was to sit in a movie theater after riding in a car all day. "No. I just want to lie down and take a nap. You buy us lunch."

The small suite held two bedrooms and two bathrooms and a little kitchenette. Alex carried in her bag and laid it on the small bedroom's bed.

"I noticed a sandwich shop close by. I'll walk around and see if it looks to be the best one. Then I'll bring us something back."

****

"That your little red convertible?" the man at the coffee shop asked as Alex circled back to the first shop he had come across.

"Yeah."

"A couple of guys came in here and asked if I knew who you were."

"No kidding."

"Told 'em I figured you were heading to Louisville."

"Thanks." Alex passed an extra dollar across the

counter as the cashier rang up his lunch order.

Alex raced back to the hotel. His heart lurched when he heard what the sandwich shop owner told him. It could be anything. They could want the truck he was waiting on, or his convertible, or Kit. My God, had someone overheard who was with him at the dealership? Kit Kittrell. He even bragged to the owner she was Tom Tanner's great-granddaughter. How stupid.

He jumped off the elevator on the fifth floor and sprinted to their room. He grasped the doorknob as he dug for his key. Unlocked. He turned the knob and stepped in. He checked Kit's room. Empty. Returning to the living area, he threw the paper bags on the kitchenette table. He moved to the master bedroom. She wasn't there. He turned down the hallway of mirrored closet doors to the connected bathroom. As soon as he entered, the plastic curtains from the shower slid back and a naked Kit stepped out. His mouth fell open, powerless to take his gaze away from her widening eyes and naked body.

"Oh," Kit squeaked and fell back into the shower, yanking the curtain shut. Alex backed into the wall, pressing his head against it. Kit reached out and grabbed a towel hanging on the rack and wrapped it around her body.

"Alex, what are you doing in here? You scared me to death."

"*You* scared me to death." His heart pounded hard. A sudden flush of warmth throbbed throughout his body. "I thought something had happened to you. And what are you doing in here? Our room was unlocked, and you didn't shut the bathroom door."

Kit walked to him. Standing inches away, she lifted her arm to the side of his head. "You're leaning against my bathrobe."

"Oh, sorry." Alex recovered enough to leave the bathroom. He stood outside the door. "You haven't answered my questions."

"I didn't know our hotel door was unlocked, and I came in here because the bathroom in the other room is only a powder room."

She exited with her hair toweled turban style and pulled her thin terry robe tighter.

"Oh, I hope those are sandwiches. I'm starving," she said, noticing the brown bags. She pulled a chair from the table and sat down. Alex stumbled, dragging out a chair. He sat, looking at Kit as she opened the bags and pulled out the grilled cheese and then the BLT.

"Yum. I could eat either. What would you like?"

I'd like to lean across this table and run my hand down the opening of your bathrobe. Then I'd like to untie the knot you so prudently tightened, then toss you on that bed over there and make maddening love to you.

He completely lost his appetite and wasn't sure how long he could sit there and watch her eat, knowing she had nothing on but a flimsy bathrobe.

"Aren't you going to eat?"

"No. Not hungry. Kit, I'm sorry. The cashier at the deli told me some men were asking about who owned the red car. I was worried. I'm sorry. I didn't mean to walk in on you. I didn't know you were in the shower."

"It's okay. Got your eyes full, huh?"

"Want an honest answer?"

"Sure."

"Not enough."

She smiled at his comment. "I better get dressed."

When she returned to the kitchen area dressed, he finished telling her what the man said at the deli shop. "I bet they are interested in the truck, not my car. I caught sight of a couple of men hanging around the garage doors earlier, and there weren't any cars in there getting their oil changed."

"Can you call the dealership and get an update?"

Alex mumbled on the phone when he called the dealer's service line, then hung up. "Thinks the work will still take a couple of hours. Why don't you take your nap? I have a newspaper—might nap myself."

After Alex was certain Kit was sound asleep in her room, he showered. Taking his time, he let the hot water beat down the back of his neck and stretched his tired body, bracing his arms against the tiled shower sides. Two people could fit into the roomy shower stall just fine. The thought that he should have stripped off his clothes and joined Kit earlier flashed across his brain.

Now, what was he going to do—knowing she had the most beautiful body he'd ever seen. He shook his head and turned off the water. He slung back the shower curtain. Kit stood three feet away. She leaned against the same wall he had earlier, staring at him. She was dressed in a little silk PJ shirt and bottoms. Grabbing a towel from its hook, he wrapped it around his aroused body. He walked to her and took her head in his hands, and he leaned down and kissed her.

"I've been wanting to do this ever since I picked you up from the train station." He kissed her again, this time hungrier. He opened her mouth with his tongue and explored her like there was no end. She wrapped her arms around him, pressing tight. His arms lowered and curved the sides of her breasts down to her hips, pulling her tighter to him. One hand crept under her top as the other continued to hold her body to him. Her knees wobbled, yet Alex kept holding her with one arm while the other undid her front buttons. He pushed the garment aside and leaned in to kiss her breast before taking a nipple inside his mouth. Kit whimpered and held on to Alex as he continued to ravage her body.

"I can't stand anymore," she whispered.

Alex lifted her in his arms and carried her into the bedroom. One yank of the covers had the two of them tumbling into the bed. He had lost his towel and pulled at Kit's PJ bottoms. He wanted both of them naked. Touching, fondling, groping, no longer lingering, Alex began his scorching trail on her all over again. He kissed her mouth, breasts, stomach, searching her out with his tongue and hand.

From the other room, Alex heard ringing. Or was his mind mingling senses? He shook his head, wincing when the ringing did not stop.

"I better answer it," Alex said with a ragged breath. *Damn telephone.* He scooted off the bed and went to answer.

"Hello." His voice was hoarse. "Yes, got it. Great. Yeah, we'll check out of the hotel, then come get it."

He came back into the room, hobbling into his pants. "That was Earl. Told me the truck was ready. Doesn't want to keep it overnight. Suspicious fellows are hanging around his dealership. Wants me to pick it up so he can close."

Sitting on the bed, he reached for her hand. She had pulled the covers over her beautiful body. He shook his head and gave a little laugh. "There's a boxing term used and now it's an expression going around with high school kids, 'Saved by the bell.' Guess that's what happened to us here. Anyway, it seems neither one of us has very good timing."

****

Kit

When Alex and Kit arrived at the dealership, the owner recounted his concerns about the unsavory characters loitering nearby. "I suspect it's your truck they are interested in, like I told you on the phone. Could have broken into my place days ago if it were something else they wanted."

Alex signed off on the work order after asking to leave his car in their parking lot for a week until he could send someone to retrieve it. As he took the keys, he asked Earl for a thin wire piece. He took the extra key and threaded the wire through its keyhole.

"Hold out your wrist." He circled the wire around Kit's wrist twice, making a bracelet, allowing the key to dangle as a charm.

They left, traveling a mere five blocks before Alex pulled into a parking lot across from the City Police Station. "We'll spend the night here and drive out in the morning. No way I'll head back to Tennessee in the middle of the night. Damn. Should have this truck back to Dillon."

"We're just going to park here?"

"Yeah. At daylight, we'll head out, not before. Sorry, not going to be very cozy."

Kit squirmed, seeking the perfect spot. She tried

making a pillow of his thigh, then settled in his arms and grazed his cheek before kissing him again. Alex pulled her away.

"Not working. Damn, Kit. With all your wriggling, I'll be turning this cab into one of those haylofts you talked about."

"Alex, do you think those men will really try to come after this truck?"

"Hopefully, they'll move on to something else." He scrubbed his hand through his hair. "Let's talk for a while. Why don't you tell me the real reason you left school?"

She scooted away from him, certain he could hear her exhale.

"That bad?"

"No. Yes. Just, I wish I could have made a difference. Disappointed in myself. Kinda sad too." She sighed.

"Okay." Alex waited her out.

"Well, no surprise, I changed majors twice. First, I was in home economics. For some reason, I thought learning about cooking would help me with our whiskey business, but I hated it. I looked at English lit. I always loved to read and write. When my mother worked in the distilleries, I remember writing on my tablets to stay busy. One day, when I was eleven, she handed me an advertisement draft. She was debating whether to use it and asked me to take a look. Afterward, I was her copy editor until prohibition shut everything down.

"But I struggled to get beyond Shakespeare classes. I was changing majors again when I enrolled in a creative writing class. The professor was awesome. His lectures were mesmerizing. He introduced us to new authors with different writing styles. He was very demanding. You couldn't write just anything and pass it off as good.

"He was a war vet. The word was he had taken a medical leave from school, then came back. One day, early in the semester, during class, a huge thunderstorm blew through." She gripped her knuckles. The image, still fresh, flashed in front of her.

"It shook the entire building, rattled the windows, the giant overhead lights sparked, and the electricity went out. It was so dark you could barely see. I was under my desk; I was scared to death. My whole body shook. You know me and storms. Then I heard some guys in my class laughing and looked up. Professor Fisher was holding onto his podium for dear life. He turned and plastered himself against the chalkboard and groped his way to the nearest door. Those same guys— young guys—not a one in the war, I bet, cheered, and clapped before grabbing their books and exiting."

"What did you do?"

"I was so mad. I grabbed my books and followed him out. When I found his office, I knocked but walked in. He had collapsed in his desk chair. After I told him I hated thunderstorms too, I revealed I had medicinal whiskey, if he wanted any."

"I can see where this is headed."

"No, you don't." She pushed away. "We became friends. He found out I loved current literature. He had an advanced copy of F. Scott Fitzgerald's newest novel and shared it. I gained enough nerve to show him the advertising copy I had written for Tom Tanner Tennessee Whiskey once prohibition was over.

"Anyway, I met the students he advised, and I brought in my roommate to his counseling sessions. We discussed and debated several topics. Our group started meeting two or three times a week. At last, school was fun."

"So what happened?" Alex asked.

"I think another prof was irritated when Professor Fisher nominated me for a writing award. And it must have got under his skin. Jealous of us meeting."

"Not jealous of your group, but of a cute, talented coed spending so much time with their colleague." He stretched out his legs. "You met him by yourself, I bet."

"I did. We'd talk about our homes, about whiskey, about hiding it. Kinda like I used to have talks with you."

"And…" Alex squirmed against her.

"You're asking if I had an affair with him? I didn't. I will not lie, Alex. I might have." She sighed. "But he never made a play for me. He could have. I was available. I was still feeling low about the whole mess I made with the raid at the Greenhouse speakeasy. He told me he'd been engaged before the war. But when he came back, he broke up with his fiancée.

"In the end, it dawned on me he couldn't…" She stared blindly out the dark window into an empty parking lot. "My roommate was a nursing student. She told me the war did strange things to men."

"Yeah."

"Alex, you and Tom and all the other boys who went off to war never talked about the truth of what happened over there."

"I got lucky. Most I saw were busted carburetors, worn-out brakes, and broken tailpipes. Your brother, though. God knows what he witnessed. The worst of it, I imagine, stuck in the operating rooms like he was."

She reached for his hand. Rubbing her thumb on his palm.

"Well, someone on campus must have complained about our meetups. The dean searched Professor Fisher's office right after I had left one night and found a Tom Tanner Tennessee Whiskey bottle. I was called up the next day in front of the dean and the school's conduct committee. They dismissed me for conduct unbecoming of a student.

"Funny, you could find whiskey bottles in dorm rooms or fraternity houses any weekday, but the implication leveled at me was I was having an affair with my instructor. They could have looked at my grade transcripts and tell I didn't need to sleep with a professor to earn good grades. Anyway, I wasn't about to tell anyone what they were implying was impossible. And why?" She took a deep breath. "I took the blame. I said it was all my fault. Then I just packed up and left. I stayed in a little apartment off campus until my money ran out. That's why I came home."

Alex pulled her into his arms. "You said you wished you could have made a difference."

"Yes. I think our meetings helped Stanley. Stanley Fisher was his name. We were kinda a therapy group. I hated the fact I most likely ended those sessions."

"I think you made a difference. In particular, if he was able to keep his job. They didn't fire him, did they?"

"No. I've thought about if I helped him or not. I hope you're right. But after I was dismissed, I felt even more useless, so aimless. And I guess everyone in town heard about me being in that speakeasy raid. You see now why I must go to Mexico."

"Yes. We'll talk about Mexico later. Kit, you matter—don't let anyone tell you any different." He kissed the top of her head. "Let's try to get some sleep." He repositioned her. "You can lay on my leg, just don't squirm so much."

Chapter Twenty-Four

Tom

Tom sucked in the chilly March night air. He stepped off the steamer and surveyed Mobile's city lights. The coolness rushed down his throat and into his lungs, making his chest expand. After seven months of exile, first in South America, then joining his dad in Mexico, he was at long last walking on US soil again.

His banishment, of course, was his own making. He could have debated whether he could have eluded federal agents long enough for them to forget about him. But when he made the disastrous decision to kidnap Cammie Johnson, he sealed his fate.

His first phone call back to the US mainland was to Hugh Thibodeaux. He passed on disturbing news. By the time his friend could leave his wife and newborn, Cammie had vanished. She remained at the Mobile townhouse for two days before disappearing one afternoon, carrying a small bag, and not returning. Hugh questioned his neighbors and surrounding shop owners. They couldn't say where the attractive young widow with the violet eyes had gone.

It seemed fruitless to retrace his friend's steps. Still, it was where he began his search. Mobile, wet and soggy, presented itself like the mainland, dreary. Tom wrapped his arms around his thin coat and headed for

Mont Street. He gave himself twenty-four hours before returning home. Hardly enough time to find leads about the only woman he ever loved.

Dillon telegrammed that Alex left to pick up their customized truck. The vehicle should be in Stooksbury's dealership garage today. Their plan to catch the whiskey thieves was set. And they needed him back in Tennessee.

On the same phone call home, his mother relayed to him about the tornado hitting downtown Nashville. Federal troops were recalled to the state's capital to help with relief efforts. With no powerful arm to back her up and increasing resentment of her presence in Oak Hollow, Beatrice Givens left town in the middle of the night, not heard from again.

Good riddance.

"I think it's safe for you to return." He remembered his mother's exact words. "Too much going on in the state for authorities to bother with you. No charges were filed against you. If there is anyone hereabouts who'd even remember what happened, I'd be shocked."

Tom wasted no time. He trekked straight to the Mobile train station to unravel Cammie's mysterious disappearance. Hugh said Cammie caught a train the afternoon she disappeared. September fifth. Did she ever try to reconnect with her aunt? Cammie did not contact his mother.

Tom paced back and forth across the train depot's floor, waiting for the night manager to come down from his office. "The only train departing in that time frame was the twelve-twenty-two to Savannah," the manager told him.

He needed more. Why Savannah? Was there

another girl's school there? Tom rubbed his stiff neck; his gaze flitted around the office. He studied charts and maps along the walls. "Can you tell me where most passengers who take the train to Savannah travel next?" he asked.

"Most travelers from Mobile to Savannah, if they aren't visiting the city, are booking passage overseas. It's the quickest route to Europe. Two ocean liners leave Savannah each week, their destination, Liverpool."

"England?"

"Yes."

"How much would the ticket cost? Could you book a passage for four hundred dollars or less?"

"Why, yes. Not if you wanted to sail first class, but if you booked steerage, you could buy a ticket for two hundred and twenty-one dollars."

"Thank you." Tom turned and left. Who would Cammie know in England? And why in the world travel there?

Damn. Tom stomped out and hailed a cab.

"Twenty bucks if you get me to a used car dealer who'll sell me a car tonight." He leaned over the front seat and waved a greenback in the driver's face. Thirty minutes later, Tom handed over two hundred and fifty bucks for a beat-up Ford that had seen better days. But had an engine that purred the minute he cranked it.

Hell of a homecoming. Just pleased to get back. It was past time for the first quarter's bottled whiskey to make it to the government pharmacy. In order to fake a delivery in the new truck, Dillon warned, it had to go out in days.

On the highway heading north out of town, Tom

racked his brain again about where Cammie might be. The night they'd spent together in Mobile, in the wee hour he had suggested the two of them might emigrate to England if she worried about settling in Mexico. Her reluctance to agree to follow him to his father's new distillery had him desperately pulling at straws of where they might escape. He'd suggested he could work at the same distillery he'd apprenticed at as a young man. However, that was in Scotland. Did she remember? And why go overseas without him? And leave no word.

Holy crap. He shook his head. To travel to Liverpool unaccompanied would be a hell of a trip. And why there? He was missing something. But he remembered the stories Cammie shared—brief sketches of what she'd endured so far in her young life. She lived through a war, lost her fiancée and parents, supported herself, and fought off a predator. In the end, she invented a story that she was a war widow. One which enabled her to survive.

Had she remembered his tales of his friend, who was now a member of the British Parliament? *Nah. Too far-fetched.* The other burning question—on the disastrous morning when they last parted, while men were waiting to sneak him onboard a ship destined for Rio. Did she remember his promise to her? He told her he loved her and would be back.

The hurt, the disbelief, had not diminished in his heart. If she remembered, if she believed him, why disappear?

****

Alex

Alex nudged Kit. "Damn, got an awful crick." He rolled his neck. The night spent in the truck was damn uncomfortable. "Go inside the police station and tell them you're supposed to meet your brother's lawyer there. Then ask to use their restroom. They'll let you."

Fifteen minutes later, Kit came back holding two paper cups of hot coffee.

"Those officers were so nice." She smiled as she handed him a cup.

"Yeah, I bet." He gave her shapely legs a second glance as he helped her into the truck.

As they crossed the Kentucky state line, Alex second-guessed his decision to travel at all. No-man's-land—the stretch they now drove between cities. He swore to himself, realizing whoever wanted this truck would figure out they were headed south and set a trap for them. They had not covered five more miles when he spotted it ahead.

Construction barrels stretched across the road. An older model black sedan with a missing headlight parked across the asphalt behind the barrels. A man waved a red construction flag, motioning Alex to pull over. The road had no shoulder to the left or to the right to pull around a barricade. They'd picked the perfect spot.

Alex counted three men and the one car. He pulled two bottles of Tom Tanner Whiskey out from underneath the seat he had stashed before they left his convertible in Cincinnati and laid the bottles on the front seat. Hidden behind the rear window that faced into the truck's bed was his pistol. The dealership had fastened a metal box right on the other side so he could reach his gun if he needed to. He did not intend to have a shoot-out with these guys and was positive the minute he got out they would frisk him and search the cab's interior.

"Out of the truck," a tall, balding man with a heavy paunch shouted.

Alex exited first, then helped Kit slide across the seat and helped her down. "What seems to be the trouble, gentlemen?"

The tall man, obviously the leader, was surprised when Kit jumped out. "Well, look what we have here, boys. I'd say it's a 'two for one' deal." He ogled Kit.

"Look here, I'm delivering this truck to a mighty important person," Alex said.

The leader looked at him.

"You may think you'd get away with a hijack—but lots of folks will be looking for this truck. What say you take this little peace offering I have for you on the seat and just let us go?"

The man signaled. "Shorty, go see what's in the truck."

Two cars drove down the highway, and the drivers slowed when they saw the barrels.

"Don't be motioning to them drivers or that will be the last breath you breathe." The leader pulled his jacket back, showing Alex the pistol he had stuck in his trousers. "Tolbert, move them two barrels and wave those cars through."

More cars would be on the road soon and, with a bit of luck, maybe a state trooper. The criminals might not be the smartest trio out there, but that didn't mean they weren't dangerous. Alex took a longer look at the beat-up car blocking their way.

"If you're after easy money, mister, why not trade her for ransom? Her family would pay big bucks to get her back," Alex said.

"Alex, are you crazy?" Kit hissed.

Alex moved in front of Kit, ignoring her seething glance. "You can call her daddy and just as soon as he hears his daughter's voice, the money will be on its way. Not even be a long-distance call."

"This is the real stuff, boss." Shorty climbed from the truck. He held up the cork of the bottles in one hand and swigged a generous sample of the contents.

"You bet it is," Alex said. "Tom Tanner Tennessee Whiskey, all legal, got the stamp on it and everything. And this here young lady is Tom Tanner's great-granddaughter for sure. The Tanner family has a long reach with folks protecting the medicinal contracts for the legit whiskey makers left to distill spirits. Politicians, police, and unsavory fellas alike want to keep the good stuff being made."

"I agree and keep the whiskey moving. That's why we want this truck," their leader said.

"I'd bet your boss knows the Tanner's first hand. Wouldn't take kindly to someone disrupting fueling their speakeasies." Alex continued holding his hands high, hoping a car traveling would see what was happening and stop. "Don't want to mess with them folks."

"Don't get ahead of yourself, friend." The man mopped his brow. "We been watching for you for two days. How do we know this young lady is who you say she is? And what if she's already spoiled goods?" the leader asked.

"Tom!" Kit's face burned.

"What are you to this missy here?"

Alex laughed at his implication. "Hey, I'm just the family mechanic. Her relatives asked me to pick her up from school after she missed her train home. They gonna be sending folks to find her if I don't hit the road soon. Speaking of hitting the road—your car has already lost a ton of oil. A heap of trouble is headed your way two miles down the road if you don't get it fixed. Most likely a loose hose."

"You talk too much." The trio's boss bent his head to glance at his car's underbelly. "So, Mr. Smart guy, how we gonna work this?"

"Same way I get paid. Just have them wire ten Cs to the Western Union office in the next town."

"Are you crazy? Don't tell them that." Kit hissed.

"After you let us go." Tom turned and winked at Kit. The men needed to think his suggestion was no big deal. He was acutely aware of their reluctance to trust anything he said.

"Why would they believe we have her?" Shorty asked.

"Phone is right next to the Western Union counter at the General Store. Have her make the call with you standing right there." The last thing Alex wanted was to surrender the truck. "Your call, easy money."

"Daddy is going to be sending out his men to look for me if I'm not home soon. I bet they are already on their way," Kit said, finally catching on.

The hijacker, who'd held the flag, tramped over to take a swig from the bottle the other man nursed. "Let me try some of that stuff, Shorty."

Two more cars approached the roadblock. Alex and Kit stood together. Their hands still in the air.

"You two get in the back," the leader ordered, motioning with his gun. "You nitwits put the hooch away and move those barrels. We don't want anyone stopping and asking questions. Wait—hey, mister grease junky—fix whatever you saw leaking from my car."

Alex popped the hood and studied the hoses. He examined each as the bald guy looked on. It was easy. He checked one hose and disconnected another.

"Let's go." The bald man motioned with his gun. "Hurry up. Let's get the hell out of here before one of these rubbernecks stops."

Alex untied the tarp at the back of the truck and lifted Kit in before following.

"Next town is Greenie. The General Store is right at the bridge. We'll stop there. Follow me," their leader said.

He jumped into his car and started his engine. His pair of underlings clambered into Alex's truck and started it. Alex moved to the window opening into the cab and watched as their leader straightened his car and headed south. One mile down the highway, smoke billowed from its tailpipe. Shorty honked and motioned his boss to pull over.

"Don't stop, Shorty, or I'll put a bullet in your head. Go around." Alex stuck his pistol he'd retrieved from its hiding spot through the opening of the back cargo window. "Keep driving." Shorty drove past his boss's smoking sedan.

Just then, a loud pop exploded. From the review mirror, Alex and the driver saw flames shoot from the black sedan. After another mile, Alex ordered the driver to pull to the road's shoulder.

"You there," he ordered the other man, "out of the truck and stand on the far side of the road." Alex gestured with his pistol for the man to get out. "Kit, get out. As soon as he's over there—you climb up into the passenger side."

When Kit was in the truck, Alex motioned to the driver. "Your time, Shorty, get out."

"Here, Kit. Get moving, mister." Alex handed her his gun when Shorty jumped out. "Slide to the driver's side. Start shooting if these fellows make a false move. I'm getting out and coming around."

Shorty stood in the middle of the road dangling a shining object. "Looks like I might have something you need, sweetheart." He jingled the truck key in front of Kit.

"Don't think you'd shoot an unarmed man, little lady. Bet you never handled a gun before," he jawed. "So why don't you just toss out the gun and I'll toss you the key before I decide to throw this here key in the creek bed over there and nobody goes anywhere?"

"Stand back. Or I swear I'll shoot," Kit stammered as the man stepped toward her.

Abruptly, the man made a play of dropping the key, and as he bent down, he pulled a small gun from his boot. He shot at Alex as he rounded the truck's side. Alex grunted and fell against the vehicle. The hijacker fired again. His next shot hit the front fender.

Kit screamed when the second bullet's ricochet smacked the hood. Aiming, she pulled the pistol's trigger. She shot two times. Shorty jumped as a bullet hit the pavement at his feet, and screeched loudly when the second struck his leg.

He cursed and threw the key into the air. Hobbling on one leg, he scampered for the safety of the creek bed and dove in as Kit fired off a third shot.

Alex jumped in the truck, shoving Kit across the

seat, and slammed the door. He grabbed Kit's hand with the wire bracelet and stuck the spare key in the ignition. The massive engine roared, and they sped down the highway.

"Like having you this close, sweetheart, but you might see if you can unwind this wire to free your hand," Alex joked as he tried to reposition Kit's body off him.

Kit untangled her makeshift bracelet. Blood oozed from Alex's shirt sleeve. "He hit you!"

"I'm okay. I think if there was a bullet in there, it'd feel different. But it hurts like hell." He wanted to puke. But swallowed hard. A throbbing pain pulsed through his entire body. Thank God, someone had a poor aim.

As soon as they stopped, Kit freed her hand. She reached under her dress and ripped her slip lace to make a bandage for Alex's arm.

"Fanciest bandage I've ever had." He chuckled as she ministered to him.

"How can you laugh at a time like this? I'm still shaking."

"Damn, if I'd known you were such a swell shot, I'd given you the gun from the get-go."

She slapped his shoulder as hard as she dared. "Shut up and just drive. My nerves are too upset to joke with you right now."

****

Kit

It was twilight when Alex drove the truck into the circle drive of Kit's home. No one seemed about. They trudged up the front steps and entered the empty house.

"Sit," Kit ordered, as they walked into the kitchen. "Let me look at your arm."

She unwrapped the blood-soaked petticoat from Alex's injury. The blood had congealed, but after she pulled off the lace, she reopened the bullet wound. Blood trickled once again.

Alex looked at the scrape. "Looks like I got lucky. He only winged me."

Kit shook her head in vexation. "You'll live," she smirked. "Wait here. I'll get some iodine and bandages."

"Fetch me a whiskey first."

"I think you've had enough."

Alex had liberally drunk from the whiskey bottle left in his truck by Shorty. They dared to stop only once on their return trip, allowing Kit to grab sandwiches and soft drinks. She offered to drive, but Alex refused.

"Bring the first aid kit into the bathroom? I want to shower." Alex didn't wait for her to leave before he started stripping off his clothes as he climbed the home's back stairs.

She left to find bandages.

"I'll leave these here," Kit said, staring at his naked backside as he stepped into the shower of her family's main bathroom.

Once in her bedroom, she removed her sweaty and blood-stained dress and turned on her shower. She pulled on a satin nightgown from her chest of drawers and was towel drying her hair when Alex appeared in her bedroom doorway.

He braced both arms on either side of the door frame. His pectoral muscles stretched as he leaned his shirtless body inward. From somewhere in her brother's room, he'd scrounged up a pair of striped pajama bottoms. The loose-fitting PJs were slung low from his narrow waist and fastened with a cotton rope cord.

"Looks like you showered too," he said, smiling.

"Alex, you bandaged yourself. Let me see."

She wrung out her damp hair once more with her towel as he walked toward her. Tossing the towel on her bed, she took his injured arm in both her hands. She gave his handiwork a cursory inspection. "Looks good."

Without releasing his arm, she ran her hand down his muscled arm, detecting his reaction to her movements. She grazed his smooth cheeks with her fingers. Smiling at the thought he had shaved for her. Warmth bathed her entire body.

He made a show of looking out her window. "It looks like we may have another storm tonight."

"Alex Stooksbury, if that is not the most pitiful excuse for trying to get me in your bed I've ever heard I don't know what is." She laughed.

He circled his good arm around her. "Can't fault a guy for trying. Most of all, an injured one. Honestly, I'm so tired I think the minute my head hits a pillow, I'll be out like a light." He leaned in to kiss her neck. With his touch, a tingling sensation coursed through her.

Kit pulled back and stared into Alex's eyes. Eyes the color of whiskey. A beautiful, intoxicating color. "Until you turn over in the middle of the night and feel a woman next to you and you show her 'what's what' before she can say her name."

He leaned back, roaring his approval at her comment with a hearty laugh. "I can't believe I said that to you. And you remembered. Did it rankle you so badly?"

"No. Truthfully, I kinda liked it. Let me know you were finally noticing me."

"Well. Yes…I was noticing you, all right." Alex pushed an errant lock of hair away from her face. His eyes were sultry and passionate. Her pulse raced and her heart thudded loudly against her chest. Pressing himself against her, he grazed her lips, then her neck and collarbone. He leaned in tighter, tilting her head back and kissing again with soft strokes. He repeated his measured crusade, intensifying it second by second, each kiss becoming more passionate than the one before.

Kit's body shivered, and she murmured, "Alex." *Was she dreaming?* Pleasure flooded her entire body. No dream. It was Alex, in flesh and blood, who was holding her so intimately.

With both hands, he slipped the straps of her gown down her arms, allowing the flimsy piece to drop to her ankles. It was all she had on.

Her hands moved to his waist, gliding across his tight abdomen, then untied the rope cord to his cotton pajamas, sliding them off. She had an insatiable desire to know him. Her hands ached with the need to touch and explore. Fluttery sensations quivered in her chest and stomach. They stood together, naked, not touching. The feeling should have been awkward but was not. Instead, every ounce of their being enveloped the moment.

Alex took her to him, pressing another kiss, tasting, pushing, quickening, their bodies growing feverish, straining toward each other. Passion burned within her. It was a heady feeling to be wanted. Each closed their eyes to better take in the intensifying emotions. Kit could not continue to stand. Pulling down her bed's covers, she crawled in and extended her hand. His rock-hard body joined her soft and welcoming one.

She had waited long enough for this moment and this man. She held him tight, afraid to let go. His mouth and fingers explored her body, further, lower, deeper. His mouth was bruising and desperate and did not break the kiss. Her arms clung to him, her fingers digging into his back. How she longed to feel the full weight of him buried inside her. His rhythmic assault on her mind and body overshadowed even the closest of dreams of this moment.

Inhaling her gasps, he closed his lips on hers. His love melded into her. Her veins, her nerves, her flesh, her heart to him. They joined together, man and woman, his body into hers, an affirmative of becoming one. He shuddered his release, rocking with her until they both ceased trembling.

She had never been so happy. Could she laugh? Would he think her strange? Alex opened his eyes, looking deep into hers, anchoring himself in her gaze. "I love you," he whispered.

She smiled back at him. Completeness, content-ness. Was there such a word? *There has to be.*

"I love you too," she murmured before they both fell into an exhaustive sleep.

Chapter Twenty-Five

Tom

Tom drove up his family's circle drive, climbed out of his car, stretched his tight muscles, and rubbed his neck. The lifting morning fog exposed the empty paddock. No new colts frisking about, no passel of beagles greeting him, eager to go on a morning hunt, and no sounds of workers hastening to their shifts. Drooping pink and white azaleas and tuffs of spring grass needing cut flanked the lawn of his house.

He tilted his head and stretched his neck. The place appeared deserted except for an enormous truck parked in front. He circled it, running his hands along the exterior. He gave a low whistle. This must be the truck he and Dillon ordered to lure Dillon's offenders. A marvelous piece of workmanship. The gleaming black paint reminded him of the giant whale that followed his boat to Rio.

He glanced at the upstairs windows again and thought he glimpsed someone. He tugged his duffle bag from the back of the used car he bought in Alabama and ambled through the unlocked front door. Alex Stooksbury hurried down the stairs in a pair of worn-out denims he suspected belonged to him. He slipped his long arms into a flannel shirt, but not before Tom noticed the thick bandage on Alex's left arm.

At the sound of the front door opening, Kit came from the kitchen dressed only in a thin cotton wrapper, holding a spatula.

"Well, aren't we the picture of domesticity?" Tom grinned as he dropped his bag in the hall.

Alex smiled. Kit had the presence of mind to blush but rolled her eyes and slammed one hand on her hip. A gesture he'd witnessed from his sister several times over the years.

"Well, come get some breakfast. I assume you're hungry," Kit said before running to him and giving him a huge welcome-back hug.

****

Dillon

"Will they like me?" Lily asked. "Your cousins, Tom and Kit?"

Dillon paused mid-stride and glanced at Lily's anxious face. They walked toward the Kittrell house for his family's planned meeting. His mind returned to the numerous occasions he had come to the Kittrells', hammering out new business propositions and celebrating entrepreneurial successes. He frowned at the burned rubble of the distillery. Irritating and infuriating kudzu vines would soon blanket the pile. He suffered a stabbing pain of sadness. A flock of birds flew off the skeleton timbers, startling Lily.

He gave her a lopsided grin. "No, they won't like you. They'll love you, silly."

Her bright eyes glimmered. She had kept her hair short, but the Florida sun had lightened her locks and given her skin a healthy glowing tan. He squeezed her hand. Would anyone mention or notice the sapphire ring she wore on her left hand? They were now secretly engaged. His two-day trip to Florida to bring Lily back for Easter became four, ending with his marriage proposal and her acceptance. The couple agreed to wait before sharing that news.

He shared with Chloe, the attorney's news of Lily's trust. Behind the scenes, so that Reggie would not be alerted, the lawyer investigated what happened. The money was gone. There would be no way to recover what Reggie had taken. He had been the legitimate designee to Lily's trust. However, her grandmother, who continued to stay in Florida, did have a safety deposit box in a bank in Lassiter. Her jewels, stocks and bonds, and the deed to her house were intact. Recovery of her family's property would wait until after his family's attempt to get their whiskey back concluded.

"Come on. I'm dying for them to meet you."

Three individuals stood around the dining room table when the couple entered. "You haven't met Lily yet, Kit, Tom, Alex." Dillon introduced her, then added, "Lily's cousin Reggie stole her money to finance the heist. She's going to help us."

Tom nodded his head, not expecting more of an explanation. "I'm pleased to meet you."

"Yes, wonderful to meet you, Lily. I've heard marvelous things about you from both Dillon and my mother." Kit reached out and clasped her hand.

Lily's cheeks pinked. There was a knock at the front door.

"And you remember meeting Marcos?" Dillon opened the door. Marcos tipped his hat as the big man entered the room.

"I've asked us to meet today to nail down a few particulars before we put my plan into action. And thanks for meeting here. I'm positive Tom Tanner Distillery is being watched," Dillon said.

"Two days ago, Marcos made sure the truck full of whiskey Reggie was delivering to his contact in Chicago never made it. It was full of half of our stolen government-stamped whiskey. We still don't know his hiding place. Luis said it might have come from a secret tunnel to the country club.

"Reggie took a phone call at two in the morning from his gangster buddy about the hijacked load. He wanted to know what the hell happened. Luis, my man on the inside, was at the country club cleaning the bar when the call came through.

"If a delivery goes bust—Chicago rules say you come through with a replacement plus double in two weeks. We're confident Reggie knows there is a fancy souped-up truck built for making whiskey runs ordered by Tom Tanner Whiskey. He just doesn't know when Tom Tanner's next delivery will happen.

"But he has to steal our whiskey to settle his Chicago contacts. He must think he can hijack our next delivery without believing it's a ruse."

"If we post our schedule, he'd suspect it's a trap. Got to make him find it out himself," Alex said.

"Exactly. Kit, this is where you come in. Saturday night, you and Alex are going to the country club, you start an argument with Alex and get Reggie's attention. Somehow you must reveal to Reggie that a big delivery is fixing to be made," Tom instructed.

"Wait a minute. He'll not know her, won't trust her. Could be setting her up for something dangerous," Alex was quick to point out.

"This is where Lily gets her grandmother's friend's

help. The little lady doesn't miss Wednesday night Bingo or a Saturday night dinner and dance. Lily is going to ask her to invite Alex and Kit to dinner before the dance, and she will introduce Kit to Reggie. It will work. He's already desperate," Dillon said. "Luis says everybody is staying clear of him at the country club. 'Fraid Reggie is going to pop one of them off any minute, he's wired so tight."

"How do we know Reggie will even be there?" Alex stalked away from the group.

"Don't know for sure, but something's keeping him there, might involve our other half of whiskey tucked away in his secret hideaway or it might be what our attorney uncovered. There's a definite link between the CBA company and Reggie Wyatt. It's a front for him and his cronies. Thanks to Lily, I found out he named it after his grandfather, Curtis Bartholomew Axelrod."

"Everything I've heard about this Reggie is he's a first-class weasel. As Luis said, he's on edge. Won't he try to stay out of the limelight for a while?" Tom asked.

"He's got to act like nothing is out of the norm. And he is a weasel. He'll try to get out of anything that remotely implicates him. I'm determined to make sure it all blows up in his face." Dillon strode to the other side of the room. "Alex, you fix the paperwork?"

"Yeah. Right and tight. Got the truck title in his name. No way he can deny it."

"Marcos and Lena have been filling bottles with rotgut for the past week. No one has a clue. We're going to stock our truck with fake whiskey. Not taking a chance, the real stuff gets into someone else's hands."

"Like the authorities," Alex suggested.

Dillon laughed. "Right. When I picture every one of those empty bottles lined up at the Playhouse—believing they are going to dilute good whiskey to double their earnings—it makes my head ache.

"Marcos, make sure Luis leaks to Reggie's favorite bartender that his cousin spotted an intimidating new truck getting prepped at Alex's dealership. Say he's heard it's going to Tanner's distillery. Guess that's it. Any questions?" He looked directly into the eyes of those present. Every head nodded.

In Dillon's mind, the whole scenario for payback was similar to a massive show being produced. Every scene and every line had to be rehearsed. No doubt the biggest production he'd ever been in. And the most important. Funny about everything ending at the Playhouse.

"Saturday night. Everything starts then." He pounded once on the table.

"We'll be ready. Okay, fellas. Us ladies have work to do," Kit said.

****

Lily

"Kit, you don't know me, but I know Reggie. You need to know the kind of woman Reggie is attracted to." Lily stopped Kit in the hall leading to the backstairs, subjecting her to a critical survey from head to toe.

"Oh, I think I can guess. And believe me, I can act the part. You'd be surprised how many of those types of women I was at school with. Come on." Kit gestured for Lily to follow her to her bedroom.

"Show me what you plan to wear?" Lily plopped down in the deep-seated pink armchair in Kit's room.

Kit pulled two silk dance dresses from her closet. They both were constructed with a drop waist design and shortened hemlines, which fell slightly below Kit's knees.

"Let's see if we can fix the neckline on this one." Lily pulled the pearl-blue silk from her hands. She inspected Kit's closet. "We need to add beads and feathers. How about your mother's things? Do you think she would mind if we looked in her closet?"

"Jeepers no. The only thing she'd be disappointed about is her not being here to help."

"And I need scissors. And makeup—can't wear too much. Your hair, Kit. Beautiful, and Alex must love it. Maybe we can do it up. We'll think of something."

****

Alex

Saturday night, Alex ambled up the front steps of Penland Kittrell's front porch and lifted the knocker. The box in his hand held a corsage for Kit. He ordered the most extravagant orchid he could find and had it made into a wrist corsage once Lily told him it was required for his and Kit's dinner date at the country club.

He grinned, the corners of his mouth turning up. Funny time to be knocking on Kit's "front door" as if it were a first date. Not like we haven't already spent four nights together and made love throughout one of those. His eyes shone with laughter when Lily opened the door. Once he crossed the threshold, he looked upward and saw the person descending the stairs.

The swaying of hips, swishing beads, and feather embellishments glittered in the hall's gas-lit sconces. He gazed, transfixed by the woman in front of him. She had mystic smoky eyes and pert ruby-red lips with an obvious beauty mark on a rouged cheek where dimples once peeked. A satin beaded headband encircled a bobbed hairdo.

It was Kit.

A flustered Alex whispered, "You cut your hair."

"Yes. Do you like it?" Kit asked expectantly.

"I... I... Yes. It's just taken me by surprise."

****

Kit

A tingling and lightheadedness encompassed Kit's whole body. Is this what every single flapper feels? This sense of sudden freedom, of imagining one could experiment and try new things without feelings of guilt or remorse. Seized by the excitement of what the evening would entail, she met Alex's wide eyes with a challenging stare of her own.

"Are you ready?" Lifting her chin, she clutched his arm. "Let's go."

Chapter Twenty-Six

Kit

Kit shook her dangling Tennessee pearl earrings,
wishing now she had let Lily put a feather in her
headband too. Maybe would have been too much. She
peered across the dining table at Alex's impassive stare.
They had joined Lily's grandmother's friend, Dotty
Dilworth, for dinner at Hillside Country Club. Kit
thought the evening would have been one for the
memory books had it not been for the rest of the night's
plans.

The tiny matron held her own throughout their
dinner. She drank endless cocktails and shocked them
both with unsupportive stories about Lily's
grandmother. She flirted outrageously with Alex, so
much so, that when Reggie Wyatt passed their table,
Mrs. Dilworth waylaying him to introduce Kit appeared
altogether natural.

"You must ask her to dance, so I might have this
young man's company to myself for a few moments."
She teased Reggie, tapping his arm with her ebony
cigarette holder.

Reggie bowed over Kit's hand in an old-world
manner. "My pleasure." She returned a shy but inviting
smile back to Reggie.

After dinner, the band's slow foxtrots tempted

couples to the dance floor. When an upbeat Charleston began playing, Kit dragged Alex out to dance. They were one of the few couples remaining on the floor and gave an entertaining version of the new dance craze hitting the country.

Kit spotted Reggie standing close to Dotty Dilworth and as the band played out the final drum melody, she made sure her energetic kicks and swivels were in Reggie's direction. The risqué cut of her silk panties flashed as she twirled about in her short dress. Over protestations, Lily made liberal use of her mother's shears to her favorite lingerie earlier in the day. The sliver of silk she wore was scandalous.

When the band began playing exotic tango notes, Kit sulked, making a show of wanting to remain on the dance floor. Alex resisted and pulled her arm.

"May I have this dance?" Reggie appeared at her side.

Kit flung Alex's arm away. "Yes," she said, turning into Reggie's arms.

The two delighted the crowd as Reggie moved her expertly around the floor. They did not speak at first, but after they locked their knees around each other, Reggie gave a pantomimed Latin lover look. "You're beautiful," he said.

"Thank you for asking me to dance." Kit blushed. "You dance divinely."

"And you, my dear, are the most exquisite partner. Where have you been hiding yourself? And what are you doing with such a local yokel?" He twirled her twice, then clasped her close.

"Alex Stooksbury? Well, he has such a swell ride. Any gal seen driving around in his luxurious car is in

Heaven. I'm sure the valet boys are still talking about it. Got mad 'cause he had a chauffeur, and they didn't get to park it." She swished her skirt and kicked out one leg.

Reggie spun her around again, sliding his hands up and down her arms. They separated for toe swirls, then arms straight, they grabbed one another and spun. Kit pivoted left, then right, before moving into Reggie's arms. When he embraced her again in the next dance move, he leaned her back with his body hovering close above hers. Kit glimpsed Alex's agitated face.

"You'd think that man with tons of cash would share it with his best gal. He promised me a diamond necklace. A big one." She tittered.

They made another turn and then parted once again before joining hands. As Reggie turned her, her back against his chest, he murmured in her ear, "And your diamond necklace—is it forthcoming?"

Kit faced him, stroking her tongue across her red lipstick-smeared lips. "We'll see. He says next Friday, I'll get a surprise."

Reggie twirled her out then back in tight to him in full upper-body contact. The music ended in a final crescendo drum beat and bead rattle flourish. The couple bowed to enthusiastic applause. She wasn't sure Reggie was attracted to her, but she was positive the man had an inflated ego. He was vain enough to want to keep a young woman attached to his arm.

"Why don't we step into the bar and get refreshments?" Reggie guided her from the ballroom into the bar area. Rather than take a table in the room, he walked her into the adjoining billiard room. He seated her on a stool near two men racking up a new game of eight-ball.

"I'll be right back." He returned in seconds and handed her a cocktail. She took a sip while watching a player attempt a bank shot. Reggie must have given them the "scram" look because they hung their cue sticks before finishing and exiting the room.

"Tell me more about this diamond necklace you're expecting, my dear." He ran his hand up her arm, stopping to trace her rhinestone armband designed like a coiling snake. There was a gleam in his eyes.

"I already picked it out, but Alex says I must wait until Friday. That's the day he gets a big bonus for helping deliver a truck he sold." She took another sip of her drink. "I know it's Friday because his secretary told me."

Reggie raised his eyebrows as if weighing the remark's believability.

"Oh darn, I have a run in my stocking." She lifted the hem of her skirt, revealing her leg up to the top of her thigh. "That's the trouble with silk."

As she bent to examine her stocking, giving Reggie an excellent view down her dress front, Alex walked into the room. It was a view she sensed Alex was the recipient of as well.

"There you are. I've been looking for you everywhere." The anger in his voice led Kit to think he was overdoing the jealous boyfriend bit. "Come on, Kit. Let's scram," Alex said, grabbing her arm.

"Wait, I don't want to leave yet." Jerking away, Kit pouted her lips.

Reggie stepped between Kit and Alex. "She says she doesn't want to leave."

"And who are you, mister, to stop us?" Alex's

nostrils flared as he glared back at Reggie.

"I think the young lady prefers my company." Once the words were out of Reggie's mouth, Alex fisted his hand and swung at Reggie's upturned nose. His aim missed its mark as Kit grabbed his arm to keep the scene from blowing up more.

Reggie rubbed his bruised chin. "Well, sweetheart—who's it gonna be?"

"Sorry, Alex." She released his arm, took Reggie's, and exited the room with him.

"Let's get my car and take a little drive, somewhere a little more peaceful." Reggie shot a glance over his shoulder. "This way."

"But the front door is this way." She pulled hard on Reggie's arm to redirect him.

"We're going out another way?"

She became flustered. She was supposed to take him out the front door. Her pulse raced. Reggie pulled her down the concrete stairs between the bar and billiard room to a walkout basement. A full moon shone through two small windows on either side of a door. Not a great escape route. It was a steep drop to the river embankment from anywhere in the back of the country club.

"Don't know what your game is?" Reggie said. "If you're trying to make your pretty boy jealous, why don't we give him something to make him really hot under the collar. You're just the diversion I need right now."

His face menaced above hers. He gave her a twisted smile.

"No, I...I can't stay." Suffocating panic swamped her.

Reggie's lips peeled back from his teeth, and he gripped her arm tighter.

"Let's not leave yet. Got me a little bachelor chamber down here. Fully stocked too, not with that coffin polish they serve upstairs." He pressed on two built-in shelves along the back wall where crates were stacked. A metallic click sounded. Suddenly, the entire shelf panel swung inward.

"No." Kit's heart pounded so hard she was certain Reggie heard it. "I... I..." Reggie flicked on an electric light. She stared into a dimly lit room. The panel was a secret door that led into what appeared to be another storage room. Crates clearly marked Tom Tanner Tennessee Whiskey were stacked floor to ceiling.

"Come on, sweetheart, it's nicer back this way."

Kit pulled back. "Mrs. Dilworth, she'll wonder where I am. If someone doesn't tell her I've left, she'll scour the entire country club looking for me. And most definitely get Alex's help. Anyway, you promised me a drive. I love fast cars. You promised." She gave her best baby talk.

He paused for a minute. Was he measuring her words? Had people been suspicious when Lily disappeared from the club weeks earlier? Was there a search for her? Had volunteers come downstairs and snooped too close to the secret door for Reggie's comfort?

"Okay, but we're going out this way." He turned and maneuvered his hideaway door shut again.

Reggie yanked the basement door open, grabbed her elbow, and pulled her down a narrow gravel path that edged the back of the club. She tripped in her high heels twice. Her limbs shook so much she feared

Reggie would notice. The instant they rounded the ivy-covered country club's corner, he whistled at the attendant standing at the valet stand.

The young man waved back, and within seconds Reggie's chrome-encrusted Chrysler roared up to the edge of the country club's west side. The valet jumped out, leaving the motor running. Reggie swung the passenger side open and pushed Kit in. Terror crept into her heart, lungs, and throat. Was it fight-or-flight time? She fumbled for the door's handle. Reggie climbed into his driver's seat and shifted the gear into first.

As soon as they shot out from the club's portico overhang, a large black Cadillac blocked their way, bright headlights blinding them.

"Oh, no. It's Alex's chauffeur," Kit said. Relief coursed through her body. "I better get out. He'll kill you if I try to leave with you."

Just then, Marcos' mammoth body exited the Cadillac. He gave a menacing look to Reggie. Kit pulled at Reggie's arm. "No. Don't even think about fighting him. He's an ex-pro boxer."

Reggie slumped back in his driver's seat.

"It's okay. I'll make up with Alex." She patted Reggie's arm and pulled on her door handle. "A girl doesn't want to throw away a chance at diamonds." She winked, hoping she gave a believable excuse. "But you can put a C note on it. I'll be back next Saturday night 'alone' with something very sparkly around my neck."

She blew him a kiss and jumped out of his car.

****

"Dang, Kit, did you need to put on such a show?" Alex scolded her as they walked to her family's front porch after Marcos dropped them off. "You might as

260

well have done a striptease right in that fella's face."

"I had to distract him. He was getting suspicious."

"Damn, I can think of a million other ways to distract a man."

"Like what?"

"Spill a drink on him or something."

"Please." She rolled her eyes, smiling to herself. *Alex Stooksbury, jealous.* She wanted to relish the moment but figured as soon as she walked through her home's front door she'd get the third degree from Tom and Dillon. Sure enough, her brother and cousin were waiting to find out how the night went.

"Tell us precisely what you saw again." Her brother zeroed in on her before she could even change out of her evening gown.

"I told you." Kit whipped off her headband. "It was a room behind a hidden cabinet behind the basement country club stairs. As soon as Reggie pushed on the shelves, I heard a click, and a door opened. The room was filled with crates of Tom Tanner Whiskey from floor to ceiling. It must be his hiding place. He must have thought I'd figure it was just another storage area, not realizing I'd know it was stolen whiskey."

"Good girl, what a find." Her brother kissed the top of her head.

"Damn, Tom, how can you say that? We're lucky she's even with us tonight, not down in a secret hideaway nobody knows about." Alex slammed his fists into his jacket pockets.

"Nobody needs to lose their cool," Dillon warned.

"She's okay, Alex. Take it easy. Now tell us again what you told Reggie." Her brother waited until she pulled out a dining room chair. She plopped down and unbuckled her shoes.

"Look, you told me to be intentionally vague. He knows Alex is getting paid for something on Friday. Right now, he thinks he might get his hands on a diamond necklace. But as soon as he puts two and two together about a delivery like you boys think he will, he'll be after the bigger prize. The whiskey. So all the other little stunts you have planned must fall into place."

"They will. They have to. Luis is at the club. He'll let me know if Reggie makes an early move. But I think he'll stick with Friday. Ole Reggie will want our truck even more now. He'll realize he must move the hidden whiskey before anyone else, besides you, finds out about his hiding place." Dillon looked straight at Kit.

"Exactly. Reggie knows she knows." The veins on Alex's neck stood out.

"Well, I'm headed to bed." Kit picked up her shoes, passing Alex on the way to the stairs. He was still mad. Maybe Tom would drop the big brother act for once and not mind Alex sleeping with her instead of down the hall in the guest bedroom. You never knew. *Men.*

Chapter Twenty-Seven

Dillon

"If I had known one call to the governor would bring enough troops to take down Reggie Wyatt and his crime syndicate, I'd done it a long time ago." Dillon laid aside the morning paper at the breakfast table.

His aunt picked up the newspaper and read it out loud. *"Nashville cops turn a blind eye to well-known bootleggers. Accusations of bribe-taking rampant. Governor vows to clean up corruption.* So something is finally being done."

"Folks are finally figuring out what they wanted, getting rid of saloons, gambling dens, and whore houses, and what they got when they voted for the Eighteenth, were two different things," Dillon said.

"I'm glad the governor has said, 'enough is enough'!" Lily poured more coffee.

"Yeah, it's all about the ballot box. Fraud, corruption, now fights between the anti-drug units and the alcohol prohibitionists are impacting elections." Dillon took a last sip of his coffee and stood, glancing outside. He spoke optimistically. "Today's the day, ladies! Wish us luck!"

"Be careful," Lily said as she and her dog followed him to the door. Charlie jumped and wagged his tail.

"I will be." He kissed her warmly and left.

The April morning arrived with crisp temperatures, and fortunately, no rain. Knowing where he'd be hiding for most of the day, he gave a swift prayer. He strolled down to the distillery, ready to receive its one-of-a-kind delivery with Charlie scampering behind him.

"Open the gates," Dillon ordered.

He stood aside as the massive truck passed through the distillery's entrance a half hour later. It had traveled from Alex Stooksbury's auto dealership down Oak Hollow's Main Street, past the Star Inn and the train station into Tom Tanner's Tennessee Whiskey compound. Anyone curious what the truck's primary purpose was could observe one hundred crates of forty-eight bottles each of legally tagged and licensed medicinal whiskey being loaded onto the monster vehicle. The rotgut liquor with its government stamp had to appear authentic for Reggie to fall for the ploy.

Dillon knew the governor and others were working hard to bring about change, but people like Reggie Wyatt had to be brought to justice. No longer could authorities look the other way.

****

Tom

Later in the day, Tom and Alex boarded the custom-designed truck with its reinforced springs and boosted engine and drove it out of the compound down the planned route. They knew the exact spot where the heist by Reggie's confederates would take place. An hour out from Tanner's, the narrow road had a solid granite high bank on the left and a steep shoulder dropping off to a creek on the right. It was the perfect place for an ambush captors thought was heading to the US government's pharmacy depot. The exact spot where Dillon was hijacked over a year ago.

At sundown, Tom rounded a long curve. A black Buick sedan parked across the road barricading access down the highway. The massive truck's headlight shone on two men brandishing long guns, motioning for them to stop.

"I see a third man standing behind the car," Alex said.

Tom braked to a stop. Both men raised their hands in surrender the minute a flashlight beam shone on their faces.

"Get out of the truck. Make it easy on us," the lead bandit in a black hat hollered.

"Don't want no trouble," Tom answered in his best Uncle Milo imitation. He and Alex dressed in tattered overalls and worn boots. Their unshaven faces and unruly hair completed their rustic look. "All yours."

The men present knew the unwritten code of hijacking alcohol. No trouble occurred if you turned over the goods and walked away. Besides, at this time of night, even in backwoods, gunshots would arouse too much curiosity. Tom and Alex, with hands still held high, ambled toward the creek side in case a dive down the banks was necessary.

With no resistance offered, the three men holding up the truck exuded an air of confidence. *Good*. The crooks would not be expecting any surprises this night. He and Alex watched the men holding shotguns hop in the truck. After starting the enormous engine, they followed the Buick to their rendezvous spot, leaving them behind.

"Glad you found a closer spot to hide our car. Don't feel like hiking a mile down the road," Tom said to Alex as the two followed the creek bed.

They approached a shallow spot where wagons and then trucks and cars shortcut through to the cornfields on the other side for generations. Within minutes, they pulled off the tree branches cut to camouflage shiny metal, which might reflect from their car on a moonlit night.

****

Dillon

Dillon studied the dimly lit Playhouse situated innocently in a dip in the hills north of the quarry town of Lassiter. Days earlier, he found the perfect hideout spot in an abandoned deer tree stand. Today, he'd left his distillery at noon, hiked a back trail, and climbed into the stand before Reggie and his collaborators converged. Once in position, he didn't wait for long.

The first of Reggie's men arrived before dusk. They headed straight for the Playhouse's cellar doors and lifted them. From a pickup truck, they carried cider jugs down the steps. Everything ready to dilute the whiskey, then tape counterfeit stamps on the bottles.

Where was Reggie? Catching low-level bootleggers instead of the person who ramrodded the entire operation was not his plan. Dillon stretched from his stooped posture and wiped his brow, his anxiety escalating with every passing minute.

Suddenly, a sleek black Chrysler with heavy chrome fenders drove into the gravel parking area. Out climbed Reggie Wyatt. Dillon's heart hammered in his chest. *Thank God.*

Reggie paused, taking in his surroundings, then lit a cigarette. A heavy truck's headlights illuminated the ridge as it rolled into the Playhouse entrance.

"Any trouble?" Reggie asked his men as they exited the custom vehicle. He blew a smoke ring, then threw down his cigarette butt.

"Nah. You know these locals. Pretty sure money already passed hands. Ain't nobody gonna turn 'em in."

"How many were there?"

"Just two."

"Seems Tanner's mighty sure of himself."

"That truck drove like a locomotive. If we'd had stopped them on a straightaway, they'd blown right by us. No way we'd have caught them."

The crook driving the Buick parked his car and walked up to join them. "Hell of a truck."

"I heard. Well, let's get to it. Got a lot of work to do. Already have Red working on the bottles." Reggie signaled at the cellar.

"Yeah, boss," one man agreed.

From mere yards away, Dillon overheard the man's smirking response. Dillon stretched his legs in the constricted space. *Bet that toad eater must feel really smart about now.*

The man who drove in the cider pulled out another lantern and lit it before setting it on the ground. The full moon, truck lights, and lanterns provided plenty of light to watch what was happening.

"Come on. It'll take us all night to dilute this stuff and get the new labels on," the man hollered.

A sharp cramp pierced Dillon's leg. When he straightened it, he kicked out a wood panel; it fell to the ground below. Dillon muffled a moan. Reggie and the man nearest him stared into the darkening woods straight at Dillon's hideaway. A night hawk flew overhead, flapping his wings, and an owl hooted nearby.

"Probably a deer," Reggie said.

The five-man crew worked nonstop for an hour toting the cases of Tom Tanner Tennessee Whiskey. From time to time, Reggie would emerge from the Playhouse's cellar to check on the crates of alcohol still in the truck. After another hour passed, he took a flashlight, climbed onto the rear bumper, and peered inside. When he jumped down, he shone his beam in the woods where Dillon was hiding. A flash of metal gleamed when Reggie reached inside his jacket.

"Butch, climb up that bank about fifteen yards and tell me what you see," Reggie ordered, pulling a pistol from his shoulder holster.

Without warning, six sets of headlights flooded the entire property. A convoy of police squad cars descended on the Playhouse's perimeter. Federal officers leaped out of the vehicles, guns aloft.

"By Authority of the United States government, you all are under arrest in violation of the Volstead Act," the lead officer shouted into a bullhorn.

Officers pointed their rifles and barked quick commands as they rounded up the hoodlums working outside the theater. Four other cops descended the cellar steps and hauled out the trio with their hands held high.

"Captain, you won't believe what's in that basement," the lead policemen exclaimed.

If highfliers like Reggie Wyatt learned anything from years of bootlegging, it was easier to surrender and agree to an arrest. Dillon knew cold hard cash was paid in bribes before, and Reggie's ability to pay for high-priced attorneys should work a deal to secure probation with no time served and a minimal fine.

"What seems to be the problem here, officers?" Reggie asked in a blameless tone. "Didn't hear you say. Are you from the Internal Revenue Bureau? Hope so. We found this stash of spirits and truck, and it appears someone's been hiding it in the Playhouse. So glad you're here."

"Stay right where you are, mister. Is your name Reginald Wyatt?"

"That's correct. And I bet you spotted two men a mile down the road. They must have been the ones who drove this here truck to the Playhouse. Never saw it before. Now, I'm a law-abiding citizen in these parts and a card-carrying gold member of the police benevolent society. Don't tell me I need to call my lawyer."

Dillon climbed down from the tree stand and trudged through the underbrush in time to hear Reggie's back peddling.

"Good evening, Captain," Dillon said. The captain touched his hat in acknowledgment.

Reggie's mouth fell open, not saying another word once he recognized Dillon.

"Lawyer's not going to be much help to you, Reggie. Chicago is gonna get word you swindled them again. And they're gonna be none too happy. Safer to stay in prison," Dillon recommended.

Reggie backed away, holding his hands high. A cry sounded from one of Reggie's men, unhappy with an overzealous cop. Retaliatory punches followed. The distraction was just enough. Reggie raced toward his car, jumped in, and gunned the engine. Shots from another officer flew overhead as Reggie skidded out of the gravel parking lot and swerved up toward the main road.

"Son of a…" Dillon cursed. "He's getting away!"

Headlights coming in the opposite direction lit up the skyline. Brakes screeched, and metal crunching against metal pierced the night. Tom and Alex, who was driving, collided head-on into Reggie's car.

Reggie lifted his head from the steering wheel and stared straight ahead. He pushed his car door open and limped out; he pulled his pistol from his holster and unloaded two shots. Tom and Alex leaped from Tom's car. Dillon sprinted up the hill, reaching the crash on a dead run.

"Duck," Alex yelled when Reggie pivoted toward Dillon. He fired two more shots. Tom scrunched behind his car door and scooped his hand down in the loose gravel, grabbing a handful of rocks. He raised and threw the stones at Reggie's car windshield. Reggie turned to shoot. He took one more shot.

"Damn." Alex yelped as his body slammed against Tom's passenger side door. "Got shot."

Reggie stood and took dead aim at Alex as he leaned against the car, holding his injured left arm. He stared at Alex, then pulled the trigger again. The gun jammed.

Dillon tramped out from behind the tree he had used to take cover. "Give it up, Reggie."

Reggie pulled his gun's trigger again. Frustrated, he swore and threw the gun at Dillon. He turned to run, but in two strides, Dillon had him horse-collared.

Tom went around the wrecked cars. "You okay, Alex?"

"Yeah, damn it, same arm." He reached into his overalls pocket and pulled out a bandanna handkerchief.

"Dillon, we'll give you first dibs at 'em," Tom said as he watched Dillon swing Reggie around.

"Nah. I want him to stay pretty, so those Chicago boys can doll him all up again for prison after they get through with him," Dillon said as he shoved Reggie forward.

"I ain't so generous," Alex said as he tramped toward Reggie. "This time I don't have a pretty girl holding back my aim." He squared off in front of Reggie and hit him with his right fist, landing a solid violent punch to his face.

"I think you broke his nose." Tom guffawed, turning to his friend.

Reggie crumbled back against the bumper of his car, holding his bloody nose. He struggled to stop the bleeding with his handkerchief. When he glanced up, the captain, who had marched uphill with his other officers to the crash scene, stood before him.

"What the hell's going on up here?" the captain demanded.

"I'll have every single one of you arrested." Reggie glared at the captain. "And I'll have your badge."

"Is that so?"

"Tell me how I should be arrested for stealing Tom Tanner Whiskey? It's in their truck. They're here. Ain't nothing been stolen." Reggie argued.

"'Fraid you're a little off-kilter, buddy," Tom said as he picked up the discarded firearm and handed it to the police captain. "We received a report one thousand gallons of Government Permitted Medicinal Tom Tanner Tennessee Whiskey was stolen from our distillery. It's why we called the law."

"Tell me again how I stole your whiskey. It's your own damn truck. I took nothing belonging to you." Reggie tried to stop the blood flow from his nose, pressing his bloody handkerchief to his face.

"That ain't my truck." Tom held out his hands, palms up.

Reggie exploded. "What, what the hell? Whose do you think it is?"

"Easy enough to find out, isn't it, Captain?" Dillon asked.

"Sergeant, see if there's a title in the glove box."

Within minutes, the young sergeant handed off a folded document to the captain.

"Here it is right here."

Reggie grinned, dabbing his nose with a bloody handkerchief.

"Truck's duly registered to Reginald Wyatt."

Reggie's body jerked in an apoplectic fit. Furious, he charged at Dillon, who grabbed the enraged man and wrestled him to the ground. Dillon pressed a knee to his back, pushing Reggie's face into the earth. "Might need to get used to the taste of dirt, Reg, where you're going."

The sergeant and another officer pulled Reggie to his feet once Dillon moved off him. They pulled both of his arms behind his back.

"Cuff him, then put that piece of crap in the paddy wagon," the captain ordered.

Dillon smoothed the front of his shirt and took a last look at Reggie while he was handcuffed. A lightness in his chest returned as he savored the moment.

Tom and Alex joined his side as they watched the

perp being escorted away.

"Been a long day, boys," Dillon said, throwing his arms around both men. "Let's head home."

Chapter Twenty-Eight

Tom

Tom paid for the cab at the corner. He preferred to walk the short distance up the narrow street in Chelsea, a suburb of London, England. He replaced his hat, covering his head. His five days onboard the *Athena* gave him back the healthy tan he'd lost since his return from Rio and Mexico to the States.

He had never hired a private detective before, but in this case, rather than go on another wild goose chase, he determined the search was worth it. Today, hopefully, those efforts paid off. His months-long search to find Cammie Johnson yielded no clues. She did not attempt to contact him or anyone else he knew since they were together in Mobile.

He went over in his mind for the one-millionth time. What could he have said or done to make her disappear? What happened in those days, hours, or weeks after he sailed on a ship bound for Rio de Janeiro?

Hadn't he made it obvious to her in word and deed he loved her? Or did she believe the morning they whisked him away she was part of an elaborate ploy used to allow him and his whiskey to slip by authorities? Did she think he left her alone to face the prohibition enforcers with the honest answer that she did not know where he was? She knew he hadn't planned to take her on the raft the day her aunt and government agents confronted him—but once he abducted her—his plans could not change. His precious cargo came first.

So did it matter they made wild and passionate love? For over a year, she pretended she was a widow. Could he not pretend he was in love for one night? Is that what she thought?

Tom checked and then rechecked the number on the house. The nondescript house was like the dozens of others dotting the streets of Chelsea, each with its colorfully painted front door and a myriad of flowering window boxes. The private investigator hired by him was certain the Mrs. Johnson he was looking for lived in the house.

The report said a female boarder received no mail and did not exit the home, except for the one day the investigator sighted her hanging laundry behind the walled rock fence. Miss Sarah Gayle Templin was, he was assured, a very respectable member of Parliament, and the home belonged to her. The investigator was confident the residents under her roof were safe.

Tom recalled telling Cammie about Sarah Gayle when they first met and talked at length about her on their raft ride down the Duck River. He told her if there was one person in the world she could count on, it would be her...and she remembered. Did she also remember his suggestion they might escape to England and travel to Scotland when he scrambled for getaway strategies for the two of them? She must have. But to try to find Sarah Gayle on her own, she must have been truly desperate. Why would Cammie disappear and leave no word as to why?

While in Rio, he assumed Cammie was safe, positive Hugh and his wife Jane would take her in. He still recalled his disbelief in learning she was not with them, the horrifying, knee-jerking fear that entered his bloodstream. When the shocking revelation faded, he sank in the belief he did not know where she was. Tom scrubbed his face. For too long, he was going through the motions of living, but no more.

Three weeks had passed since he'd received the detective's report, including time to book passage and sail across the Atlantic. In Liverpool, he caught the train to London. Twenty-four hours later, he was standing on the sidewalk staring at a painted blue door. His heart beat harder. He took a deep breath. Was this another dead end?

His family bestowed their wholehearted support when he dropped the bombshell he was sailing to England when he revealed he hoped to find Cammie. With Reggie in jail awaiting trial and Dillon overseeing the recovery of their stolen whiskey, his relatives sent him off with their blessings on what they hoped would not be another dead end.

Prohibition continued back home in the United States. But the needle was moving in the opposite direction of the drys. Strange bedfellows were joining to repeal for the first time a constitutional amendment. As with all political movements, it would be a slow crawl.

He knocked at ten Primrose Street. A young housemaid answered the front door. He asked for Mrs. Johnson, adding he was a family friend. She curtsied.

"I believe she is outside. She takes a nap at about

this time of day. Shall I wake her?" the young woman asked as she took his hat.

"No. I'll go if you show me the way. Thank you."

Tom walked through the narrow house and out through the back door. He spotted a bench with cushions under a tree, but no one was about. A gust of wind blew across the yard, billowing white cotton sheets on the clothesline.

"Oh."

He heard a voice and then spied an arm reach to reclasp a clothespin. The woman must have sensed his presence because she stepped around the flowing linen. It was Cammie. It would be hard to say which one of the two was more shocked.

Tom's muscles went numb. He could not move. Not knowing where to look, his eyes wandered to her swollen belly and then back up to her widening eyes. She took a step back, pressing her fist to her mouth. Her frozen stature wavered, and she grabbed a flimsy sheet for support.

"Oh, my sweet angel. Why didn't you tell me?" Tom gathered her in his arms as she released her hold on the unsupportive fabric, his nonsensical question not deserving an answer. He kissed her forehead, her hot cheek. With care, he walked her to the bench but dared not release her hand.

"They told me I'd never see you again if I didn't help," she whispered as she laid her cheek on his jacket.

"Who?"

"The men who came and looked for you the next day. There were no abduction questions, nothing about me. All they wanted was the whiskey. And they threatened me." Cammie shuddered in his arms.

"My God." An abhorrent thought entered Tom's head. "They, they didn't hurt you?"

"No. But I panicked. I didn't know what to do or where to go. Not back to my aunt. She had no concern for my whereabouts. Hugh was so kind. He sent Naomi back down to care for me. But those men, Tom, they said they would be back. And they made it clear they would make me help them find you. I heard them talk. One of them indicated they could use me as a hostage to draw you out. I left straightaway, not even telling Naomi where I was going. I was afraid for her as well."

"Why didn't you go to my mother?"

She looked at him, shaking her head. "Tom, I couldn't run to your mother. I was the very reason she would never see her son again." She pinned her arms against her stomach, shielding her body.

Tom wrapped his arms around her and, with a shaky laugh, said, "If you only knew my mother. And let me tell you, she'd swap a grandchild out for me any day."

Cammie brought her hand up and ran her fingers down the side of his face, smoothing his sideburns. Did she notice the gray? He took her hand and kissed the inside of her wrist.

"I guess I have a lady inside the house I need to thank," he said as he looked back at Sarah Gayle's house.

"Oh, Tom, she was everything you said she'd be. I was uncertain if I could find her, much less if she would help me. But she did. I was lucky. I caught the train to London. Parliament was in session. Sarah found me sitting outside her office after her secretary told her an American wanted to see her."

Tom winced, tightening his grip on her hand. "I can't believe you made such a frightening decision to come here by yourself. You are so brave, my love." He hugged her to himself once again before releasing her to look into her violet eyes.

"But Sarah knows me. Why did she not write to me and tell me? Why, once you realized a baby was on the way, why did you not write?"

"Whom would we write to?" She grimaced. She moved away from him. "I had no idea where you were. And I made her promise not to."

"Of all the…" A painful tightness constricted his throat.

"Tom, we don't live in the Dark Ages, but I could not show up in Oak Hollow pregnant years after my husband was supposed to have died. This way, I can have my baby and find a family who will hire me as their nanny or governess. I don't want to leave my baby for adoption."

Tom embraced her. "You'll do no such thing." He shuddered at the idea of finding her before it was too late. He reconsidered the hurdles, the obstacles she must have met to bring her to this point in her life. Scattered thoughts raced in and out of his consciousness, his relief in finding her, the gratitude he felt toward his friend for helping Cammie, and his immediate desire to bring about a solution.

He glanced at his wristwatch. It was only three o'clock in the afternoon. "We'll get married today."

"Tom."

"No excuses. Come—we'll find Sarah. Let's not delay." He almost said we don't have much time. Cammie was without question in the last stages of pregnancy. And what little he knew of pregnancy, he was quick to calculate in his mind that this baby was due.

What an absolute idiot I am. He took her hand and then kneeled on one knee on the ground.

"Cammie Johnson, will you do me the honor of marrying me?" He gazed at her glistening eyes, waiting for the answer he desired to hear.

"Yes, yes," she said breathlessly.

He stood, pulling her into his arms. The negative emotions of emptiness, heartache, loneliness, and even fear dissipated. Joy and happiness found a home in his heart, leaving him feeling connected for the first time in months. His breath caught in his chest as he lowered his head and kissed her tenderly.

Chapter Twenty-Nine

Kit

"They're coming!" The entourage waiting to meet the Kittrell clan waited outside the train terminal instead of inside the stuffy station. Fragrant rose and camellia scents from the nearby gardens on the town green permeated the May mid-morning. Spring's last dogwood blossoms fluttered on their branches. Birds flew overhead, circling the antique weather vane of the Victorian train station, the site of many Kittrell and Tanner homecomings.

"I'm so glad Dad met them in Atlanta. And they could travel in together." Kit bounced on her toes. "Isn't this exciting?"

Almost a year had passed since her father left their home and family to start a new rye whiskey distillery in Mexico to save Penland Kittrell's whiskey brand. Her mother had stayed behind to help run Tom Tanner Tennessee Whiskey. However, when her only son sent a telegram from London a month ago requesting her presence, she dropped everything and left, leaving complete management in Dillon's hands.

Dillon's new bride, Lily, waited alongside Kit in anticipation. They both danced in place, twisting and turning in their identical cloche hats and filmy, short summer frocks. Their pouty lips were smoothed with

Earth and Fire red lipstick, and each sported a strategic beauty mark on their cheek. Reservations had been made for lunch at the Star Inn before they'd separate and go in different directions from Oak Hollow.

Dillon and Lily would head to Tanner House. The newlywed couple had taken up residence in the big house since their marriage and converted the manager's cottage into a home for Tena and Marcos. She still lived at the family's home but was happy to crash at Alex's bachelor apartment whenever the two needed stolen moments.

"I think I see your father," Alex said as he wrapped his arms around her. She was ready to run up the steps to the terminal when Alex pulled off her hat and sneaked a kiss on her neck below her ear. She turned in his arms to kiss him back at the same time her father walked through the double doors.

A gentle breeze swooshed across the town's green mussing Kit's bobbed hair. Her father froze when he recognized her. She snatched her hat back from Alex when her father turned to hold the door open for her mother.

Kit remained motionless. Her mother walked out carrying a baby. Whose baby? A small infant. Tufts of downy brown hair blew in the breeze as her mom hugged a blue blanket tighter around the child.

"Mom?"

Tom followed their mother outside. Her brother tugged on the hand of a slender woman drawing her outdoors. She wore a pink dress with a matching jacket and hat that topped long brown curls. She had huge eyes and the sweetest smile. Kit watched her turn and take the baby from her mother's arms.

Kit stood dumbfounded on the sidewalk with Alex, Dillon, and Lily, returning the stares from the four adults standing at the terminal exit doors. Her father continued to frown, his stern gaze fixated on his daughter's shortened hair. Alex's arms dropped from his tight embrace.

Oh, gosh. I can tell Dad is wondering why Alex has his arms around me. But Mother. Her mom was dressed in the most exquisite designer suit, which must have come straight from Paris. A stunning art nouveau pin, stuck in the side of her smart hat, glittered in the midday sun. She looked so beautiful. Kit wondered for the millionth time how her father could stay away for so long. But it was not only her family, but families everywhere were undergoing upheaval throughout America.

Everyone spoke at once. "A baby!" The girls scampered up the terminal steps together, oohing and aahing over the bundle.

"This is Cammie, my wife, and our son Tanner," Tom said proudly.

Kit hugged her brother. Her eyes teared as she stepped back to look at her family.

"Mother, Tom, how could you keep this a secret?" She hugged her mother, then her father, before allowing them to answer.

"Looks like someone else has been keeping secrets," her dad uttered as he returned her hug.

Kit shook her tousled head. "We have tons to catch up on." She clasped his hand.

Dillon came forward and introduced Lily as his wife.

"Congratulations. Chloe wrote me about your

news." Pen glanced at Alex.

"I'll go see about your luggage. You all go on to the Star Inn." Alex looked at Kit. Her father was still scrutinizing her from head to toe. He went inside the depot to help without even squeezing her hand.

****

Dillon

After lunch at the hotel, the women surrounded Cammie and the baby while Dillon took the men out on the back porch to update them on the family business.

"Alex got our truck back at the municipal dealer's auction," Dillon told them.

Alex grinned. "Yeah, a shame we had to pay anything for it, even a reduced price. But I'd say it was well worth it, sending that popinjay to jail. Hell of a truck. Dillon already paid me back," he said.

"Sorry to have missed the trial." Tom clapped his hand on Dillon's back.

"I was able to provide most of the evidence the federal government needed to indict Reggie. Took the jury less than four hours to convict him. The counterfeiting got him more years than the stealing of whiskey. Go figure. Everyone said it took the jury as long as it did cause they were holding out for another free lunch." Dillon passed his flask to his uncle-in-law.

"Went to Brushy Mountain?"

"Yeah. And I still have some friends there. I heard they gave him a real nice welcome." Dillon guffawed.

"Even the London papers carried stories about the shenanigans going on in our state," Tom said. "Can't believe the drama involving bootleggers, undercover cops, and society folks."

"Those Nashville folks can have all that publicity.

Takes prying eyes off us." Dillon shook his head.

"So, is public sentiment shifting?" Tom asked.

"I think so. Don't get me wrong," Dillon answered. "Folks are still being arrested; lots of plea bargains. But not for our friend Reggie Wyatt. We've got him put away for years."

"I'll go bring the cars around to the front of the hotel," Alex said before heading back inside.

"I wouldn't be surprised if prohibition went on five more years," Tom said.

"Don't say that." Pen took another swig from Dillon's flask.

"Can't help it. Our state is more fixated on overturning the teachings of the origin of species than on overturning the Eighteenth Amendment. That upcoming trial with William Jennings Bryan and Clarence Darrow is in all the headlines."

"Surely things can't get any worse before they appeal the Eighteenth?" Pen handed the flask to Tom.

"Crime's one thing. But when life hurts people in their pocketbooks, it will get overturned."

Pen rubbed his chin. "Looks like the economy is still roaring."

"Yeah, and that can't last forever, either." Tom gave a sarcastic laugh.

"Give me another swig. Damn, got a grandchild I didn't even know about, and my daughter's out there hanging all over the town's bad boy like there's no tomorrow."

All three men laughed. Dillon gave Pen a commiserating pat on his back as they returned to the ladies.

****

Alex

With everyone's luggage loaded, the group walked to their cars. They said another round of goodbyes before heading home. Alex caught Kit's eye and pulled her aside.

"I can drive over tonight to talk to your father. Don't want your dad to think my intentions are not honorable," he whispered.

She sent him a melting look. "I'd kiss you right now, but Daddy might notice my lipstick on you. I think he has enough on his plate right now. And don't forget he's seeing my mom for the first time in almost a year."

Alex glanced at Mrs. Kittrell. She was still a woman who stopped men in their tracks. "You know, you are a duplicate version of her. Yeah, if I were your dad, I'd want to get on home too and not be disturbed." He ran his hand through his hair. "Damn, I need a whiskey."

Epilogue
Oak Hollow, Tennessee, June 1925
Tom

"Mr. Tom, hand me your baby. Don't want him throwing up all over your tuxedo," Tena fussed at Tom before taking Tanner from his arms. "We don't need to spend another half hour buttoning Mrs. Cammie's matron of honor dress if she has to nurse him again. And we sure don't want to delay Miss Kit's wedding."

"Lord, no. Don't want to do that. Tena, what are we going to do without you?" Tom kissed his son before handing him over.

She gave him an exasperated look. "I'm staying right here while Marcos goes down to help your father." She tightened her arms protectively around the baby and strode back the incline to Tanner House, leaving Tom with Alex and Dillon.

"Stroke of luck, your father being able to take Marcos down to Mexico to run the distillery," Alex said.

The men moved into the giant tulip poplar's shade. Two girls in ruffled dresses with trailing ribbons raced in front of them.

"Yes, but we'll miss Tena when she joins him. She has been a world of help with Tanner to Cammie and me."

"Sounds like your father will come on back and leave Marcos down there as manager," Alex said, adjusting his boutonniere.

Tom saw Alex peek at his watch and then at the upstairs windows of Tanner's Victorian mansion. He smiled and gave Alex a reassuring pat on his back, relieved he didn't have to suffer the chaos of a traditional wedding. "Mother wants to merge the Tom Tanner and Penland Kittrell brands," he told his future brother-in-law. "We want to be ready once prohibition ends. Whatever the future brings—we'll face it together."

Alex nodded in agreement, then sighed. "Guess conversations away from whiskey in this family are going to be scarce. By the way, Kit says the family business is going all legit now. Getting out of the bootlegging business for good."

"Yeah. No more loads down the Duck River or elsewhere. The profits from that last run helped finance our Mexico branch. So we're done. We are old married men now. Wives don't take kindly to jailbirds. Not that we wouldn't help a neighbor out if they came calling." Tom winked.

"Well, if we come up short of funds, we can always ask for a loan from the ladies. Kit and Lily's own advertising business is off and running, thanks to someone." Dillon clapped his hand on Alex's shoulder.

"Well, you're the one who showed Lily those old lithographs. Seeing those prints and Lily's sketches gave Kit the idea of starting an ad agency."

Tom cut in. "It's been a tough battle with the prohibitionists. Don't think we'll be using pictures of alluring women to sell whiskey anymore. The concept of prohibition needs to stay buried."

"Got both women working on my auto ads.

Already have an office for those two at my dealership. Monthly installment payments, going to be a game changer," Alex said. "But folks in these parts have a fear of putting anything on credit. Looking to those two to help me with messaging."

"Heard your parents invited the governor?" Dillon asked.

"He sent his regrets. Said it wouldn't be good to have his picture taken with so much whiskey flowing around." Tom grinned. "His wife is coming, though. She wants to meet Kit and Lily."

"Lily worried you wouldn't have anyone on your side at the ceremony, Alex," Tom told the groom to distract him. "I reassured her there would be a swarm of women present, mourning the fact you were off the market."

Alex gave Tom a simulated punch. "Ouch, remember you only have one good arm left. Getting close. Here comes the minister now," Tom said.

"How's the groom feeling?" the minister asked when he reached the trio.

"Just glad it's not raining. When Kit told me she wanted to get married outdoors, I thought, 'Oh Lordy.'" Alex chuckled at his inappropriate reference in front of the clergyman.

"No worries there. If that's what she wants, she's gonna get it," her brother chimed in. "Kinda like she wanted you!"

Music began playing from the quartet positioned on the edge of the terrace. Soft melodies floated down to where the men stood.

The minister shook Alex's hand. "I think we're ready to begin."

****

Kit

Though early summer weather in Middle Tennessee could be unpredictable, her wedding day turned out blissfully fair. Kit stood staring out at Tanner House's second-story window. The Tanner House gardens had never shone to such an advantage, making the spot chosen a perfect site for the wedding.

She surveyed the area, focusing on where the vows would be exchanged beneath the majestic magnolia trees. White folding chairs lined two sides, forming a center aisle leading to a lattice arch decorated with rose blossoms and gardenias serving as the altar. Overgrown blue hydrangeas blooms mixed with wild honeysuckle scented the air. Up on the flagstone terrace, Tena and Marcos created a canopy of lights to hang above where the reception would take place. For dancing, they laid a section of an old parquet floor down, surrounded by small tables decorated with candles and scattered rose petals.

She watched as guests trooped in. "Has anyone seen Alex?" Kit asked in a panic.

"I did when I first got here," Lily said.

"I could kill my brother. He told me yesterday they were kidnapping Alex from the bachelor party last night, but not to worry."

"Oh, my lord. " Cammie fanned her face.

Her mother stepped into the bride's dressing room. "I've talked to the minister. Everything is fine. They found the flower girl by the creek. Her shoes are a little muddy, but everything will be all right once we find her rose petal basket. Darling, you look lovely."

Kit twirled around in her white silk drop waist

dress with cap sleeves designed with embroidered beads and silver rhinestones in geometric shapes. Her tie-on sash and circular flounces draping down at the back tickled her skin. A beaded headband in the same design framed her short hair bob and secured the wispy, gossamer veil brushing her fingertips.

"I thoroughly approve of these short wedding dresses. Oh, the miles of silk and taffeta we dragged around at weddings in my day." Her mother tucked an errant curl under her daughter's headband.

Kit gave a nervous laugh, and Lily rolled her eyes.

"Mother, you look fabulous, too." Her mother wore an elegant navy silk dress with a cape that extended to points at her back. She arranged her hair in a stylish chignon, although she confessed to Kit she was tempted to cut her hair in a bob too.

Cammie and Lily, Kit's matrons of honor, stood smiling in their matching dresses in light blue silk. Each wore broad-brimmed straw hats decorated with ecru ribbons and blue cornflowers.

"Mrs. Kittrell, did you find the flower girl's basket?" The minister's wife poked her head into the dressing room. Kit sent up a small prayer as her mother hurried off to help in the basket search.

Cammie puffed out Kit's veil and tucked another flyaway lock under Kit's headband. "I feel like we're sisters now."

"I'm so glad to have you in my family. My brother does not know how lucky he is," Kit said.

"Oh, yes, he does. Tom practically drools when she walks into any room he's in. And did you glimpse those beautiful pearls she's wearing?" Lily teased.

Cammie pressed her hand to her necklace, blushing

from her neck up.

"I'm just glad you didn't wait another month to get married." Lily twisted in front of the dressing room's full-length mirror, pulling at her waistband. "I'd never be able to squeeze into this dress if you'd had a July wedding."

"Lily?" Cammie and Kit exchanged looks. "Are you saying…" Kit grabbed Lily's arm.

Lily grinned in answer.

"Congratulations! This is so exciting. Do Mother and Father know?"

"Heavens to Betsy, no. Your parents have had enough on their plate these past months. Dillon and I will tell them after you and Alex have left on your honeymoon. Maybe help get their minds off you."

Both girls kissed Lily. "A cousin for Tanner. I'm so happy for you." Cammie squeezed her hand.

The dressing room door opened, and Kit's mother and the minister's wife reentered.

"You must make your father laugh," Kit's mother said as she clutched tight to her handkerchief. "If not, he will tear up, and he'll be embarrassed." She dabbed her eyes.

"Mother of the Bride. Time to leave. Ladies, please take your bouquets."

Chloe blew her a kiss as she left. Downstairs, her father waited while her two matrons of honor hurried ahead. He lifted his eyes to Kit and watched her descend.

"You look beautiful." He kissed her cheek before tucking her arm in his. "Are you ready?"

"Yes," she answered breathlessly.

Her father shook his head. "I can't believe I'm

giving my only daughter away today. And to a man obsessed with fast cars, now fast airplanes."

"Dad, we've already talked about this. You must admit, flying will be the quickest way for us to get to Florida." As a wedding gift to the young couple, Alex's former commanding officer in the war and his car dealership benefactor gifted them two weeks at his palatial Palm Beach mansion for their honeymoon.

"But why must everything be so fast with him?"

"Not fast enough. I would have married Alex at fifteen years old if he had asked."

Her father gave a perceptible shudder. Kit kissed him on the cheek. "So, in reality, he gave you six more years with your adorable daughter."

Her father grinned broadly. Recalling his role, he patted her hand. "You will always be my little girl."

He swung her about and escorted her outside to the terraced lawn. Approving and admiring smiles greeted them as they walked down the improvised aisle. How lucky she and Alex were to have the support of so many friends and family. Had anyone besides herself imagined this day? That she would marry the man she picked out to marry as a young girl. She smiled to herself.

Her heart leaped when she saw him. The handsome groom waited for her with the most heart-melting gleam in his eyes. Her knees weakened, and she steadied herself on her father's arm. At this moment, they only had eyes for each other. When she reached Alex, her father released his hand and placed hers into her groom's before joining her mother.

They chose a traditional marriage service, yet each wanted to affirm in their way their commitment to each other.

"Katherine Regina Kittrell—'Kit'—do you take…'"
Kit's mind wandered for a few seconds from the
minister's homilies. Did anyone know her real name?
She was named after her two grandmothers. Family.
Tradition. That's what she wanted with Alex. Her chest
swelled with pride. No matter what the world threw at
them. Separation, war, prohibition—they were
determined to stand together, stay together, support, and
love one another.

"I never wish to be parted from you from this day
on." The line Kit selected was from one of her favorite
authors.

"You have made me stronger, loving you," Alex
said, his voice steady and strong.

Rings were exchanged. A flock of birds flew
overhead as Kit heard the words for which she was
waiting.

"I now pronounce you husband and wife."

Alex kissed her until their breaths became one.

"Ahem." The minister cleared his throat and then
announced, "May I present Mr. and Mrs. Alex
Stooksbury."

Cammie handed Kit back her bouquet, and the
guests clapped in approval. The music resonated as the
newly wedded couple traipsed down the grass aisle.

"Did you ever in your wildest dreams picture this
day?" Alex asked.

"I did," Kit answered. Alex kissed her again. Her
eyes glistened. "Was it a beautiful wedding?"

Cammie and Lily surrounded her in answer when
they reached the happy couple, hugging Kit and
congratulating Alex. They giggled and laughed until

Alex pulled her away. The two of them turned to greet the other guests coming up from the lawn. Kit held tight to her bouquet. Poor Alex, his hand would be sore tomorrow after shaking so many hands.

After photographs, Alex led Kit to the open dance floor. He took her hand and twirled her once under his arm before taking her in his arms to sway to the music. Guests crowded around to watch the newlyweds dance together for the first time as husband and wife.

Alex leaned his forehead against Kit's. "I am the luckiest man alive."

When the song ended, he relinquished her to her father for their traditional father-daughter dance. Out of the corner of her eye, Kit spied Alex inviting her mother to dance. Once the bride and groom surrendered the dance floor, popular tunes started. Foxtrots, Charleston, tangos, and "Yes! We Have No Bananas" played through the night.

Marcos manned the outdoor bar set up on one end of the terrace. Pen made sure he had everything he needed for his specialties, from popular fruity cocktails to nonstop shots of Tom Tanner Tennessee Whiskey. There would be no government agents raiding Tanner House property tonight.

To the delight of the crowd and the disappointment of a swarm of young women, the flower girl snagged Kit's bouquet as soon as she tossed it, scampering off, with no one daring to stop her. Everyone joined in to sing "Ain't We Got Fun!" before Kit raced up the stairs with Lily and Cammie to change into her going-away outfit.

Fireworks and sparklers lit the sky above the wrap-around porch as Alex retrieved Kit. At long last, time to escape in their getaway car. White shoe polish covered the windows with "Just Married" scribbling, ribbons fluttered, and a ruffled garter dangled from the car's door handles.

Kit kissed her parents goodbye as tons of rice showered the departing couple. "Goodbye" and "We love you" shouts intermingled with the fireworks' blasts.

Alex assisted Kit to his car, then jumped in and zoomed off down the drive. At the property's gate, he stopped and drew her to his side. "I've wanted to kiss the bride properly all night long."

Kit turned into his embrace, not caring for the crush of her over-the-top "going-away" corsage. The kiss was long and passionate. Alex reached to smooth his hand down Kit's short knit skirt, then traveled up the length of one slim leg.

"You know, it's almost two hours to Nashville. I wished I'd booked a hotel room closer, rather than one, by the airport." He sighed as he pulled her in tighter. "But I know every back road into the city, even the deserted dirt ones."

"Is it faster if we take them?"

"No." He laughed. "However, it would allow us to test out the theory of making love in the back seat of a car."

"There's a theory?"

"I'm not sure; then I always want to learn more about cars."

"Alex, you are incorrigible."

"Uncertain what that means, but if it means I'm hopelessly in love with you, then I'll agree, Mrs. Stooksbury."

"Umm, I love the sound of that," she said as she leaned on his shoulder.

"Mrs. Stooksbury, Mrs. Stooksbury…"

A word about the author...

As the daughter of a United States military officer, Joy Allyson grew up loving travel and deeply appreciating history. A former teacher-turned-writer, she has an unquenchable thirst for historical romances in her reading choices. Her favorite characters – are rebel heroines and salvageable scoundrels. Joy believes the best romances are the ones you want to read over and over again.

She and her husband call the beautiful hills of Tennessee home, and her two daughters and six grandchildren are nearby.

Visit her at:

www.JoyAllyson.com

Printed in the USA
CPSIA information can be obtained
at www.ICGtesting.com
LVHW011453120424
777220LV00001B/154